I0687249

LEAP INTO THE DARK

Dark Sons Motorcycle Club - Book Five

ANN JENSEN

Published by Blushing Books
An Imprint of
ABCD Graphics and Design, Inc.
A Virginia Corporation
977 Seminole Trail #233
Charlottesville, VA 22901

Ann Jensen
Leap Into the Dark

Print ISBN: 978-1-63954-154-6
v1

Chapter 1

Making new friends is easy, it's not killing your old ones that's hard.

Jade

Jade arranged the mats for the private group that was coming in with a sense of pride. Her Parkour gym, Leap, was the physical manifestation of a long-held dream. The last two years she had spent getting established had been a rollercoaster of success and struggle. Finally, she was making a steady profit.

For her, Parkour wasn't only a job or a way to make a living, it was a way of life. Something amazing that she loved sharing with anyone with an adventurous spirit. It was an out of the box way to look at the world in which you learned not just how to overcome obstacles but to do it with flare.

Jade's phone buzzed, letting her know someone had come in the front door. She pasted on a smile and jogged to meet her newest students. The hilarious Southern lady she'd spoken to on the phone said she and her friends were looking for something fun to do together every week. She planned to take them through the basics of Parkour, Mountain climbing, and maybe the trampoline if they had time.

The five women were an interesting mix of people, ranging the spectrum of body shapes and sizes. A woman came towards her with a big smile, teased up red hair, and a t-shirt with the words, 'Namaste, y'all', printed in glitter. Jade had to hold back a laugh at the unique image she pulled off flawlessly. Something about the sunny personality that exuded from this woman's pores reminded her of the person she'd spoken to on the phone."

Making a guess, she held out her hand. "Are you Val?"

"That's me." Her southern accent was unmistakable. "These are my girls." Pointing to the closest woman, she smiled. "The tiny one is Pixie. To her right is Tari, Cami, and my best girl, Jojo."

"You just say that because she knows where to buy all the clothes that glitter," Pixie teased.

Jojo winked and struck a regal pose. "A drag queen without sparkle is like a flower without scent."

Jade laughed. These were definitely an eclectic mix of women. Pixie looked like her namesake, though she was probably the same height as Jade. The woman had blonde hair and a much more delicate build. The tall, elegant woman next to her, Tari, looked like a runway model hired to display the yoga gear she was wearing to perfect effect. Cami was a medium tall, curvy woman with bright purple hair who stood arm in arm with the African American drag queen. Jojo was impressive, her top a sparkly riot of color. She topped over six feet, and had muscles that impressed even Jade.

She gave them her best professional smile. "It's a pleasure to meet you all."

"Oh my god, you're Jade!" Jojo squealed. Jade blushed. Now and then, people recognized her from the 'Parkour

Warriors' TV show. She had been on the show for almost six years but hadn't become a featured contestant until year three. "I've watched every single one of your episodes. You are one badass bitch." The way the woman snapped on the last word made her laugh.

"Yeah, that's me. I'm glad you liked the show."

Jojo turned to Cami and grabbed her hands. "Seriously, you don't recognize her? She's Jade, the tiny one that kicked the asses of all those guys on that show. She's like, part monkey, part Hercules."

The purple-haired girl turned with wide eyes. "Oh my god. I loved w-watching you. You put that big, trash-talking m-muscle-head to shame. What was that, in the semifinals?"

Trash-talking wasn't usually a part of the sport, so Jade knew the event she was talking about. Sometimes new competitors tried to make a name for themselves by hamming up for the camera. Luckily, the fans of the show wanted nothing to do with drama like that.

They preferred to focus on possible love connections or stories about overcoming difficulties. They had loved to drag out the video of the injury that ruined her Olympic chances. They would praise her for overcoming adversity. No one had ever understood how painful it was to be reminded of her unrealized dream.

"Yeah. He didn't believe that muscles, when they're too big, are a hindrance in Parkour." To do well in the sport, you had to be strong, but there was a balance that most people didn't understand.

"I don't think too many muscles are ever a problem." Pixie waggled her eyebrows.

Jade shook her head. "Well, it's not the muscles, so much as the mass that comes along with them. A lot of the challenges require you to hang by your fingertips, and there is only so much strength you can build in your hands." They were veering way off topic. "So, Val told me you all are interested in a more non-traditional workout. What made you guys think to try here?"

"Well, Pixie and I," Val gestured between herself and the small blonde woman, "we've recently had babies. We were talking about wanting to get a couple of baby pounds off."

Jade looked over at the two women with surprise. Sure, maybe they were a little softer around the edges. But there was no extra weight on either woman.

"She said something where our men could hear and they thought it would be a good idea to take us down into their gym." Pixie laughed. "I don't mind watching my man lift those heavy weights. But after about ten minutes, I was bored out of my mind."

Cami laughed. "So then I started teaching them p-pole dancing. It is wonderful exercise. But since the only poles we have are at a strip club or in the m-middle of the Clubhouse, our men would interrupt and we got distracted." The woman had a slight stutter, but no one seemed to notice. Her eyes sparkled with mischief. "One night when we were w-watching that Warrior show, Jojo suggested it would be fun to do something like that."

Val spoke up. "So I looked around, and I found this place. I didn't have any idea you were on that show."

"Yeah. I was on pretty regularly for four years. When Eric, the co-owner, and I, won the team competition over in Japan and got that big payout, we decided to open up this gym." Jade gestured around the large warehouse area. "I still do competitions if they're local, Eric travels anytime he gets a sponsorship or finds a way to finagle it. But I prefer doing Parkour more for fun than for competition. I enjoy teaching others."

"That's fantastic," Jojo said. "I hope I don't sound like a crazy person, but do you think it's a good workout routine?

Some of their men thought it would be a fun waste of time."

"Oh yes, it's definitely a full-body workout. Today, I'm going to run you through a couple of the basic activities we teach. We offer several styles of training here. If this is going to become something regular, then you can either focus on one thing, or cycle through the different activities we offer. Any of them will build your stamina and strength."

She didn't think any of them needed to lose weight, but a woman's self-image was a funny thing. The group followed her from the front, into the first area she had set up with a couple of easy portable obstacles.

"We're going to start with some basic Parkour moves. I'll teach you the most efficient way to get over obstacles. Then, if you are interested, I can show you some moves you could learn to give it a little more flair." Jade gestured up to the far wall. "Over there we have mountain climbing, with courses from absolute beginner all the way up to extreme difficulty down at the far end."

"Oh my god you have your own P-Parkour Warrior set-up in here!" Cami bounced on her toes with excitement.

"Yes, the majority of the space is taken up by the obstacles that you see on the TV competitions. We try to switch those up about every four months to give it variety. The harder ones are over the foam pits, but we still ask that you be careful and get supervision, or a harness, before trying them. We also have a large trampoline at the far end."

Pixie clapped her hands. "Are we going to try that?"

"Sure. We offer gymnastics classes for the little ones, but nothing like any of the more structured student gyms have." A sense of pride filled Jade as the women explored the different areas for a few minutes.

She and Eric had designed this place themselves from the ground up. It was the size of three small warehouses, side by side, with long foam pits that were able to be covered or opened, depending on the obstacles that were over them, and what kind of safety was needed.

"This is a lot more impressive than I thought it w-was going to be." Cami had her hands on her hips. Her eyes were wide as saucers. The women looked ready to start, so Jade moved them back into the open area she had set up.

"All right, if you guys are comfortable, how about we get started on some stretches?"

Pixie and Tari pulled off their long sleeve t-shirts to expose the sports bras underneath before lining up with their friends on the mat in front of her. Jade started them off with some simple leg stretches.

"Stretching is critical when you are doing Parkour. You'd be surprised how many muscles will thank you for it afterwards. Most people don't realize that as we get older, our bodies settle into a routine. Once the exploration and learning we do in childhood is done, our muscles get set into patterns because we repeat the same motions over and over. So, if you don't get yourself properly stretched before we start, you're going to be hurting tomorrow."

Jade led them through her usual warm-up routine and was pleasantly surprised at how flexible they all were. She caught sight of some gorgeous artwork on Pixie's shoulders. Unable to resist she moved closer to get a better look.

When she could finally get a good look at Pixie's shoulder, the depiction of an adorable fairy entranced her. The color and details were astounding. The watercolor effect on the shading wasn't unusual, but the mixture of the intense detail on the outline made her think she knew who the artist was. The hyper-realistic depiction of a screaming demon on the woman's other shoulder was a shocking contrast. It looked so real Jade could almost suspect a photo transfer rather than a tattoo.

Those contrasting styles could only be achieved by two men whom she had been virtually stalking for almost two years. Excitement bubbled in her stomach as she wondered if Pixie might have met her celebrity crushes. Would it be rude to ask? If she kept herself in check and didn't fangirl too hard, then it shouldn't be an issue.

She could wait till the lesson was over. They were done stretching, and it was time to start running them through the courses. It would only be another hour, then she would have her curiosity assuaged… Nope, she had to find out if she was right.

"Pixie, I hope you don't mind me asking. Do you have a tattoo from both Hannibal and Ink?" Jade knew her voice was pitched a little too high, but she couldn't help it. Those men were the Michelangelo and Van Gogh of the tattoo world.

Pixie's light laughter filled the room. "How did you know that's who did my tattoos?"

It was their work. She knew it! "Oh, you have no idea how much I love their work. I think I've studied every one they've done that is out there on social media." Joy bubbled in her stomach. "Hannibal's mixture of soft and hard lines and insane amount of details makes it look like the tattoo could float right off the skin. I don't think there's anyone in the country who can match his style. The demon woman on your shoulder had to be one of his."

"It's a Banshee." Pixie smiled.

"Oh, that's awesome. Is it like an angel demon thing?"

"Yes, exactly." The woman tilted her head. "What about my Fairy? How did you know Ink did it?"

Jade shrugged and shook her head at how silly she was being. "There's maybe four people in the United States, who do work like that. He has a gorgeous watercolor style that feels soft, but then uses sharp line work that keeps it from looking blurry. All of his artwork has a touch of fantasy made into reality. When you add in the fact that the subject isn't something that could have actually been a picture that was transferred into a stencil, you're down to like two people in the US who could have done it. Put the two tattoos together and the fact that we are in Denver, well, it seemed obvious to me."

Jojo crossed her arms and smiled. "Sounds like you know a lot about tattoos."

"You know how you watch the Parkour Warriors show? Well, I love all the tattoo reality shows. Doesn't matter if it is about coverups or who is the best artist, I can't get enough of them. I might also read blogs and the magazines."

Jojo laughed. "You're a tattoo superfan."

"You could say that." Jade blushed. "When we set up shop here, I was excited that Dark Ink was so close. I've always wanted to get a tattoo from both of them. But they are not cheap. I've been building my business for the last two years, but I finally put aside enough money to get my name down on their list last month. I have my initial consultation appointment with Hannibal this week, but they couldn't schedule the actual work till later." It would be almost five months before she would have the finished products on her skin, but it would be worth it. "I can't wait. Seriously, to meet someone with talent like that is going to be a treat. It would suck to find out that they are actually jerks." She knew she was fangirling and tried to pull herself together. "Well, enough about my celebrity crushes. How about we get started on the fun part of the lesson?"

Chapter 2

I don't come on demand.

Ink

I nk was not a fan of being summoned. Especially not by a three-word text followed by an address. Sharp's Old Lady was an adorable woman, with an ability to cook that rivaled five-star chefs, but she could also be as crazy as a coon dog after being trapped in a kennel all day.

After receiving the words *'You owe me'* he had attempted to call Pixie back. Of course, the minx's phone rang straight to voicemail. Tonight was one of his rare nights off from both business and Club responsibilities. Ink's plans had included practicing his whip work on some targets in the backyard of his and Hannibal's house, which they'd bought together a few years ago.

The relationship between Hannibal and him was one people rarely understood. They had met up in the Rangers when Ink had been assigned to be Hannibal's spotter. The large, over muscled black man from Louisiana had practically adopted him, dragging him home to meet his crazy Cajun family.

Ink hadn't seen his own parents since he had escaped them at eighteen, and being thrown into the middle of a large close family had been amazing. They had stayed together for the rest of their time in the Rangers and lived through the nightmares of war. Over time, they had grown closer than brothers. Joining the Dark Sons MC together had been a simple decision and now they shared everything from their house, their business, and their women.

A few months ago, their regular hookup, Didi, had moved away for work. Since then, the two of them had been in a bit of a dry spell and that night they had plans to remedy that. The two of them had agreed to meet up at their favorite BDSM club to find a willing woman to share. Depending on what Sharp's Old Lady wanted, they might still get a few hours at the club. He would have to text Hannibal soon if he was going to have to cancel completely.

Ink pulled into the parking lot of the address, frustration at possibly losing out on a relaxing night souring his mood. From the brightly painted signs on the building, Pixie had summoned him to some sort of gym. The large warehouse didn't look like it would hold any sort of gym he was used to. It wasn't a surprise to see one of the Club's Prospects, Decaf, already parked in front of the building. He would be there on guard duty with at least one Old Lady inside a business they didn't own.

His mood lifted when he saw Hannibal parked next to him. Ink pulled up next to the two men and shut off his bike.

Ink chuckled and shook his head. "Did the little pickpocket call in a marker with you too, Brother?"

The girl had often conned them into betting for favors. Calling one of those in was the only thing that could explain why Hannibal was here rather than at their business, finishing up the monthly paperwork so they could have a night out for a change. Hopefully, the man had finished before coming here. Ink sighed. When had he become the type of man who worried over paperwork?

He needed to ease up. The night out was now a priority. Ink needed the relaxation working over a willing sub would have given him. To remind him, he wasn't a buttoned-up businessman.

Hannibal snorted. "You know she did. What do you think the little troublemaker has going on in her head?"

"I don't know why she called you two. There hasn't been any trouble." Decaf shrugged. "But you know when the Old Ladies get together chaos follows."

Ink couldn't agree more. "They do keep their men on their toes. No way through but forward."

The two men nodded in sync to Decaf and swung off their bikes. They fell in step as they approached the warehouse as they always did since the first time they teamed together in the Rangers. War had forged them into a unit, and Ink never wanted that to change. Sometimes he wondered if they would die side by side.

Living and working together was as natural as breathing now. They were a team closer than their other Dark Son Brothers could understand. Together, the two of them owned Dark Ink, their habit of using drawing to pass the time while on deployment, had transitioned into a good business once they were out. Now, business was doing so well that soon the two of them would only need to work a few days a week.

The idea of cutting back was tempting, but what would

they fill that time with? Shaking off the dark thoughts, he stepped inside the warehouse.

Hannibal's low whistle summed up his surprise at the impressive sight in front of him. Large wooden and metal structures filled the cavernous area. Obviously intended for use as obstacles, they ran the length of the building and spanned over foam pits. Covering the walls of the building were outcroppings and handholds that looked like they could be the ultimate mountain climbing set up. There was even a giant trampoline off to the right.

Ink had seen enough of those Warrior competition shows to guess that was the purpose of this place. Rangers did obstacles during their training in the military but nothing quite like this. What had that crazy woman brought them here for?

"I think I've died and gone to heaven." Hannibal's shoulder bumped his, and Ink noticed the group of six women further inside the building.

Four of the Club Old Ladies were looking up and shouting encouragement to Jojo, the crazy drag queen the women had adopted a few months ago. She was high up on one of the mountain-climbing obstacles, reaching out, trying to make it to the top.

Hannibal's gaze wasn't on the booty short wearing climber. Holding Jojo's safety rope was a woman drawn straight out of his fantasies. The harness she wore hugged a heart-shaped ass that should have monuments constructed in its honor. The goddess who owned that perfect anatomy was tiny, but not in the way that made Ink fear she would blow over in a brisk wind. Her dark chestnut hair was swept up into a ponytail, exposing olive skin and a graceful neck that he wanted to nibble.

Her long sleeve t-shirt hid what were probably luscious

curves and was tucked into shorts that highlighted her muscular shapely legs and tapered in waist. She had a well-done vine tattoo climbing up her left leg. He traced each tendril of the ink-work with his gaze as it slid under the tight cotton.

For the first time in his life, he was jealous of another tattoo artist. The urge to have her under his needle was almost overwhelming.

Ink shook his head to try to clear his thoughts. "Heaven indeed."

Hannibal crossed his arms with a small smile. "I don't know why the little bit called in her marker, but I know I'm not leaving until we get that beauty's number."

"What's the play?" Years of approaching women both together and separately had proven Hannibal was the expert in the art of capturing a woman's attention.

The two of them were different sides of the coin when it came to their personality. People saw Ink's country boy looks and Hannibal's harsher dark features and mistakenly assumed the light and dark of their skin tones matched their desires. Truth was, his Brother from Louisiana was the sensualist, a complete opposite to his own sadistic nature.

Ink hoped Hannibal wasn't about to suggest they work separately. While occasionally they would be with a woman without sharing, that was for the rare occasions when their tastes did not line up. It was obvious they both desired this gorgeous woman. It was easier to approach women, either at the BDSM club or the Dark Sons Clubhouse. Here, without the safety of knowing the woman was kinky or understood the score, Ink needed to rely on his Brother's Cajun charm.

"We find out what Pixie wants. Then distract and overwhelm."

Ink's step stuttered, and he paused. Hannibal faced him

with a grin. Distract and overwhelm was a technique they usually saved for a woman they knew was submissive. Hannibal would charm the woman while he loomed and crowded her. It was his job to throw her into submissive headspace while his Brother lulled her into feeling safe. Ink looked at the woman, and tried to see what signals he had missed. She was vibrant and smiling, not the usual shy bird that needed this sort of approach.

Hannibal's eyes twinkled. "Look at her inner thighs and back of the knees."

The woman's legs were gorgeous, but he had already noticed that. It took a few moments before he understood what he had been looking for. Most women who had leg tattoos stuck to the outer thigh, calf, or ankle. These zones were the least painful for getting intricate art. This beauty, however, had as much ink on her inner thighs as she did the outer. There was also a full color flower on the back of one of her knees.

No one got tattoos there without a high level of pain tolerance. It was a clue that this was a woman who might crave what they could give her. Society looked down on people who enjoyed mixing pain with pleasure. It often led to people repressing and denying what made them feel good.

Ink didn't care what most people thought about the kinds of things he and Hannibal did in the bedroom. He had decided a long time ago that if a woman was ever going to be their Old Lady, she would need to have a unique blend of strength and submission. That combination was as rare as water in the desert, and he had accepted that they wouldn't find anyone, but Hannibal still held out hope.

It was an interesting risk they were about to take. If all they wanted was a single night with this woman, the gentle seduction angle would have been more likely to succeed. Ink guessed Hannibal was as tired as he was of ending up with women who only enjoyed what they could give as a novelty, not as a way of life.

Apparently, his Brother intended to push this woman to find out if she might be good for more than just a single night.

Chapter 3

Always run away from temptation, but slowly so they can catch up.

Hannibal

Hannibal couldn't take his eyes off the absolute beauty in front of him. Her tattoos were only the start. The firm muscles hugged by the tiny little shorts made everything inside him sit up and take notice. It was all a trap.

Hell. He was a red-blooded man, and it was easy to picture her pinned between them. So tiny, yet strong. She would be gorgeous splayed out, begging for their touch. The woman tilted her head back and let out a laugh that was full of joy. The sound had his dick swelling from half-mast to full on excitement. She tossed her ponytail, dark hair whipping across her shoulders.

He wanted to see his hand wrapped in the long length as he pulled her head backwards. The sounds she would make when she was at his mercy would be filled with the same joy. Ink and he would push her until she was lost in the throes of passion. They would use every bit of their skill to bring her pleasure higher with bites of pain.

The image of her whimpering as her knees shook and her core dripped with honey was already playing across his mind. He loved the confused expression a woman got as the line between pain and pleasure blurred so much that she didn't know what she was asking for anymore. Bringing her to that blurred line would be his privilege.

"Oh my god. I'm so glad you're here!" Pixie bounced over to them with a big smile on her face and mischief in her eyes.

Hannibal loved the waif-like woman whom his Brother Sharp had been lucky enough to patch. He executed a fake courtly bow. "The mighty Banshee has summoned us here. We didn't dare refuse. What's so important that you are calling in your markers?"

The twinkle in her eye usually meant trouble, so Hannibal braced himself. "Well, I've got someone who wants to meet you. After I introduce you, I think you guys might give me back those markers."

Hannibal's eyes flicked back to the one person in the room he didn't recognize and chuckled low in his throat. "You called your markers just to get us to meet a girl, *cher*? Seems like an awful waste. You could have just brought her back to the Clubhouse."

Pixie rolled her eyes. "Not just to introduce you to a superfan. I'm calling them in to ask you guys to move up her tattoo appointments. This place is awesome." She gestured to include the warehouse. "Jade's finally shown me a fun way to work out. So I thought it would be a nice gift, to show how much I appreciate not having to lift heavy weights, to get you guys to fit her in sooner."

"She's a superfan?" Ink's eyes twinkled at the strange term.

Sure. Both of them had plenty of people who admired their work. Over one-hundred-thousand people followed the shop's social media, but the two of them left that to the person they had hired to run it. He guessed it made sense that they had admirers since they both had waiting lists for new customers that were over six months long.

But a superfan? Did the beautiful woman feel strongly enough about their work to call herself a superfan, or were those Pixie's words?

"Jade! I have some people here I want you to meet." Pixie was bouncing on her toes like an excited toddler.

The gorgeous woman, he had been having trouble keeping his eyes off of, turned her head and he couldn't help but smile when he saw the moment that she caught sight of them. Recognition was like a light passing over her face. Her eyes went wide and her jaw dropped.

Jojo was returning to the floor, and the woman worked a buckle on her harness. The webbing dropped to the floor, and she hurried over to them like she was barely restraining the urge to run. The gait caused her hips to swing in a tempting rhythm that emphasized her slim waist. Her full chest pushed against a long sleeve t-shirt emblazoned with this place's logo on it.

No makeup marred her natural beauty or was needed to draw focus on plump pink lips, or to brown eyes that sparkled in the light. Her breathing was fast, and he doubted it was from the quick trip over to meet them.

"Pixie said she knew you guys. I never thought she'd call you. I'm such a fan of your work. I'm Jade." Her words were hurried with an edge of nerves as she stuck out her hand to shake.

Ink moved faster than him and took her hand up to his lips in his charming Southern way. He pulled her a touch closer, and Hannibal watched a slight flush as it worked its way up her neck and to her cheeks. Ink's action allowed Hannibal to step up behind her, unable to resist the urge to get her between the two of them.

"Happy to meet you, darlin'." Ink's voice was filled with the Texas charm he so rarely shared.

He could see her pulse fluttering in her throat and enjoyed the startled way she looked up between the two of them. Like she didn't know where to rest her eyes. They weren't touching. But his dick was getting painfully hard.

The two of them had left her enough room to move out from between them if she wanted to. But she stayed still, where a slight movement would have her brushing against one or the other of them.

"How do you know our work, *cher*?" Hannibal smiled at her small intake of breath.

She swallowed, and he studied what he could see of her face from above. Lips parted, breath short, which caused her chest to rise up and down beautifully. If she had shown a single sign of fear, he would have stepped back and given her some space. But she didn't.

"I saw your work three years ago when you were featured in 'Inked'. The follow-up videos your shop did on YouTube were gorgeous, though the word doesn't even cover how wonderful they were. Since then, I've followed you on social media. Your work is so unique." She looked up. "Both of you."

Hannibal wanted her to stare up at them like that, but without so many clothes on.

"Is it me, or do they look l-like they're about to kidnap our instructor?" Cami's badly whispered words broke the moment, and Jade quickly slipped out from between the two of them with a pretty blush coloring in her cheeks.

"Sorry, ladies." Her words were breathy, making both men smile.

"It's all right, honey," Val said. "We know a Dark Sons man can be as distracting as tits on a pig."

Jade clapped her hands together. "All right, let's finish up this workout. Then you ladies can tell me whether you want to come back again. If this was a unique enough workout for you?"

Ink chuckled next to him.

"What's that laugh for?" Cami put her hands on her hips with a scowl. Of all the women here, she was definitely the biggest spitfire.

"Nothing." Ink shook his head. "I think it's adorable that you guys think this is a workout."

Hannibal winced at the condescending tone that came out of his Brother's mouth. He might agree that this was better described as playtime than a workout, but insulting someone's business was never a good idea. From the displeased looks on all the women's faces, it seemed they agreed that Ink was being an ass and disagreed with the validity of the statement.

"Not a workout? What do you think a 'real' workout is?" Jade put her hands on her hips and gave his Brother a scowl that should have warned him he was on shaky ground.

His Texan Brother's raised eyebrow stated clearly he wasn't planning on backing down. "Weights, running, I guess biking or swimming. That's a workout. This might be enjoyable exercise." Hannibal was glad to hear him pause and hoped it meant he was really considering the words that were coming out of his mouth. "I wouldn't call it exactly a workout."

She crossed her arms. "Not a workout. Huh? Since this is all I do, I guess you think you're in better shape than me?"

Hannibal groaned and tried to rescue the situation. "I know I like your shape a lot better than his."

She didn't appear like she was interested in his flattery.

"Personally, I think weights are a nice warm-up for a real workout." Jade raised her eyebrow and gave them an adorably challenging look. "Something that works the whole body." The way she said those words had dirty images flicking through his head. "I mean, what's the purpose of a workout? If not to get you ready for action?" She turned back and faced the women. "See, that's the problem with most men. They are so focused on making themselves attractive that they forget the practical reasons behind a workout. So they bulk up. But what good is strength if it isn't put to use?"

Hannibal shook his head as the challenge lit up his Brother's eyes. He had no idea where this was going. But it was going to be one hell of a ride.

Chapter 4

There is nothing more satisfying than beating your personal best, except maybe beating an arrogant man who thinks he is better because his reproductive organs are on the outside.

Jade

J ade smirked as Hannibal dropped off the rope that was the final obstacle on the easiest of the gym's courses. After goading them into the challenge, she'd let them pick which of the many options, they would use for their competition. It wasn't a surprise they picked the one most resembling those used by military and police personnel.

The terms were simple. If they won, she would go out with the winner. If she won, they agreed to move her tattoos up to their first available slot and do them for free. That last part had been Pixie's doing. The idea of being able to use the money she'd set aside for the tattoos on something else thrilled Jade. Or she might think up a second tattoo for each man to do for her.

Watching the two men navigate the phase one obstacle course had her heart racing. Her panties were also embarrassingly damp. Which confused her because she watched at least twenty people traverse it a day and had never once found it sexy.

Newbies trying to navigate the cargo net at speed was always good for a smile. The next obstacle wasn't difficult, but the height of the monkey bars over the foam pit could cause people to balk at navigating the thirty rungs. After jumping down, the final obstacle, a climbing rope, reminded most people of their elementary or middle school gym days. Training or incredible upper body strength was the key to success with that. She often found joy in teaching someone to overcome what, for some, was a childhood nightmare.

Jade fought to keep a smile off her face. She was overly excited, but Hannibal and Ink were here in her gym. She was competing against them. The number of hours she'd spent staring at photos of those two men and their work was slightly embarrassing. Seeing them in person was so much better.

She'd almost groaned out loud when they had taken off their leather cuts. Her secret dreams were becoming reality. In her mind, they hadn't stopped at the one article of clothing. Watching their muscles move as they worked their way through her obstacle course would fuel her fantasies for a long time.

Hannibal was pure power. His large muscles bunching and flexing through the shirt he wore, sparked the desire to trace every bulge on the man's body. His hair was shaved close to his head, and he gave off a powerful, almost intoxicating sense of barely contained strength. Unfortunately for him, he had very little technique. But there hadn't been a single moment where she worried he wouldn't power his way through whatever obstacle lay in front of him.

Ink, on the other hand, was grace and sleek strength. He had a slow, lazy movement style that matched his dirty-blond country boy good looks. Everything he did looked effortless. Like waves in the ocean, his power was deceptively calm until it pulled you under.

Their completion times weren't exactly bad. The two men had done better than most newbies on their first try. However, she ran through these obstacles all the time. The time they had spent on the cargo net alone guaranteed she wouldn't have any problem beating them.

And that was the problem. She was competitive by nature. The idea of throwing a race had never crossed her mind until now. The terms of their bet had her so tempted to fake a bad run.

The opportunity to go out on a date with one, or both, of these men had an ache starting in her most intimate parts. Jade shook her head, and muttered under her breath, "Pride and free tattoos or dates with the two sexiest men I've ever seen. My life sucks."

Jojo's bark of laughter made her blush as she realized at least part of what she'd said had been overheard.

Cami smirked. "Are you w-worried you're not going to beat them? Or that you are?"

Jade shrugged. "Beating them is not going to be a problem."

The woman's smile grew sharp. "So what's the p-problem?"

With a sigh she confessed, "I've never been so disappointed to win a bet."

She looked over at the two smiling men across the foam pit and up at the times displayed on the race board on the wall. Maybe one of them would still be interested in a date without the bet? Men's egos were a delicate thing in her experience. If she stalled enough to make it a close call, then there would be a better chance. Right?

"How badly are you going to beat them?" The sinister look on JoJo's face made her nervous.

Jade considered. The cargo net was the time suck for most people. Without the right technique, the obstacle was still easy, but you ended up spending twice the time and energy needed to complete it. That, along with her practice and experience on the rope at the end, meant she would come in almost a minute before them. More if she really pushed herself. But she didn't want to embarrass them. She could slow herself down without taking too much of a hit to her pride.

"At least thirty seconds."

Cami rubbed her hands together. "Let's m-make this interesting." The mixture of laughter and groans from the surrounding women made Jade's stomach flip. The woman cupped her hands around her mouth and shouted to the men, "How about we up the stakes?"

The smiles the two men gave did something evil to her insides. Hannibal and Ink strode around the edge of the pit and back towards the group of women. Their movements held a predatory air that had her shivering. It was unfair. How was she supposed to remain focused when they moved like that? Jade's imagination conjured up images of the two men surrounding her in ways that had nothing to do with competition.

Never had her fantasies included two men, but something about these two had her remembering some of the dirtiest scenes she had read in romance novels. Heat flushed her cheeks. An hour ago, she wouldn't have imagined she could tempt one of these men. Now she wanted both of them. Together.

Hannibal's smile as they finally reached them caused her nipples to tighten. "What are you lovelies thinking?"

Jade thought she would die of embarrassment until she realized the question was to Cami.

"If she beats your time by over thirty seconds, you b-boys admit she's in better shape than you and agree to come train with her for a m-month."

Jade wanted to groan. Sure, she was competitive, but she wouldn't rub a win in someone's face. However, the idea of a guaranteed month with these men had her throwing out the idea of losing on purpose. A whole month versus a single date. This woman was going to be her new best friend.

Ink's smile went wide. "So you think you're going to win, darlin'?" His voice was like smooth whiskey.

Screw it. If she was going to do this, she was going all in. She stepped forward, the movement forcing her to look up at the two men who were unwitting participants in so many of her nighttime fantasies.

"Well, it's not like you gave me much of a challenge."

Hannibal chuckled and circled her. She turned to follow his movement. She found herself between the two men and wondered if this was a dream.

"And what do we get if she doesn't?" The way Hannibal said *we* had wicked images playing through her mind.

It was obvious that these two men were close friends. Not only business partners but part of the same Motorcycle Club. The idea of the two of them together with her was almost more than her brain could handle. Things like that didn't happen in real life. Porn and romance novels aside, two over the top sexy men like that couldn't possibly come as a package.

Not that she wanted them to come as a package. That was insane. She was barely able to handle dating one man at a time. Two would be overwhelming. Wouldn't it?

Truth was she had never really had much luck in love. Men on the Parkour circuit seemed to come in one of two varieties. Party boys who didn't take anything seriously or cocky assholes. Neither of which interested her.

She couldn't even search for her perfect man based on her reading preferences because that would require us to make contact with aliens. Jade shook her head, clearing the wayward thoughts. She crossed her arms over her chest.

"What do you want?"

Ink's chuckle was right in her ear and she tried to spin, but he had stepped closer, almost pinning her between the two of them. She let out a small groan, and both men laughed.

The sound of their amusement was almost intoxicating. Ink whispered in her ear, "Not sure you can handle what we want."

Hannibal nodded. "How about: If you lose, you admit we are in better shape and come train under us?"

Jade's nipples tightened, sending a jolt of pleasure to her core. Why did she think that training under them would have very little to do with physical fitness? There was no way to lose at this point. Every outcome guaranteed she got to spend more time with these gorgeous, talented men of ink and muscle.

But she had to admit, she liked the idea of them having to come and train with her for a month. Less pressure and it would give her the opportunity to get to know them, and either get over her crushes, or maybe, if she was exceptionally lucky, convince one or the other of them into a little more personal training.

Heat flushed her cheeks at that thought. When had she become such a little slut? Jade snorted at herself. She had always known that her sex drive far exceeded those of the woman she hung out with. But she wasn't about to let anyone here know that.

This was her business. No matter how much fun she had had tonight. She needed to keep some semblance of dignity.

"You're on." She turned her head between the men, giving each one a nod.

She gathered her courage and stepped out from between them, only slightly disappointed they didn't stop her. Jade pulled out her phone and used her app to set the wall display to a countdown timer. She adjusted the time so it was thirty seconds less than the faster of the two's time.

Jade handed the phone to Pixie and moved towards the start line. "Simply hit the button when you're ready." The system was programmed to give a three beep count down then start the time. "Once you hear me ring the bell at the top of the rope, hit the stop button."

Pixie giggled. "This is going to be so much fun."

Jade smiled. She pulled off her long sleeve shirt and revealed the tank top she wore underneath. The loose material of the shirt was likely to get in her way as she climbed. Her choice to take off her shirt had nothing to do with the hope they would be watching her with the same distraction she had watched them with. The whistles that came from the women behind her made her smile.

Val's laugh was almost musical. "Girl, do you have those guns registered for concealed carry?"

Jade burst out laughing. She knew her arms were more muscular than the average woman's and sometimes felt self-conscious about it. Especially around men. But these women somehow made her feel confident.

She wasn't as bulky as a bodybuilder. But years of concentrated training, first in gymnastics, then in Parkour and mountain climbing, meant that every muscle on her upper body was well defined and visible. Many men were intimidated by the fact she had biceps, and not just when she flexed.

Luckily, genetics had also gifted her with enough curves to ensure she was never mistaken as masculine. But the truth was, most men hesitated to date someone possibly more in shape than they were. And she couldn't count how many times people tried to imply that she had done steroids or some other performance-enhancing drug in order to get her muscles.

Standing there in bike shorts and a tank top meant there was no way to hide her body. She refused to be embarrassed by the muscles she worked so hard to maintain. But she wasn't brave enough to look at Ink or Hannibal to see what they thought. Not yet.

Jade smiled over at the southern woman. "Every girl has to have a secret weapon or two."

"Fuck."

Jade wasn't sure if the groaned word came from Hannibal or Ink, but the admiration in the tone gave her courage to look at them.

The two men were moving towards her with heat in their eyes. There was none of the shock or wariness she was used to seeing. Neither man was trying to hide their appreciation of her body. Unsure of what they wanted, anticipation sent adrenaline shooting through her system.

"I think we should give our girl a kiss for luck." Ink's voice was heavy with what she had to believe was desire.

The temptation to pinch herself was almost overwhelming.

"Agreed." Hannibal stepped in front of her and her brain seemed to scramble.

"Don't you want to win?" Jade's voice was more breath than sound.

"Oh, I think we all are going to win," Ink said.

Was this really happening to her? She tilted her head up, planning to question them, but the moment her lips parted Hannibal lowered his head. Her breath left her in a rush as his mouth brushed against hers.

She groaned and leaned into him, unable to resist the pull of this large man. His kiss was warm like a fire on a chilly night. It filled her up with a slow desire that danced through her limbs until she felt like she was going to burst. His tongue flicked against her lips and she shivered.

"My turn."

Ink spun her around and before she knew what was happening, his mouth was claiming hers. The difference between the two men was overwhelming. Ink was like a forest fire, ready to burn her up in its intensity. Lightning pricks of pleasure shot down her spine as he took her with his kiss.

Where she had wanted Hannibal to lay her down and devour her slowly, she felt the overwhelming urge to climb Ink and ride him till she found release. His kiss was a challenge that demanded an answer.

He pulled back, almost ripping them both away from the kiss. Jade tried to catch her breath, stumbling back a few steps. The beeps of the timer were an unwelcome interruption when all she wanted was more of their kisses.

She glared over at Pixie as the third loud beep echoed in the room and indicated the start of the countdown. How the hell was she supposed to do anything with her legs weak with desire? She took a deep breath and narrowed her eyes at the two smug men chuckling over her lack of movement. She would see who was laughing in the end.

She turned and launched herself up the twenty-foot cargo net, barely pausing on each rung. If they thought losing a few seconds of time would mean she would lose, they were about to find out how wrong they were.

Every obstacle in this building was like a part of her. She

had designed them, constructed them and run through them more times than she could even count. Every day she trained other people on the best ways to conquer them. She could probably navigate the entire building blindfolded.

This place called out to the young child within her who had loved scrambling through the woods and reveled in racing for the sheer joy of it. Adrenaline filled her system as she cleared the top of the net and scrambled up onto the platform.

She leaped out to start the hand over hand four rungs out without a pause. The quick slap of the metal into the palms of her hands as she swung across was like a heartbeat. Steady and calm. She smiled as she swung off the last rung and bounced quickly down the platforms to get to the base of the rope.

Almost thirty seconds left on the clock. Hannibal and Ink were standing on the other side of the mat. The mixture of shock and admiration in their gazes fed her soul. The rope was twenty feet tall and wouldn't take even half that amount of time. She gave them a cheeky wink.

Having them training with her here at the gym was going to be so much fun. She leaped up at the rope, not bothering to use her legs, and pulled herself quickly hand over hand to the top. Jade slapped the bell at the top of the rope, and laughed at the jangle.

She wrapped her legs around the rope and slowly let herself down, hand over hand. She dropped to the mat just as the loud tone marking the end of her time sounded. Happiness and the thrill of winning bubbled through her. This night had turned out differently than she originally imagined.

Jade had hoped these women had enjoyed their time and signed up for more sessions. Now she was going to have time alone with two sexy men, teaching them about something she loved. Getting to meet Hannibal and Ink would have been amazing on any night.

Winning free tattoos from them as well as the training seemed too good to be true. Nervousness flooded her stomach as she walked over to the stunned men and cheering women. Hopefully, they wouldn't be sore losers. She doubted these two were used to losing at anything.

Chapter 5

The worst kind of block is a cock block

Hannibal

It had been a long time since Hannibal had been shocked by anything. This woman had managed to surprise him in several ways in the last few minutes. Ink and he had never been shy about what they wanted from women. But they usually kept their fun confined within the Club, where their proclivities were well known.

Coming onto this woman earlier had been an unexpected impulse. She was temptation wrapped up in a tiny little package. What had started as a teasing kiss, egged on by Ink, had turned into so much more. Jade's lips had been like velvet. Her body was a fascinating contrast between hard and soft.

He had never really considered muscles on a woman, but damn, Jade made everything in him stand up and pay attention. Watching her she practically floated through the obstacle course was a turn on. He hoped the small signs of submission, that both he and Ink had picked up on, weren't imagined. The idea of the strong, capable woman choosing to give herself over to them was a seductive prospect.

It was a shame they hadn't won the second half of the bet. They all would have enjoyed the type of training he'd had in mind. But he'd learned long ago that losing the first battle didn't mean that the war was over. Between the two of them, they would find a way to seduce this little firecracker. And if nothing else, he was going to get her under his needles soon.

The thought of marking that lovely woman permanently with his ink made his cock painfully hard. Hannibal stood next to his best friend and Brother and they watched as she basked in the congratulations of the Club's Old Ladies. She seemed to fit in well with them.

"What are you thinking, Brother?" Ink's voice held a note of hesitation that he didn't like.

Knowing his Brother the way he did, the man was already second guessing everything. "Thinking about getting her under my needles and getting her between us." His words were designed to keep things light even though his thoughts were wandering down more serious paths.

"Do you think she can handle that?"

Hannibal chuckled. "After watching that, I think she can handle anything."

Ink's face was a blank mask as he watched Jade laugh and tease with the other women. "Not sure this is a good idea."

For a minute Hannibal studied Ink's face, trying to figure out where this hesitation was coming from. "You sore that she beat our time?"

Ink frowned. "No, it's not that. We barely know this civilian and we're already committed to spending a month with her. What if she isn't interested in what we want?"

"You didn't seem to have those concerns before she beat us."

Ink ran his hand through his hair, one of his few tells that he was nervous. The man was usually all confidence, especially about women. His Southern good looks always drew in the women. He didn't usually worry about whether they would stay once they realized he and Hannibal were a package deal.

The funny thing was, once a woman saw past the surface, it was usually Ink's indifference outside the bedroom that kept a woman from returning a second time. Ink would make sure their partners enjoyed themselves physically, but it was up to Hannibal to show them any sort of emotional care. Over the last few years, the women they had shared had been submissive but hardened by life.

Women looking for a good time, but not ready to settle down. Hannibal enjoyed edging women, tattooing them, or piercing them. He loved watching them give themselves over to him, as he used a mix of pain to heighten their pleasure. Ink didn't seem to see the need for the gentle to soften the harsh. He pushed a woman's boundaries and enjoyed walking her right up against the edge of any limits she set. It would take a unique woman to handle both of them in the bedroom as well as outside of it.

Jade finally broke away from the group of Old Ladies and came over towards them. She was an interesting mix of giddy excitement and an almost shy smile. "Your friends have decided to set up twice a week private sessions."

Hannibal was tempted to continue the teasing from earlier. "Is that so? When do we get our private sessions?"

"I suppose that depends on your schedule. We can do your training while the place is open, or if you want, I'm willing to come in early or stay late." Her tone was completely professional, even if her words gave him so many dirty ideas.

"Are you now?" Ink said.

Color rose in Jade's cheeks. Hannibal considered the question. They had a pretty flexible schedule for everything except when they were doing tattoos at Dark Ink. Without looking at both of their calendars, there was no way to make a commitment. He would have to get back to her, even though he really wanted to lock her down now.

"How many sessions will you need to whip us into shape?" Hannibal loved the way that she didn't back away from both of their obvious flirting. He could see her nipples tightening underneath the tight little tank top she wore. It was his deepest wish at that moment that she would be up for what the two of them wanted.

"You don't have to come train under me." She looked up at them, a teasing smile tipping her lips upward. "If you don't think you can handle it, we can stick to the original bet. I'll admit it would have been fun teaching you how to conquer the cargo net the right way. I get if I'm too much for you. But I've dreamed of having your ink on me, so I guess I can settle for that."

Ink's eyes sparked and Hannibal wondered if Jade understood how big of a challenge she was throwing down. "You think you can handle both of us at the same time? Because we don't really do one on one. Better be sure you understand what we're offering, darlin'."

Her quick gasp of breath and the way her eyes lowered was so fucking attractive. Hannibal wanted to lay her out right there on the floor and see if she tasted as sweet as she looked. Would she be fire or honey once the clothes came off?

He followed her quick gaze over at the women and saw

that the Old Ladies were packing up and waving their goodbyes.

"I–" She cleared her throat with an adorable little sound. "Both of you. You mean together. At the same time. Isn't that painful?"

Hannibal studied Jade's body language. Her breathing was quick and her eyes were dilated. All signs she understood and was interested in what they were offering. However, it never hurt to be crystal clear. He ran a finger along her jaw, tilting her face up to look at him. "We do our tattoo work separately, beautiful. But everything else we like to share. If that's something that interests you, all you need to do is say yes."

Ink stepped behind Jade and ran his fingers over the gorgeous woman's shoulders. She shivered and swayed between them. She tipped her chin up, looking at him. Her lips quirked up into a little smile. "I think joint sessions might be fun."

"Might be." Ink's chuckle was a low rumble. "Oh, there is no, might be, about it. We always make sure everyone has fun when we're together."

Hannibal cupped her cheek while Ink ran his hands down her sides from the back. They both stepped closer, pressing her body between theirs. Letting her feel how turned on they were. It was tempting to start stripping off what little clothing she wore right there. The feel of her tight body against his trapped cock was a painful little tease.

Jade's eyes glazed, and he hoped she was feeling the draw as strongly as he was. God, it would be so disappointing if she wasn't up for the kind of games that he and his Brother enjoyed. Wanting two men to share her didn't mean she would be interested in fulfilling their other needs. Not that he wasn't ready to take her up on whatever she was ready to offer.

It was obvious there was a submissive spirit in this woman from her reactions to them. But some instinct told him she wasn't experienced in the kind of games they liked to play. Introducing someone completely vanilla into the world of BDSM wasn't something he had ever considered doing. He and Ink had always preferred experienced subs to remove any misunderstanding. But the beautiful Jade tempted him.

The idea of being her first in so many things, was an exciting prospect. A game plan began to form in his mind. "How about we get started tonight?"

She took a shaky breath in. He enjoyed the sensation of her trembling against him. Jade's body jerked, her gaze locking on something over his shoulder. Hannibal turned and surveyed the room. He didn't see anything out of order. Just the empty warehouse full of obstacles. The only other thing in that direction was a set of stairs that led to a room marked Office. A dim light was barely visible through the frosted glass.

He turned back to look at her and quickly realized that something had changed. Her lips were tight and her shoulders bunched. She looked angry as she shook her head, and stepped sideways, slipping out from between them. Hannibal backed off, puzzled by the strange reaction.

"I'm sorry I can't tonight. I've got things I've got to take care of." She began moving away. "I'm open to any other night this week. Your friends have my cell number if you want to text me. I'm sorry, I have to go." With those strange words, Jade took off at a jog, heading through the obstacles towards the office without even a glance back

"What the fuck was that?"

Chapter 6

If you're not losing friends then you haven't grown up.

Ink

Ink watched Jade's heart-shaped ass as she strode off as if on a mission. She had been right there with them. Everything about her body, her pulse, her breath said she was ready for whatever games they wanted to play. Then something happened that snapped the mood.

Ink shook his head. "I don't know. Did we push her too fast?"

Why was he so concerned that she had walked away? She was a distraction for the evening, not someone who should make him question his actions. If she didn't want what they were offering, there were plenty of women at the Club who would be happy to be between him and Hannibal.

Ink wasn't the type of man to question his moves. Hesitation wasn't something either of them bothered with. It had been a long time since they had tried to connect with a woman anywhere where the women didn't know the score. Maybe he was rusty?

Hell, going after a woman who they just met was a stupid risk. But something about Jade had them both acting as if she was already theirs. Not that they had any intentions of claiming her. No, he didn't intend to claim anyone.

Settling down was for men who had more vanilla tastes. What woman dreamed of having to put up with two men with their tastes in the bedroom for the long term? Sure, there were plenty of women willing and eager to join them for a night or occasionally several nights on the dark side. But after the initial thrill of walking on the edge wore off, they all wanted a single someone who they could be proud to take home to the family.

What he enjoyed in the bedroom wasn't something he was willing to give up in the long term. Not only the BDSM, but sharing with Hannibal. When he was alone with a woman, he felt like he needed to be on guard. His voyeuristic tendencies weren't the only reason he enjoyed sharing women with his Brother. It was the ability to trust that between the two of them, not only would the woman be satisfied, but that there was a second person there to keep them safe so he could let go of some of his natural wariness.

Hearing a woman scream from pleasure with a bite of pain was intoxicating. The absolute surrender and trust in her eyes fed a necessary part of him. Watching as their partners gave over and allowed the two of them to push past the edge of what they thought they could endure, an almost addiction.

Hannibal was the only man he trusted to be at his side in moments like that. In the Rangers, Ink had been the one to watch out for his Brother. As a spotter, he was the one to make sure that they never got in too deep or were taken by surprise. But in the bedroom, their roles reversed.

Hannibal never lost himself in the moment. The hyper aware senses he had learned as a sniper took in every detail and he often knew long before Ink did if their partner was in trouble. It sometimes bothered him knowing that his Cajun Brother would have probably settled down with a nice woman if it wasn't for Ink's need to share.

Ink pulled his thoughts back to the present. "I don't think so. Her mood changed faster than a jackrabbit in the brush."

Hannibal nodded to where Jade was now rushing up the steps to the office. Her smaller legs didn't even seem to strain as she took them two steps at a time. It was hard to see Jade's expression, but the way the woman's body radiated fury set off alarm bells in his head.

Ink started walking towards the Old Ladies, who were making their way slowly out of the building. "Let's make sure the women are off and see what's got our little Jade all worked up."

Ink waited at the entrance door of the gym to make sure they could get back into the building while Hannibal walked the women out to their SUVs. Decaf gave him a chin lift as he followed the women's cars as they drove out of the parking lot. It was a comfort knowing they would be guarded all the way home. Some people would have called it paranoid, but he called it good sense.

A red Ferrari GTB was now parked in the lot that hadn't been there when they had arrived. The expensive car looked completely out of place. Not only because it was too high end for the area, but because with plenty of other spaces available, the owner had parked diagonally across the handicapped spots.

Hannibal gestured to the sports car. "Looks like she's got company."

Ink nodded, and they both headed back into the building.

Almost immediately after they cleared the front entry, they could hear shouts coming from inside.

"This is my business, too. If I want to take cash from the safe, I can!" Anger was obvious in the unfamiliar male voice.

"No, Eric, you can't." Jade's clipped voice matched the volume of the other speaker. "As of the contract you signed two months ago, you are only a twenty percent stakeholder, not an owner. That means you get your checks every month for your portion of the profit. You do not get to use this place as your personal piggy bank anymore."

"Get off your fucking high horse, Jade. This place wouldn't exist without me. You had no right to change the safe combination. The deposit you put in my account last week was a joke!"

"That's because I took out the money you stole from the safe last month."

Ink glanced over at Hannibal, his lips tight with anger. There was obviously a lot of history between these two, and it sounded like things were escalating quickly.

"Can't steal what's mine. That's not how a business works."

"You signed the contract when you sold me back thirty percent of the business. You no longer have the right to access anything but the financial reports and monthly dividends."

"How the hell am I supposed to live on that bullshit number?" The man, Eric's, voice held equal parts anger and whine.

He and Hannibal reached the top of the stairs. By unspoken agreement, they paused to listen. Ink was pretty sure he should feel guilty about listening in on a private conversation. But the man's angry tone and ridiculous demands pissed him off.

Owning your own business was hard work and could

easily crumble if not handled correctly. It had taken months and help from their more business minded Dark Sons Brothers for Hannibal and him to get the finances of Dark Ink under control. How much harder would it have been if they both hadn't been committed to making it work?

"You said you wanted out and I'm buying you out. That takes time." Jade's voice was tired. This was obviously not a new argument.

"I need money now." Eric's words were tight as if spoken through gritted teeth.

"What the hell did you do, Eric?"

"That's none of your business."

"It is my business if you're trying to come in here and rob the place again."

"It's not stealing! I'm taking what's mine." The man's deep breath was audible even through the closed door. "I need another $1,000 Jade."

"No. I'm not doing this again. You will get more money next month."

The loud crash of something being thrown against the wall had both him and Hannibal moving. They opened the office door and stepped quickly into what was a small office. Jade stood stunned behind the desk. At their entrance, the man, Eric had spun to face them. A computer was lying on the floor along with scattered paperwork and a toppled chair.

Eric was a lanky, blond man who stood slightly over six-feet tall. Anger and a wild sense of desperation danced in his eyes as he loomed over Jade. She stood with her back against the wall, arms crossed with an expression of fury on her face. Both of them now stared at Hannibal and Ink.

"Who the fuck are you?" Eric snarled.

Hannibal got a lazy smile on his face that Ink knew meant trouble. His Brother had an extreme dislike of bullies, especially ones who thought they could use their size to intimidate women. If this prick pushed too hard, neither of them would hesitate to push back.

"We're friends of Jade's. And we don't appreciate you trashing her office." Hannibal's Louisiana accent was thick, showing how angry he was.

It was a southern thing. Ink knew, he did it himself. The angrier the two of them were, the thicker their accents got. Their speech slowing and full of fake cordiality.

"Bullshit. Jade doesn't have any friends I don't know about."

"Reckon you're out of the loop. Maybe she stopped sharing when you started stealing from her," Ink taunted.

Eric's face went red and his fists clenched. "This is my business, and I can do what the fuck I want. Now get out of here."

Ink had to give it to the guy. He had a set of brass balls on him. The man might be tall, but he had a lanky, slim build. When faced with Hannibal's bulk, most men lost their spine. When faced with both of them dressed in their motor-cycle club cuts, his attitude was reckless. The idiot wasn't even smart enough to know when he was out of his weight class.

Ink took a moment to look at Jade. Her face seemed to teeter between embarrassment and anger.

"Is that what you want, darlin'? You want us to leave?"

She took a deep breath and crossed her arms. "Eric was just leaving, Ink."

"No, I wasn't. Wait…" The guy snorted with laughter. "Ink. This guy is Ink?" The man looked between the two of them. "Let me guess, that's Hannibal. These are the guys you are always panting over. Isn't it? That's priceless."

Ink made sure he hid his inner smile at knowledge that this woman talked about them. So Jade panted over them?

They would have to find out how deep this beautiful woman's fantasies went. But that could wait until after they got rid of the dickhead.

Jade's face blushed a lovely shade of red. "Get out, Eric. You got your check last week. Your next check will come next month. That is all you are getting out of me."

"Until you buy me out completely, Jade, this is still my place. And I want my money available now."

Ink had had enough. It was easy to see from this asshole's body language Eric had no intention of leaving on his own. Hannibal moved and Ink shadowed him. They both closed in on the guy.

"The lady said leave," Hannibal growled.

The guy looked between the two of them and finally seemed to realize he was at the disadvantage. Eric stood straighter and puffed up his chest. The move was comical, seeing as he was facing off against Hannibal. His Brother was a giant of a man who many described as a tank. It would take very little effort for either of them to make it so the guy didn't ever walk again, let alone threaten Jade.

"You try anything I'll call the cops."

Ink snorted. "If you think the cops would stop us from doing anything, you're sadly mistaken, little boy."

"What did you call me?" The look Eric shot him was probably supposed to be intimidating, but it didn't even ruffle his feathers. He knew men like this. Men who thought their size meant they were important or scary. Idiots who thought the world owed them something. When, in reality, they were simply pieces of shit.

Ink smirked. If this man got sensitive about a man ten years his senior calling him boy, then all the better. "I suggest you do what the little lady's said and get out, because me and my Brother here would love to show you where the door's at, the hard way."

The man glared at the two of them. It was obvious he knew this wasn't a fight he could win, but he didn't want to leave. He looked back at Jade and seemed to deflate. "I need the money. You don't understand."

Jade's shoulders slumped, and she shook her head. "No, I do understand. I understood last month and the month before, and the month before that. This time, though, I'm not giving in. Get out yourself or get taken out."

Ink was proud that not only didn't she cave under the pressure, but she had given them permission to help.

Eric's angry gaze hit each of them a few more times before he said, "Fine. This isn't over."

Hannibal and Ink didn't block the man as he stormed out of the office. They heard him stomping down the stairs, like a child having a tantrum. They watched through the windows of the office as he made it through the building until the front door clicked behind him.

The silence in the office was still tense, as he and Hannibal turned back to look at Jade. She had her chin up and her eyes were bright, as if she was daring them to question her. But he and his Brother had patience she couldn't imagine.

Silence was nothing to the two men who had spent days waiting for a target without uttering a single word. Slowly her bravado seemed to slip and her shoulders slumped.

As always, Hannibal was the first to act, knowing exactly what to do. Ink watched as he opened his arms to her. Much to his surprise, Jade stepped around the desk and folded herself against the big man's chest. As if needing the affection, the comfort he offered. Ink watched, not sure if they were doing the right thing.

What the hell had they gotten themselves into?

Chapter 7

Some days you just need a hug, on the butt, with a paddle.

Jade

There is no greater reality check than having all of your dirty laundry aired in front of two men you've secretly idolized for years. Jade didn't know why she'd accepted Hannibal's offer of a hug. But wrapped in his arms, it was like everything from the last year came crashing down on her at once. He held her while she gave in to all the emotions that had been locked away for months.

She was a world-class athlete, a businesswoman who was succeeding despite all the shit her partner was throwing at her. In that moment, none of it mattered. All she wanted to do was lose herself in the warmth of the arms of a man she'd met less than two hours ago. How screwed up was that?

She couldn't even stop the tears flowing down her cheeks. She was tired. Tired of having to stand strong. Tired of having to make all the decisions. Tired of having no one on her side but herself.

It took a few minutes, but she managed to wrangle in all the emotions. Push them back. Down into the mental boxes where she kept them normally stored. She stepped back and wiped her cheeks with her fingers. The disappointment at how easily Hannibal let her go was silly.

"I'm sorry you had to see that."

Hannibal's hand came up and lightly brushed against her cheekbone. It was ridiculous, but the thought that he was wiping away the last of her tears was a more intimate action than kissing him had been earlier. Not as exciting, but more personal.

"It's not our business, *cher*. But if you want to tell us what that was all about, we'd be pleased to listen."

If Hannibal's face had held pity, she probably would have clammed up. But there was no trace of that in his face or voice. Only an interested concern. She looked over at Ink. His face was a closed off mask. What did he think of her?

These men were a mystery. It was interesting, she would have thought the sweet-looking cowboy would have been the gentle, comforting one. Instead, it was the big bruiser. She shouldn't share her problems with people she'd just met, especially ones whom she had hoped to seduce at one point.

But the truth was she didn't have anyone in her life whom she could share these problems with. Her mother had died a few years ago from cancer and her father had been distant since her parents' divorce when she was a child. She didn't have any siblings. The few friends she'd made while she was on the Parkour circuit had all dried up when she had stopped competing.

She hadn't even known Eric was bad-mouthing her to their old friends until recently. The sad fact was he had been her only close friend for so many years and she didn't even know how to get new ones.

Why not share? It's not like it could hurt anything except her chances of being in the middle of a Hannibal and Ink sandwich. They had been flirting pretty hardcore earlier. But after they saw what a mess her life was, they would probably want nothing to do with her.

The men were gorgeous, successful artists and businessmen who belonged to the largest motorcycle club in Denver. They probably had women throwing themselves at them. Would they have really wanted more than a night with her?

From what she could tell, they had lots of loyal friends. Would they even want to be with her once after this? Hell, everything she'd learned about them was garnered off of social media. So who the hell knew what was the truth? But they were offering to listen, and she needed someone to talk to. Maybe it would be better to gain them as friends than one shot lovers.

"Eric and I have been best friends since childhood. When I got pulled off of the Olympic Gymnastics team because of a knee injury. He was there for me." Memories of the dark depression that had settled over her were something she fought with still. Her best friend had dragged her back into life, kicking and screaming. Showed her that there was something other than gymnastics that she could be good at. "When we turned eighteen, we decided to try our hand at the Parkour Warriors circuit. I don't know if you watch that show, but we were a pretty big deal for a while. We had lots of sponsors, enough that we both made a pretty good living."

Though not at first. For over a year, the two of them had lived out of a van scrounging for side jobs and barely able to feed themselves. When the show gained popularity, everything changed. It was hard to explain how crazy they had gone spending the money they earned at first, like it would keep coming in forever. Eric still believed that he could get back to that place where people dumped money on them to show up and support an event.

"I've heard of the show," Hannibal said. "Now that I know you are on it, I'll have to go back and watch."

"I think you can get most of the episodes for free on the internet now. Anyway, a few years ago, I decided I wanted to settle down. I knew the fame and money wouldn't last and I wanted something stable. Eric said he wanted to support my dream. So we went 50/50 on this business."

"I thought he only owned twenty percent?" Ink asked.

"That's all he owns now." Jade laughed, even though it wasn't funny. She wished she could go back in time and take out the loans so that this place hadn't ruined their friendship. "It only took a month or two for him to realize that my dream was not his dream." How could she explain the care-free spirit that her friend had been? "He likes life on the road. The wildness and the excitement of traveling and meeting new people every month was perfect for him. Settling down in one place hasn't really worked out for him."

"It seems like more than a case of wanderlust. If he needs more money, he should sell that car of his," Hannibal said.

"Oh, what was he driving this time?" Jade shook her head. "Doesn't matter. He doesn't own it. One of his few regular gigs is as a spokesman for a car dealership. He sweet talks them into letting him drive some of their top end inventory in return for doing social media on the car each week till it sells."

Ink raised a disbelieving eyebrow. "They let him drive a

car worth over three-hundred-thousand dollars so he can post pictures of it?"

"You'd be surprised how many people will buy an expensive car because someone supposedly famous drove it and raves about it."

It baffled her as well, but she had seen the truth of it too many times to ignore. She had never been big on social media herself, preferring to look at others instead of promoting herself. Eric had been the one to handle that end of everything.

"So he's been taking money from you?" Hannibal's displeasure at her friend's actions wasn't unwarranted, but she wanted to explain.

"Since I stopped touring with him, the sponsorships have dwindled off. Together, we were unique. My story of being an Olympic competitor and him helping me find another outlet, something they could market. Alone, he's one guy among many. There are lots of younger, better competitors starting the sport every day. It's only been recently that he has turned bitter. We got an offer on the land, the building and the business about six months ago. And Eric wanted to take it. I had no interest. I mean, the offer was good. But it wasn't enough for me to start again by myself."

"What did he do?" Ink asked.

"The partnership contract we drew up said that we both had to agree to sell the business. So there wasn't much he could do. He was pissed. I felt guilty but not enough to give up on this place. So I took what little savings I had, and I started buying out his half. Every month I buy a little more, but it's going to take another couple months before I can fully buy him out of the business at the rate we set."

"He didn't seem to want to wait." Ink's observation was the truth. Eric hadn't been happy with her, but he had been willing to wait. At least at first.

"A couple months ago, he started taking money out of the safe without asking. I wouldn't figure it out till I went to reconcile the next day. The first time I let it slide. Asked him about it. He apologized and said he had a sponsorship fall through and he needed travel money." She'd believed it to be a one-time thing and let it go. "Then it kept happening. He stopped even bothering with explanations. The last contract I had him sign, when I bought more shares, clearly outlined that he no longer had access rights to the working capital. So a couple weeks ago, I got the safe combination changed."

"And he discovered that tonight." Hannibal's smile was pleased.

"Yes, I guess the extra money I gave him to buy more shares and the dividend check ran out. I have an accountant sign off on the amount he gets so that there can be no argument that he is getting his fair share. I hadn't seen him in those few weeks. I'd hoped he was off finding another way to bring in money, but when I saw the light on up here earlier, I knew it was him." She remembered the fear and anger at seeing the light on when she clearly remembered turning it off before coming down. She wasn't sure if it was a good or bad thing that it had interrupted whatever had been happening between her and these men. "He can't get the money anymore, but I wasn't sure what he would do once he figured that out."

Ink scowled. "Why didn't you tell us? We would have come up here with you."

Jade laughed at the serious expressions on the men's faces. "We met less than an hour ago and I'm supposed to say, what? 'Hey guys, we've been flirting pretty hard and I think my business partner is upstairs about to flip out. You look big and burly, want to come be my backup?'"

She didn't think it was possible, but Hannibal looked

even more upset than when he had burst into the room earlier. "We would have done that."

They both looked deadly serious. She smiled, glad they weren't looking at her like she was crazy. "I think you would have, but I wasn't comfortable asking you to." Jade took a deep breath and admitted, "I am glad you came up. He's never been that aggressive before. He's never physically gotten violent. Smashing the stuff on the desk isn't like him." The doubtful looks on their faces forced a bit more honesty out of her. "Yes, he can be an asshole, but I'm used to that. Maybe I should have given him the money."

Guilt pricked at her conscience. Eric had always been there for her emotionally. Did she need to be more understanding?

"If he needs money that bad, he could come in and work like you do." Ink obviously had no sympathy for her old friend.

She nodded, not able to argue the sentiment. "I offered, we have several people who would happily pay for individual lessons from him. But he said he's too busy. I can't help but worry. Our friendship has deteriorated over the last six months and I honestly don't know what's going on in his life. We don't talk anymore."

"Were the two of you an item in the past?" Hannibal asked.

"No, though he wanted to be." Jade shrugged. "I never saw him that way. The TV liked to paint us as a couple, though. And I kept my mouth shut for the sake of marketing. He's not the type of man I'm attracted to."

"And what type of man is that?" Ink stepped closer. She had slowly been leaning against her desk in an attempt to create distance. In this small office with these two men, that wasn't really possible.

"I like my men with a bit more ink." Both men laughed

and seemed surprised by her attempt to lighten the conversation.

"Is that so?" Hannibal traced his fingers up her arm, his voice dark with suggestion. She wasn't sure if the shivers that ran up her spine were from his words or his gentle touch. "You're playing with fire, Jade."

The conversation had taken a quick turn, she didn't mind. Worrying about her dissolving friendship was hard and drained her emotionally. Flirting with these two men, while outrageous and almost surreal, was something that made her feel empowered. "I've been known to take a few risks."

She looked down, blushing at her blatant offer. People on the Parkour circuit and here at the gym all marveled at the risky stunts she was willing to attempt. Truth was, she was never happier than she was when she was pushing herself to her limits. Her body, her mind, all of it.

It wasn't the adrenaline so much as the freedom she found when she was trying to do something that didn't allow her to be anything but present in the moment. Whether it was racing across the rooftop doing flips and tricks, or climbing an impossible mountain and hanging on by the tips of her fingers. That was another thing Eric didn't understand. How she could love pushing herself like that, but not want the spotlight or the attention.

How for her it wasn't the rush, but the pure focus of pushing yourself to your absolute limit. Knowing that each time she could go a little bit further, do a little bit more. Mentally, she had never competed with other people. That wasn't the point of it all for her. It was about being in competition with herself. However, she had never taken those kinds of risks with a man.

"Just how wild are you willing to get?" Ink pushed her

hair behind her ear, his finger catching slightly. "Think carefully before you answer."

It took little thought. Reckless as it might seem, she knew she would regret it if she didn't experience what these men were offering. "Well, apparently I'm willing to offer myself to two men I met only an hour ago because I like their artwork."

Hannibal's chuckle was like warm velvet against her skin. "Is that all you like about us? Our art?"

Her cheeks heated. "No. I like the packaging too."

The two men exchanged a look that had her insides heating. Hannibal nodded and turned her to face him. "I'm gonna get real with you, *cher*. What my Brother and I like is not what you would call vanilla."

She couldn't help but laugh. Her mind was racing at all the distinct possibilities. She'd had partners try different things with her. Some of them even tried dominating her. The idea of a man taking control turned her on, but she hadn't found one who could pull it off. She thought over their interactions so far and felt herself grow wet at the idea of these two men doing things she had only read about to her body.

"Two bad ass men who obviously like to share. I wasn't thinking we were going to be lying down in a bed of roses."

Ink nipped at her ear. The sharp bite seemed to travel right down to her clit. "Darlin', sharing you is the most vanilla part of what we like. How much do you know about BDSM? Do you have any of those naughty books hidden away somewhere?"

Jade's heart raced and her nipples tightened almost painfully. Her e-reader was overflowing with stories about BDSM. The fictional men in those books had fueled almost as many fantasies as these men had when she stalked them on social media. The ability of the women in those stories to give over control sounded amazing. But could that ever happen to her?

Her past lovers had been good enough, but outside a slap on the ass or two, none of them had been particularly creative. Her fantasies fell on the spicy side of the spectrum. Since she was usually single, she had an extensive collection of toys ranging from the basic to exotic to help make her solo adventures worthwhile.

She cleared her throat. "I might have read about it."

Hannibal's breath skimmed along her other ear. "Are you a dirty girl?"

She blushed and fought the urge to look down at the ground. Focus was so hard with these men surrounding her, causing her imagination to run wild. A small jolt of nerves warred with her desire to jump in with both feet.

Jade needed to push herself if she was ever going to experience, even once, some of the things she'd dreamed about. She didn't believe for one moment that these men would be interested in making a long-term commitment, but maybe, if she played her cards right, she would be able to tick off a few of her fantasies before they got tired and moved on.

"I've never considered two men. But I think that's because my imagination was severely lacking." She gasped as her arms were pulled behind her back. The urge to struggle was overwhelming, and she pulled against Ink's tight grip. A strange sense of peace poured over her at the knowledge she couldn't move.

She arched back and looked up into Ink's eyes. They showed desire, strength, and the ultimate knowledge that he had her trapped. Hannibal's eyes held a wicked gleam as his gaze took in her body. She settled into the embrace and her pussy clenched, wanting more.

"I think you'll like that, Jade," desire filling Hannibal's

words with a growl. "If you've read the dirty books, you know about the stoplight system." She nodded and Ink pulled her arms tighter.

He leaned his body against hers. The movement pressing her between them and stealing her breath. Her breasts throbbed against her tank top. The fabric of her bra rubbing against her nipples and causing a jolt of pleasure to shoot down to her core.

"Tell us what it is, use your words." Ink's voice rumbled through her chest and it took a moment for her to remember what he wanted to hear.

"Red means stop. Yellow, slow. Green, good. I'm so green right now I'm soaking my panties."

Hannibal's hands came up and cupped the undersides of her breasts. His thumbs ran slow, lazy strokes across the bottom swells. A jolt of pleasure caused her to buck when he flicked over the tips of her nipples.

"You're so green, what?" Ink's last word was almost a whisper.

Her brain struggled to function as Hannibal slowly moved back and forth over her tightened nipples with his thumb, and Ink somehow made his grip tighter. How did they expect her to think at a time like this? Inspiration struck, and she almost laughed, which would not have been a good idea.

Not wanting to ruin the moment, she answered, "So green, Sirs."

Ink's breath was hot on her neck. His voice rumbled against her throat. "That'll do for now. But when we really play, I prefer Master."

The statement should have been ridiculous. She was an independent woman, not someone's slave. Jade's body seemed to disagree as every part of her practically vibrated at the idea of these men controlling her to that extent. A sweet jolt of pain raced through her body as Ink bit her neck at the same time Hannibal pinched her nipples.

She groaned her pleasure, not sure if she should press back into Ink or forward into Hannibal. Eyes closed, she lost herself in the sensations as the two of them alternated between gentle caresses and quick flicks of pain. Back and forth they took her and Jade's core dampened. She tightened her thighs as her clit pulsed in time with the pressure on her nipples.

Her eyes shot open at a sharp sting to her thigh. "None of that, little Jewel. Your pleasure is at our command. You don't get to sneak and play with yourself." Jade didn't consider what she was doing as playing with herself, but Hannibal's words had her wanting to clench harder.

"Yes, Sir. Sorry, Sir." The words were so natural, like they could be nothing else but Sir in that moment.

Ink nipped her throat. "You don't know our rules yet, but I don't care. I want to punish that gorgeous bottom pressing so temptingly against my cock. Lean forward and place your hands around Hannibal's neck. Stick that ass out for me."

Her mind whirled as the grip on her arms released. Hannibal raised her arms until they stretched around his neck. How was she supposed to bend over? The man was almost a foot taller than her. Ink gripped her hips and pulled Jade backwards until she was stretched, but barely bent.

Hannibal winked. "She's not quite tall enough to make this work. He grabbed one of the two chairs in the room and sat down. Not letting her hands move from around his neck for even a moment. The position held them intimately close, face to face.

Bent at a ninety-degree angle her face next to Hannibal's and her ass out towards Ink. She licked her lips. As if he felt the same draw, Hannibal leaned in the last few inches and claimed her mouth with a fiery kiss. She felt Ink's hands on her shorts and soon cool air sent shivers up her spine as he pulled them down along with her underwear.

She moaned, loving the kiss and the exposed feeling of being half naked in her office. The anticipation of the spanking that was to come as much of a turn on as the man in front of her mouth. Pain didn't scare her. But not experiencing this would be something she regretted her whole life.

The first smack had her yelping, but it quickly morphed into a warm heat that she knew had her slowly dripping down her inner thighs. She moaned in frustration into Hannibal's mouth as light tap after tap landed on her ass. The blows were barely hard enough to give her the jolt of adrenaline that she'd expected.

Hannibal reached between them and scooped her breasts out over her bra and tank top so they were hanging down towards the ground. He began playing with both her nipples and his kiss grew rougher.

So did Ink's strokes. Finally, he was giving her what she wanted. None of it made sense in her head, but that didn't matter. She knew she wanted even more and would not try to puzzle out why.

Should she push back her ass, hoping he would pick up on her need for more? Or did she push forward and try to encourage Hannibal to play harder with her nipples? The pleasure built slowly, but not intense enough to push her over the edge of orgasm. She groaned and wondered if they were purposefully keeping her so close to the edge as torture.

Hannibal pulled back. An evil smile tipped his lips. "Problem?"

"More please." She wasn't sure exactly what she was asking for, but she wanted it. "Sirs, please."

The spark that flared in Hannibal's eyes gave her chills. "I think our little Jewel is saying you're going too light on her, Ink. She's dripping for you."

Ink's hand slipped between the folds of her pussy. There was no hiding how turned on she was. His finger brushed the edge of her clit and she bucked against his hand. If he would stop and focus there for a bit, she knew she would explode. His hand pulled away, and a blissful shock pulsed through her as he slapped her right on her pussy.

"Yes! Thank you, Sir."

Her cry was something almost animalistic. The next slap came down on her ass so hard she saw stars behind her eyes for a moment before the pain settled into a blissful heat. Her moans must have told them how she felt because his next slap matched the first.

Hannibal's grip on her breasts grew more brutal as he twisted her nipples. She squirmed and screamed, letting herself fall into the sensations. Every minute of it was Heaven. The men matched their rhythm in a dizzying frenzy. She couldn't anticipate the blows that came down on her thighs, ass, and clit. All rational thought fled before their coordinated attack.

Jade dug her nails into the back of Hannibal's shoulders and tried to hold back the orgasm that built in her core and filled up her insides. As the tidal wave of pain and pleasure morphed through her body in ways she had only imagined, she somehow knew she had to ask to come. She needed it so badly, but she couldn't even form the words to beg.

She whimpered and pushed against both of their hands, hoping they would understand just how desperate she was. It had been almost a year since she had an orgasm by anyone's hand but her own. She needed this release after the crap Eric had made of her day.

Jade needed them to chase away all her worries in a tidal wave of pleasure. Force all thoughts from her head and let her fly.

"I'm going to be kind, little Jewel." Ink's voice was a

grounding force in the swirl of emotions. "I'm gonna give you five slaps to your naughty pussy and then you can come. I want to hear you scream for us. Do you understand?"

"Yes, Sir." The words were a gasp between blows because he hadn't stopped peppering her ass with sharp little strikes. She moved her feet slightly wider apart to give him better access. Wanting to feel everything.

She barely fought back the orgasm as the first blow landed directly on her pussy and vibrated through to her clit. The wet sound was obscene, but the sting was so wonderful she didn't care. Jade was alive with sensation and vibrated with tension. The second strike sent stars shooting across her eyes. The third and fourth slaps were back to back and had her moaning. Not in pain, but in release.

Every emotion she held inside of her poured out through her primal groans. Before she could catch her breath. The fifth blow landed right on her clit. She teetered on the edge of orgasm, whimpering with need. She whined as his fingers rubbed between her lips on either side of her clit with an expert touch.

Ink's growl was like a sensual touch. "Come for me."

His fingers pinched either side of her clit as he bit down on her ass. She exploded into a shaking orgasm as Hannibal tightened his grip on her nipples.

She screamed for them.

Chapter 8

Fugglesnuck: Vb. When the snuggling and fucking is over and you're back to snuggling and thinking about sneaking in another quickie.

Hannibal

I t took all of Hannibal's focus not to come like an untried teen when Jade exploded into a bucking orgasm in his arms. He never could have imagined how perfect she was. The first time he and Ink played with a new woman, they were always careful to go slow. Testing their limits before pushing too hard and ruining the fun before it even began.

He had hoped she would be interested in exploring the kind of games they preferred. In his most optimistic thoughts about what they were going to do, he never considered what they had discovered. It was one thing to take a woman and slowly expose her to the beauty that was the pain and pleasure of BDSM. To take the time to watch her blossom under the control and freedom found under a skilled dominant's care.

But to discover Jade was an untried masochist, who had never explored even the smallest bite of pain in her sexual encounters, was a treasure. It had been obvious that their starting light touch had done nothing but frustrate her. When Ink had given her the hard warning slap, it was supposed to bring her back in line. Instead, she had melted under it.

The fire in his Brother's eyes as he let the leash go and stopped worrying about pushing her too far had been intense. It had been the perfect moment. His Brother unleashed, Jade lost in the ecstasy, and all three of them connected by pleasure. Paradise. Hannibal looked down at the beautiful woman and saw her pupils blown wide.

Jade's smile was floaty and her gaze, not tracking. Their little Jewel had found subspace on her first try. He stood up and gathered her into his arms. She cuddled instinctively against his chest.

They both knew play was over for the night. Sure, they could continue and she would, by all appearances, be willing. If they'd played before and discussed it in advance, they definitely would have. But it wasn't worth the risk.

The beautifully submissive woman had reached the point where consent was no longer possible. He didn't want to blow their chances of another night with Jade by pushing it too far. Hannibal looked around the office and there wasn't really a good place to sit them down. Ink and he locked gazes, and he nodded toward the door. They would have to take her downstairs to the comfortable matts.

Ink's expression was as gentle as it ever got. "I've got my aftercare kit in my saddlebags. I'll be right back."

Hannibal carried Jade down the stairs to the soft mats that were piled up in the corner. As he sat down, he arranged her on his lap so the least amount of pressure was being placed on her ass. A few minutes later, Ink returned with a fuzzy blanket, a couple of bottles of water, and a chocolate bar.

Hannibal raised his eyebrow as he took the items and wrapped the blissed out woman in the comforting blanket. Ink shrugged. "There's a vending machine in the lobby."

Hannibal smiled, realizing that his Brother had gone out of his way to ensure Jade had what she needed. There is no way a candy bar would survive any length of time in a saddlebag, so he'd sought out chocolate another way. Ink sat down next to them and moved her feet onto his lap. He stripped off her socks and shoes and slowly rubbed along her arches to help bring her slowly back from subspace.

The two of them had done this countless times. But something about bringing this beautiful woman back down to earth in a gentle way was special. Hannibal knew better than to say anything like that out loud. The man next to him had an absolute terror of getting serious with any woman.

He was the dreamer of their partnership, believing that someday they would find the perfect woman to complete them. Years of the women they played with scoffing at the idea of a long-term menage had taken its toll. But he didn't give up hope.

He wasn't ready to say that this woman in their laps was that one, but he thought she had the potential for more than a one-night stand. Hannibal rubbed Jade's back gently, enjoying the warm, small, feminine form in his arms.

The truth, he only admitted in the privacy of his own mind, was that he was ready to settle down. Constantly changing partners was exhausting and growing almost as old as they were. The thrill he had gotten from wild nights and new women had long since lost its luster.

Their last partner, Didi, had been their regular girl for almost a year. Unfortunately, even he had to admit there wasn't any sort of connection outside of the bedroom. When she had announced a couple months ago that she was moving back east, the parting hadn't even been sad. Honestly, all he had felt when she told them was exhaustion at the knowledge that they would have to dive back into the pool of random women.

Jade stirred. Her body going from the languid motions of someone flying high in subspace to the squirming movements of someone feeling their ass burn after a good spanking. Hannibal cracked open one of the waters and held it up to her lips. "Drink deep for me, little Jewel."

Her eyes fluttered open, and she didn't resist as he brought the water up to her mouth. After a few sips, he pulled it away. Jade flinched as she adjusted her position slightly and her ass brushed against his outer thigh.

"That was amazing." She groaned as Ink pushed his thumbs into the arches of her feet. "No. That feels amazing."

Ink chuckled. "You like that word?"

She tilted her head a bit. "What word? Amazing?" Her laugh turned into a groan as Ink continued to rub her feet. "Well, if the word fits I don't see why I need to pick another." Jade looked up at him and then over at Ink. "Amazing is a pretty perfect word to describe how I'm feeling."

Hannibal opened the chocolate bar and broke off a piece. "You should eat this."

She opened her mouth and chewed on the chocolate with a smile. "Not that I'm complaining, but why should I be eating chocolate?"

"It helps with sub drop."

"Sub drop, what's that?"

Hannibal fed her another piece of the chocolate. "After the endorphins of an intense scene start to wear off, subs can experience mood swings or a drop in emotions if you don't slowly ease them out of subspace."

"Hmm. So you send me flying, give me orgasms, and take nothing for yourself. And I get foot rubs, water, and chocolate after? I think I like this arrangement."

Hannibal couldn't hold back the laugh that burst out of his chest at her sassy words. "Glad to hear that."

Her fingers danced a lazy circle over his name patch on his cut. "So you don't want to…" her words trailed off.

He didn't like the uncertainty in her tone. Hannibal tilted her chin up, so he was looking her in the eye. "We want to. But we're not going to. Not tonight."

"But another night?" She looked away, as if afraid of the answer.

Ink tapped her foot, causing her body to shake a little. "There will definitely be another night. But I think we need to lay out the ground rules first."

The way Jade's nose scrunched up in confusion made him want to tap it. But instead he brought the water back up to her lips and made sure she drank some more before he continued. "We're gonna get all your contact info, Jewel. Then we're going to send you a limits list."

She jerked in surprise and winced. "A limits list? Is that really necessary?"

Her voice was small and almost scared. It was hard for him to remember that she was so new. To have this kind of relationship communication was essential, and he had found a limits and desires list to be essential. "Yes, it's a sort of contract that sets limits and expectations so that there's no confusion between the three of us as to what we all want."

"Oh, it seems so impersonal. Shouldn't we just see where this goes?"

"It's anything but impersonal." Hannibal teased as he rubbed her back in a soothing circle.

"What kinds of things are you talking about with expectations and limits?"

Hannibal enjoyed the fire that lit in Ink's eyes as he looked over at Jade. "It will spell out what we are and aren't allowed to do to your body, as well as what things you want us to do to your body. It will also tell you the kinds of things we want you to do with us."

Her pulse raced against Hannibal's skin and her breath quickened. The way her still exposed nipples tightened showed she wasn't as averse to the idea as her words implied.

"No other men except us." Hannibal's words held a demand that surprised even him. They usually shared their women with anyone and everyone who was interested. But there was something about the brunette in his arms that brought out a new possessive side.

Ink's raised eyebrows showed his surprise, but after a moment his Brother nodded. It was easy to see that they were going to be having a long conversation once they were alone. Hannibal rarely made unilateral decisions for the two of them. Making this one was a risk. The request for exclusivity might end up being the sticking point that sealed the failure of the relationship before it ever began. Not because she wouldn't agree, but because the implied commitment would send Ink running.

"No other women for you?"

Hannibal nodded, but Ink's shrug was tight. He glared at his long-time friend. Luckily, Jade didn't see his glare before his Brother grudgingly said, "No other woman for us either. But your orgasms belong to us. You don't get to come. Unless one of us says you can."

The little squeak she gave was adorable, and he didn't think she knew she had made it. The way her thighs tightened told them how much she liked the idea. "Even at home, by myself?"

Her question was so innocent Hannibal had to shake his

head. "If you want to play with that pretty little pussy and we're not there. You have to call one of us to get permission."

"Okay."

Hannibal knew what he was about to say was pushing the line so hard it might break. There was one thought, though, that had been playing over in his thoughts from the moment he saw her glistening pussy, so he couldn't resist the temptation to ask. "Are you on birth control, Beautiful?"

Both Ink and Jade gave him surprised looks. His Brother's was tinged with anger and hers with wariness.

"Yes." The word was drawn out, filled with hesitation. So Hannibal forced himself to temper what he was going to say next.

"I wanted to know our options and risks." He paused and didn't see a delicate way to state what he wanted, so he powered through. "If this gets serious. I'd like us all to get tested."

The quiet of the room was absolute, though he could almost feel Ink's anger vibrating through him. They'd never gone bare with any woman in the decade-plus they had been sharing.

Jade's body danced with tension. "I'll think about it. At some point, maybe."

Hannibal let out his breath in a sigh. His Brother was going to have harsh words with him later. Birth control was one-hundred-percent required and long ago, they'd both agreed not to risk trusting a woman to be the one responsible for their primary form of protection. Ink trusted no-one and children were not something they'd been ready for.

None of the old arguments kept him from wanting to be able to fuck this woman with nothing between them. His dick was so hard from just the possibility that he was pretty sure the zipper was going to leave an impression on it for several days.

"That's all I ask." For now, at least.

Jade shook her head and smiled. "I'm starting to think you're the optimist." She nodded her chin at Ink. "And he's the pessimist."

"He's something all right." Ink's words were an annoyed growl. Thankfully, that was all he said.

Hannibal tried to appease them both by giving them a partial truth. "I'm the planner. I like knowing all the options. I can't wait until you fill out your limits list, so I can start planning all the dirty things we are going to do to your body."

Hannibal enjoyed her shudder. Ink's body next to him was as stiff as stone, not distracted at all by his attempt to lighten the mood. Hopefully, his last question and the risk Hannibal had taken to push for exclusivity would be worth it in the end. The last thing he wanted was Ink throwing on the brakes before they got to explore any of the possibilities he saw so clearly with this beautiful woman.

Hannibal knew in his gut that this woman was worth taking all the risks for.

Chapter 9

It's okay if you disagree with me. I can't force you to be right.

Ink

Two days of uncomfortable silence were about his limit. Ink sat at the bar in the Dark Sons' Clubhouse sipping Jack Daniels, contemplating if he should strangle his Brother in his sleep. The argument after leaving Jade's gym had been one for the record books. This was the longest the two of them had stayed mad at each other in ten years. It was his fault, not the argument, but the fact it was still unresolved.

Two days was all he had left to get over his frustration at Hannibal's high-handed declarations of commitment. Then Jade was scheduled to come to their house. He had to decide if he was willing to live up to the level of commitment Hannibal had implied, or if he needed to lay down his own truth. It wasn't that he didn't want to see the woman again. His fantasies were running wild at the idea of introducing her to their private playroom, and it would be a shame not to try out at least a few of the toys. He'd been jerking off so often to images of her in his mind that it felt like he was a teenager again.

The idea of finally getting a taste of that beautiful treasure stirred something inside him. He needed to figure out how to let go of the anger. Why had Hannibal pushed so hard? The exclusivity thing should have bothered him, but the truth was, it didn't. It was the rest of it he wasn't ready for, and it wasn't fair to even pretend that he was.

Going bareback was something he'd never even considered with a woman. It meant something above and beyond the ability to fuck without latex. Trusting that a woman didn't lie about birth control, that it would work or, if it didn't, committing to becoming a Father. Christ, he couldn't even begin to consider that.

His own father was an alcoholic asshole who loved to use his fists. Ink had inherited his temper. He channeled his desires into consensual BDSM play, but that didn't make him any less of an asshole. If kids and settling down were what Hannibal wanted, was it time to tell his Brother he was on his own?

If he was a good man, he'd let him go and find his own happily ever after. Ink tried to picture it. Could he watch as Hannibal and Jade grew closer together while he stood back? His knuckles popped, and he realized he had been gripping the glass so hard that it was on the verge of cracking.

No, he wasn't willing to not be part of the sweet sounds she made as she fell apart under his hands. He might not be ready to settle down, but he definitely wasn't ready to let her go. What the fuck had changed? Hannibal had always been the one making sure they took things slow. Ensured that whoever they were with understood they were liked but not loved, so things didn't get messy.

His calm patience was the primary quality that made the

man one of the best snipers around. He didn't rush. One time in the Rangers, the two of them had sat in the same position for over seventy-one hours. Hannibal was the one who didn't twitch, even when Ink had been sure he was going to die of boredom.

Ink was supposed to be the one who had to be reined in. The one with impulse control and a temper, while Hannibal acted as his safety net. He was not supposed to jerk the net away and leave his partner dangling, not knowing what to do.

It wasn't even that he'd asked about getting tested that bothered him so much. The way Hannibal had snapped at him when they'd gotten back to their house meant his Brother was more invested in Jade than he had ever been in another woman. Ink had been ready for a quick argument about not discussing things first that would have landed them back on solid ground. Before he could even say anything to call his Brother out for going off script, Hannibal had snapped, *'It's not like I asked you to put our patch on her back, Ink! Grow up, get over your issues because I'm not in the mood to hear them.'*

The shouted words were a slap to his face, and he'd lost his shit. He couldn't remember a single time his Brother had shouted at him in their entire friendship. Their arguments were always with him shouting and Hannibal patiently calming him down.

Ink took another sip of his drink, and let the burn ease down his throat. The front door to the Clubhouse swung open. Feminine laughter filled the room as several of the Old Ladies practically danced into the room. They were all dressed in workout gear. Highdive following them, looking like he had survived a prolonged battle. The expression was all too familiar since every Brother had worn a similar one at least once after being on protection duty for the Old Ladies.

He hid a smile behind his drink. They must have come

from Jade's gym. Had his girl put the Marine through one of her courses? The Enforcer for the Club wouldn't like being shown up, especially not by a tiny thing like Jade. But he would have put up with it for the sake of the crazy women under his protection.

He loved his Club. The Dark Sons were a brotherhood of trust. They would always have his back. A group of men brought together because of their common belief in a cause bigger than themselves. Each one of them had served their country in one way or another and found when they came back that civilian life was no longer to their liking.

Ink had been one of the founding members of the Denver chapter. Joining up with Hannibal because he wanted a set of good men at his back. Ones he could trust. They'd helped him and Hannibal start their business and seen it thrive and succeed. They partied at each other's sides, and had been through wild and dangerous times together.

Over the last couple of years, some of the Brothers had settled down with Old Ladies. While there were still wild times and the loyalty of his Brothers was unswerving, these women had given something new to the Club. A poet would call it a soul, or a grounding influence that balanced them all out.

Not a single one of those women tried to hold their men back. Instead, they acted like an anchor in the storm and gave them all something to protect, something to fight for. 'It's not like I asked to put our patch on her back.' Hannibal's words echoed in his head.

Was his partner ready to find his own anchor? Could he settle? If it wasn't for the fact that he never planned to be a father, maybe he might consider it. If the woman was anything like these ladies. He needed to get on the same page as his Brother and he didn't know how.

"I'm so glad I went with you this time! Did you see her

on the Salmon Ladder?" Cheryl, Deep's Old Lady fanned her face. "Seriously, that was the sexiest thing I've seen in a long time. If I wasn't married to Deep, I would so be trying to get in her pants."

Val's musical laughter rang across the room. "Who are you kidding, girl? Deep wouldn't mind if you got in her pants. But I think she has her sights set on double trouble."

Ink turned around and raised his eyebrow at the women as they walked by. It was a poorly kept secret that the Old Ladies called him and Hannibal double trouble, but they usually tried to hide it. He could only guess that the 'her' they were talking about was Jade.

"I reckon you ladies had fun at Jade's gym?" He sometimes played up his good ol' boy roots around these women just to see them smile.

"Yes," Val said and winked. "We had more fun than a kid at a county fair. Highdive tried to race Jade on the Salmon ladder."

"Salmon ladder?" Ink looked over at his Brother.

The Sergeant at Arms shook his head, his amused frustration plain on his face. "It's like a pullup bar on steroids. You have to hop the steel bar up the ladder."

Now that he heard the description, Ink was pretty sure he knew what they were talking about. "I'm guessing it's not as easy as it looks?"

Highdive shook his head and gestured for a drink of his own.

Pixie giggled. "She beat him almost as bad as she beat you and Hannibal. We are hooked on that place. If she can teach us how to do half of what she did today, I'll be happy. You are having so much fun you don't even notice you are working out till your body feels like jelly."

Cami bumped her hip. "Amen to that. So much more f-fun than lifting and running. Have you and Hannibal started your t-training sessions with her yet?" The woman's devious smile was dangerous, so Ink ignored the question.

He turned his attention to Pixie. A question had been bothering him for the last few days. "Why did you use your marker to get us over there? It's not like you needed to get leverage with Jade for something."

Pixie's eyes held a mischievous glint. It was hard to remember that behind her innocent looks was a very devious woman. "Any woman who talks about a man with that level of excitement in her voice deserves a chance to see if the reality can live up to the fantasy."

He had almost forgotten that Jade had said she was a fan of their tattoos. It was easy to forget details like that when his brain constantly replayed the image of her shattering under his touch. What had she said to provoke the interfering instinct in Pixie?

"What did she say?"

"Looking to get your ego stroked?" Pixie teased.

Val laughed. "I don't think it's his ego he wants stroked."

"Never mind." Ink shook his head and turned back to the bar, knowing engaging would only lead to more trouble. The Old Ladies' laughter as they walked away made him question his own sanity.

Highdive sat down next to him and sighed, probably imagining the good-natured ribbing he was going to endure.

"Hey, Brother. They are in fine form today." Ink decided not to tease, since he had been beaten by the woman as well.

"That they are."

Highdive's role as Enforcer for the Club meant he appeared distant at times. Having to be the one to enforce rules inside and out of the Club wasn't something Ink envied. While the other Brothers formed close relationships, his friend was forced to stand on the outside. The feeling of isolation among such a close group had to be difficult.

Because of mutual interests outside of Club business, they had grown close. They spent a lot of time together at the local BDSM club. Highdive was a master of Shibari and had taught him and Hannibal the basics of the art of rope bondage. The ways his Brother could tie up a woman were beautiful and often pleasurable for whoever he chose to be his sub for a night.

His brother's body was tight, and it was unlikely to be the result of spending a few hours on guard duty. "What's on your mind?"

Highdive took a deep breath. "You're going to be hooking up with Jade again."

The man's words were a statement, not a question. He wondered if she had mentioned it and why that would cause his Brother stress. Did Highdive want Jade for himself? Ink's muscles clenched as a wave of territorial anger spiraled up from the darker parts of his soul.

"We are. How did you know?"

"Her gym is the Old Ladies new interest. So, we're tapped into her security. She only has cameras in the main gym, but Hannibal carried her down missing some pieces of clothing."

Anger and relief simmered in a strange mix in his stomach for a minute. Highdive didn't want Jade. Knowing they were invading her privacy like that bothered him. He took a sip of his drink and fought back the unreasonable feelings.

It only made sense. The Dark Sons were protective of their women. If Ink had taken a minute to think about it, he would have realized that his Brothers would have already done everything in their power to make sure the place was safe. Hacking into her security and computer systems would have been the least they would do.

"Is us seeing her a problem for the Club?"

Highdive took a long drink. His hesitation raked along Ink's nerves. "I don't like to interfere, but I'm not sure you want to get wrapped up with her mess."

Ink finished his drink and pushed the glass away. "What's that supposed to mean? Exactly."

"The place is safe enough for the ladies to go visit, get their workout, and leave. Jade's another story."

What could the little bundle of gorgeous submission be involved in that would cause his Brother to not only hesitate but bend the rules to tell Ink about it? "That's not enough to go on." He tried for levity. "What is she, a secret cannibal?"

"No. She's as straight and narrow as a woman can be."

"Then what?"

"That partner of hers, he's in a mess pretty deep."

"What kind of mess? What kind of blowback are we talking about?"

After meeting the guy, it wasn't hard to imagine the fucker getting himself into a mess. Entitled assholes believed the world owed them something and never looked too closely at any deals that came their way. When their mistakes came back to bite them, they would blame everything and everyone but themselves.

"If it is only the women going there and having fun? The worst blowback on the Club is that the place goes under and we have some disappointed women."

"And for Jade?" He shouldn't be worried about her already, but he was. He didn't want to see her lose her dream because of some bad choices she had nothing to do with.

"The man's up to his eyeballs in all sorts of debt. Both with the banks and alternative lending sources. She probably doesn't know he's used the business as collateral with some people who won't care if he doesn't legally have the right to do so."

"That man's slicker than a slop jar and she doesn't know it."

"Yeah. He's got a gambling problem, and your woman bails him out every time."

"Not my woman." The response was instinct, but if she was in trouble, he wouldn't be able to stop himself from getting involved.

"Of course not." Highdive snorted. "Guess you don't need to hear the rest then."

Ink growled and glared. "Tell me."

"The rumors say his non-traditional debt has expanded to an uncomfortable level and they're going to start collecting."

Non-traditional. What a polite phrase for loan sharks who didn't mind breaking bones if it was necessary to ensure a person paid. "So you think she's gonna get pulled into his mess."

"Unless she has almost a 100k sitting under a mattress somewhere to bail him out, they are going to come after him and the business he used as collateral."

Ink ran his hands through his hair in frustration. "She can't know about this."

"Do you think the collectors are going to care if she knows or not?"

The idea of Jade getting hurt because of her friend's debts sent his blood boiling. Dammit, they barely knew each other. And even if he didn't see a long-term prospect between them, that didn't mean he wanted to let her go and leave her to have to face this kind of shit alone.

The look Highdive gave him was intense. "It's too late, isn't it?"

"What do you mean?" Ink wished he had another drink but stopped himself from asking for another.

"Swear to God, you all live to make my life hard. I love all my Brothers. But you fuckers can't seem to pick uncomplicated pussy to save your lives."

Ink leaned back, considering the last few Old Ladies who had joined their ranks, and he had to agree. But he shook his head. He needed to make things very clear. "I never said she's going to be our Old Lady."

Highdive's eyebrow raised. "That look of anger on your face when I told you she might be in trouble. That tells me otherwise."

"Just because I don't want to see a woman hurt, doesn't mean I want my patch on her back."

"You keep telling yourself that."

Anger and frustration roiled in his stomach. Ink gripped the edge of the bar and tried to maintain his calm.

"Brother, you know what I like. Do you see any woman settling down with two men who have our temperaments? Do you think any woman wants to live the rest of her life with men who get off on sharing and controlling her? Sure. We're fun for the short term. The long haul, white picket fence, two kids and a dog, that just ain't me."

"Wow, I didn't realize this was a pity party I'd been invited to. I would have brought something."

"Fuck you, man." Ink didn't enjoy cursing. It was one of his hang-ups from childhood, but sometimes they were the perfect words for the situation.

"Cut the shit. Look around this place. There isn't a man here who doesn't like control. Those Old Ladies." Highdive gestured in the direction the women had gone. "Each one of them is happier than a civilian woman with their supposedly enlightened men. We both know plenty of happy poly couples at the Club. So what is the actual issue?"

What was the issue? Ink wasn't ready to dig down into his feelings. "Didn't ask for a psych eval."

"Doesn't take a doctor to see someone making excuses and avoiding the issue. You think we haven't noticed you and Hannibal are on the outs?"

No. He didn't. "When did my life become fodder for a Club hen party?"

Highdive ignored his jab. "Do you think your girl doesn't like pain? Afraid you'll have to hang up your bullwhip?"

He didn't actually, though enjoying a spanking was a far cry from wanting to feel the kiss of a whip. People feared his favorite implement, picturing the kind of lashing that tore open skin and left scars. In the hand of someone skilled like him, the whip could deliver anything from gentle taps to flashing bites of pain that would leave small welts for days.

"You saying she does?" He wasn't going to admit what he knew, but wanted to know what his Brother thought. "You met her once and magically have the inside scoop?"

"You met her once and are acting like a protective guard dog. But no, I actually read her bio."

The fact his Brother might know more about Jade than he did was disconcerting. "And something in it makes you think she likes pain? What, has she been secretly attending BDSM clubs? Because I'm telling you, she's a novice."

Her reactions that night had been too genuine to be practiced. Her joy in discovering something new and exciting too real to be faked.

"Oh, I don't think she's been to a BDSM club a day in her life, but she trained to be a world class gymnast, from childhood. She climbs some of the most dangerous mountains that are out there. And that Parkour crap?" He shook his head. "She has had more physical pain in her life than ten other people. If she didn't get off on that shit, there is no way she could have become as talented as she is."

Highdive's words were an uncomfortable revelation. It would have been easier to believe that she wouldn't want anything long term than to think that his own issues would be the ones pulling them down. There had been too many times in his life where he had believed that there might be a woman interested in them for the long term. But time after time, he'd been proven wrong.

All of that aside, he needed to go home and settle things with Hannibal. Let him know what he had found out about their Jewel. Then he could decide if the risk of disappointment was worth putting himself on the line.

Chapter 10

Friends are like boobs. Some are big, some are small. Some are real and some are fake.

Jade

The long, nighttime drive to Dark Ink Tattoo Studio gave Jade too much time to think. Music filled the car, and she tapped the steering wheel to the rhythm of the beat, trying to burn off some nervous energy. She was a coward and hadn't called Hannibal to tell him about the appointment she'd set up for today.

When the three of them exchanged contact info and set up plans to meet in a few days, she had assumed they would call or text. But the men had gone radio silent. She'd expected them to at least reach out about coming into Leap to train. She tried not to be too mad. The phone went both ways and she could have reached out even if they hadn't. Her appointment today with Hannibal would have been the perfect excuse to do so.

Instead, she obsessively checked her phone for messages

while at home and at work. Work had kept her relatively busy. Training the women from their Club earlier had been fun. Becoming friends with them if this thing with Hannibal and Ink didn't go sideways would be easy. They seemed like a tight-knit group of women who wouldn't want to make things awkward by continuing a friendship after things fell apart.

Now she was driving down the road with her nerves eating at the sides of her stomach. Should she have called Hannibal and let him know she would be at Dark Ink? It wasn't like she was an unwanted interruption. She had a legitimate appointment, made over a month ago, but a heads up probably would have been respectful. Would Ink be there?

Flashbacks of the scorching events in her office replayed in her mind too often for comfort. Ink's no orgasm rule was one of the hardest she'd ever had to follow. Sleep the previous night had eluded her and the temptation to call them was intense. The idea of asking for permission to play with herself both excited and embarrassed her. Even worse, every time she sat down and tried to work in the office, her whole body came alive with reminders of their time together.

They'd seemed interested in continuing things and taking them further, but the two days of silence had eaten away at her confidence. She tried to strengthen her spine. She wasn't a teenager praying for the attention of the cool kids. If they wanted to play it so relaxed, they didn't bother to call or text, then she would be an adult and tell them that wasn't acceptable to her.

She'd state clearly that she was not okay with being forgotten. If they couldn't be bothered to even send a single text after playing her body like an instrument, then she didn't need their kind of relationship. She would tell them that she wanted the tattoos but possibly anything else was a mistake.

Her phone rang. She looked down at the console on her car dash and groaned. Eric was calling. She didn't want to have to deal with him when her emotions were already bouncing all over the place. But if she put him off, things would escalate and get worse.

With a deep breath, she hit the hands free ACCEPT button.

"Hi Eric. What do you want?" She was proud of how neutral her voice sounded. He needed to understand that she was done with putting up with his bullshit. He'd damaged the close friendship, and she doubted it would ever recover.

"Hey Jade. I'm sorry I've been such an ass."

Hope, that stupid emotion, fluttered in her at his opening words. They'd been friends for so long that it was hard to match the man he'd been for the last year, with the over a decade friendship they'd had before it.

She missed the Eric who had been her rock through some of the hardest times in her life and wanted him back. Hell, she would have even accepted if he turned back into the fun, carefree party boy he'd become while they'd been on the TV circuit. The surly, angry version of him hurt her heart every single time they talked.

"I'm not sure what to say to that." His sigh through the phone was loud.

"Yeah, I know. I am sorry. Things are really rough right now."

"Are you ready to tell me what's going on?" Her navigation system told her there were fifteen minutes before she would arrive at Dark Ink. Her appointment wasn't for another thirty minutes. She hit the blinker, moving into the slow lane so they could talk longer.

"Are you in the car? I thought you'd be at the gym."

Jade rolled her eyes. She did spend most of her time there, but the place closed over two hours ago. If it hadn't been for the private lesson, she would have been back at her apartment. He should know the gym schedule as well as she did.

"Gym is closed, Eric."

"Then I'll come by your apartment so we can talk."

"No. I'm not there." Suspicion filled her response.

"Then where are you?"

"What business is that of yours?"

"It's after eight on a weeknight."

"What are you, my dad?" Not that her dad had ever cared enough to check up on her.

"Where are you going?"

She was not going to put up with him, even pretending he had the right to question anything she did. "I'm an adult and can go wherever I want when I want. I don't have to check in with anyone, especially not you. You have five seconds to tell me what you want before I'm hanging up."

"Jeez, where's the love?" He took a deep breath. "I guess I deserve that."

"You do. What do you want?"

Seconds ticked by and she clearly pictured him searching for the right words to get what he wanted from her.

"I need money."

The bluntness of his words was so unlike Eric, she took some time to process them. She was so used to the excuses and stories designed to tug at her heartstrings. Jade wasn't stupid. She knew her friend sometimes played her, even outright lied to her. But he'd worn away at her goodwill until there was nothing left. She was worried about him, but that didn't stop her resentment at the fact that she was nothing more than a piggy bank to him anymore.

"Of course, that's what this was about. You couldn't just be calling to apologize. That would mean you actually cared that you'd done something wrong."

85

She smacked the steering wheel in frustration, tempted to hang up on him.

"Jade—"

"We've talked about this." She cut him off. "Next, check comes in three weeks. I should have the rest of the money to buy you out in four months."

It was going to take her scrimping and saving every penny she had. But she was determined to get him out of the business. Maybe then their friendship could recover. People had warned her from the beginning that going into business with a friend was a bad idea.

In her worst imaginings, she couldn't have pictured things turning out like this. Over a decade of friendship, torn apart. She only needed $50,000 more to buy him out. Then she would be done with him.

No more money fights. No more pretending, phone calls, to try to sucker her out of more cash. Their entire friendship flushed away because he wouldn't live within his budget and thought she should fix all of his problems.

"Can you give me an advance on next month?" Desperation was clear in his voice, even through the car's speakers. "I'm in a tight spot. I need you."

Jade sighed, hardly believing she was even considering it. "How much are we talking about?"

"I need at least five grand. Ten would be better."

Shock made her voice harsh. "Eric, your portion of the profits this month was only two-thousand dollars. That was before taxes. What you are asking for is at least three months' worth of advances."

She had a personal account where she'd been saving to buy Eric out that held almost thirty-eight-thousand dollars. It was her personal safety net as well for emergencies. It was possible to do it without breaking the bank, but when would it stop? Would he ever learn to handle his own finances?

"I'm desperate. You have to help me out."

Jade tried not to grind her teeth at his demanding tone. "Tell me what you need the money for, and I'll consider buying a couple more of your shares from you. But no more advances. Any money you get outside the regular cycle goes against the $50,000 dollars to buy you out."

"You can't be serious. I'm not selling any more of the business to you."

Jade was stunned. "Did you even read our last contract? You agreed to sell the rest of your shares to me if I came up with the money within a year. I have ten months and believe me, I plan on buying you out."

"What am I supposed to do without the dividend checks?"

The ones that he did absolutely nothing to earn. That had been part of the deal when he'd agreed to the buyout price. "That's not my problem. If you wanted more money, you could come in and take some personal training sessions. I don't know, earn your paycheck."

"You don't have to be such a bitch."

"I'm not being a bitch, Eric. Just not letting you walk all over me anymore."

"Fine, then give me the five grand."

It was tempting to give in, but a part of her knew she needed to know what was going on in his life before getting any more involved than she already was. "No, you tell me what you need it for. Then I'll get the contract drawn up, and you can stop buy in two days."

"What do you care what it is for? You abandoned me and ruined my career with this bullshit. You owe me."

Guilt and anger flooded her system. What he said was technically true, but she didn't owe him the rest of her life. It was an unpleasant reality that Eric had capitalized on her story to bring them both into the limelight. She had the right to not want to be in it anymore.

"If you don't tell me what it's for. No contract. No money."

"Fuck you, you ungrateful manipulating bitch–"

Jade hit the end button on her phone. She wasn't going to listen to his curses or insults. Within a few seconds, he was calling back, but she'd had enough. She switched her phone to silent. It took a few minutes, but by the time she reached Dark Ink's parking lot, her breath and temper were under control.

Jade wasn't going to allow anything to ruin what was supposed to be a dream come true. Not Eric's bad mood, or the uncertainty about her and the guys. She had been planning the tattoos she was going to get from Hannibal and Ink for almost five years.

The picture of what she wanted on her back was so vivid in her mind that if she had had any artistic ability, she would have been able to draw it up herself. When she had imagined getting this tattoo designed, she had always known that it would take both of them to make what was in her mind a reality.

Her fantasies about meeting them occasionally took an erotic turn where one or the other of them seduced her. The dream versions of the men had nothing on the reality. Admittedly, she hadn't considered that both of them might want her at the same time.

What they had done to her body should be required teaching for any man who wanted to please a woman. They had known exactly what to do to push the pleasure into mind numbing territory. Of course, they in turn needed to take a class on how to keep a woman more than twenty-four hours.

She wasn't saying she was definitely calling off between them. Because the idea of more encounters like the one in her office was honestly worth a little frustration. But she had her pride.

She intended to make sure two things were clear before opening herself back up. One, that regardless of how things worked out, she could get her dream tattoo. The second was that they understood if they wanted to play more bedroom games with her, she needed to feel respected.

She might be willing to give up control to them. But in return, she expected to be treated the way she deserved. No more disappearing without a word.

Walking inside Dark Ink was slightly surreal. She had seen hundreds of photos of the place, but none of them fully captured the retro beauty that was inside the building. Chrome and black and white decorated every part of the shop. The only colors in the place were the gorgeous photos of what she imagined were some of Hannibal and Ink's best work.

The muscled back of a man was larger than life on the wall right inside the door. The tattoo on his back, an absolutely gorgeous rendition of a motorcycle in the Colorado mountains backdrop. Arching over the scene were the words 'Dark Sons for Life'.

Who could be the owner of that masterpiece? It would be amazing to get to meet him so she could see it in person. Photos couldn't fully capture the beauty of a tattoo.

There were five tattoo stations in the front area of the shop. With three artists working hard on customers. A bored young woman, with almost every inch of visible skin covered in tattoos, sat at the front desk. An annoyed scowl filled her face as she took Jade in.

"Do you have an appointment?"

Jade wanted to roll her eyes at the snippy tone in the woman's voice. She was glad her own employees had better customer service skills.

"I do. Nine o'clock with Hannibal."

The girl glanced over to her left at a computer screen. "Hannibal's nine o'clock is a guy named Jaden. We don't allow appointment swaps."

That was an odd policy. "My name is Jade. They must have written the name down wrong."

"Well, he is expecting a guy."

This woman had obviously not been hired for her cheery personality. Jade held out her arms in frustration. What did this woman want her to do? "As you can see, not a guy. Though I'm not sure what difference that makes in a tattoo consultation."

The girl looked her up and down. Jade was wearing a short jean skirt and crimson scoop neck t-shirt. She wouldn't admit it out loud. But she'd picked out the outfit specifically to show off her best assets.

The girl's eyes finally lost a bit of hostility when she looked down and studied the vine tattoo on Jade's leg. Her gaze followed the path of the design from her ankle until it disappeared under her clothes.

"Nice ink."

"Thanks."

"Jade!" Hannibal's deep, rich tone pulled her attention away from the receptionist's odd attention. The warmth of Hannibal's smile relaxed something inside her.

Maybe he hadn't been avoiding her on purpose. It had crossed her mind a few times that it was possible the guys had regretted hooking up with her. In moments, his long strides closed the distance.

She was shocked when Hannibal wrapped a hand around the back of her neck and pulled her in for a kiss. It only took a moment for his skilled mouth to start her toes curling. Jade melted into him, forgetting where they were.

The heat of his mouth on hers was intoxicating. All the

stressful thoughts from the day scattered through her mind. His hand slid down her back and over the swell of her ass.

She moaned, and he pulled back from the kiss, a small smile tipping up the right side of his mouth.

"It's so good to see you, *cher*. I wish I could break away but I've got someone coming in for a consult any minute."

"She's your nine o'clock." The annoying voice of the receptionist cut through Jade's lust induced haze.

She had forgotten for a minute that she wasn't there to make out. Hannibal looked down at her, a wicked thought sparkling in his eyes.

"Is that so?"

She nodded and tried to gather her thoughts. "It is. I've had this appointment for almost two months."

"Well then. I guess you'll have to follow me into the back. I can't wait to find out how you want me to put my mark on your body."

His words were so wonderfully dirty they sent a shiver across her skin. Giving herself a mental slap, she followed him. She couldn't wait to see what he thought of her ideas either. Jade bit her lip as she watched Hannibal's ass as he led her through to the back of the shop.

Hopefully, this was going to be a more unique consultation than she had imagined.

Chapter 11

If I had a dollar for every time I got distracted, hey you look fucking hot.

Hannibal

Hannibal had been surprised by how much seeing Jade at the front of his shop lifted his mood. The last two days of silence between him and Ink had been rough. The fight was his fault, but he wasn't sorry.

Backing down wasn't an option. He loved his Brother in a way few people understood. And while he was willing to make allowances for Ink's issues, he was tired of not even being able to discuss what they wanted in the future.

It wasn't solely about Jade. He wanted him to be open to the possibility of something more. This beautiful, dynamic woman was only the catalyst to make him wake up and realize that if he kept putting off the discussions, the two of them would end up old and alone.

Over the last two days, he'd learned everything he could about their precious Jewel. When he hadn't been losing himself in work, he'd been watching videos and reading blogs about her. She was incredibly strong in both body and soul.

What she could do on a Parkour course was nothing short of amazing. There'd been a couple of videos of her doing tricks that he'd had to watch several times before he believed it wasn't special effects.

The girl could run up a fifteen-foot wall, leap and flip over gaps and heights that would have left normal people shivering. Her showing up at his shop had been a wonderful surprise. His first thought when he saw her was that she'd gotten tired of waiting for them to contact her. That she'd come here to yell at him and Ink.

He wouldn't have blamed her for being upset. Hannibal had thought about texting hundreds of times. Hell, he'd wanted to see her. Every time he watched a new video of her, he'd had the urge to text and tell her how unbelievably talented she was.

He'd held back, not wanting to talk to her until he'd worked things out with Ink. It wouldn't be fair to her to give false hope. When he wasn't sure if his Brother was even willing to still meet up with her that weekend.

Finding out that not only was she his next appointment, but that she was his last appointment for the night, made him come to a decision. He wasn't gonna hold back anymore. Ink was either going to pull his head out of his ass or get left behind. They never had rules about playing with a woman alone, so he would not hold back.

That thought pulled him up short. No, he would never abandon Ink. But that didn't mean he couldn't indulge his fantasies. Really get to know this woman and figure out why she drew him in so strongly.

Hannibal guided Jade through the black velvet curtain that closed off the back private tattoo stations from the front of the shop. Then down the hallway and into his and Ink's office. Well, they called it an office. But it was more where the two of them hung out when they didn't feel like dealing with customers or the other artists.

The room held a big comfortable couch, perfect for catching naps. A large table was in the center where the two of them sometimes did their sketching. There were no desks or usual office furniture.

Prints of drawings lined the walls, not only their art, but of other tattoo artists as well. Jade smiled as she walked in and immediately started studying each and every one.

Along the back wall were the high-end printers they used to create stencils for their work and two large, closed cabinets. One held back-up supplies for either drawing or tattooing. The other held their back-up BDSM gear that they kept here because it was closer to the city than their house. They'd learned to be prepared if either of them got the urge to play with a willing sub.

"That's not your work." Jade pointed to an intricate tribal pattern running down a masculine arm.

"No. Only about half of these are ours. The others are some of our favorite artists. Inspiration for us. Maybe a little competition." He winked at her.

She laughed. "So being in the top five percent on the 'best of' lists is not enough for you guys?"

He clutched his heart in mock horror. "Are you saying we're not in the top two percent?"

She laughed. "If they judged by talent alone, probably. But you don't pander to the celebrity crowd or social media. So I doubt they'll ever rank you that high."

Hannibal found it amusing how some artists jockeyed for position on the lists that the different magazines put out. Like any form of media, they liked drama as it fed their sales. Reporters would drop rumors during interviews trying to foster rivalries.

He knew and respected many of the people who hit the top 100 lists every year, along with him and Ink. Most of them thought the whole thing was as silly as he did.

"You can't rank art. It's about what a person wants and what they're feeling at the time. Finding the perfect combination between talent and vision. I do some tattoos that are completely from my own mind, but most of them are collaborations between the person whose body is going to be the canvas and my vision of what they want. How can you rank that?"

"That's beautifully said. I prefer tattoos, that mean something. Don't get me wrong, I obviously want them to be beautiful as well. But I think a simple tattoo that holds deep meaning is more precious than something elaborate that's only purpose is to feed someone's vanity."

"Is that what you want from me, *cher*? Something simple."

"Oh no. I want the best of both worlds. That's why I wanted both you and Ink to do a back piece for me. I want something beautiful and elaborate, that means something very important to me."

A lock of her hair had fallen in front of her face during her impassioned speech. Hannibal couldn't resist brushing it back and running his thumb down her soft cheek.

"Let's sit down." He gestured at the couch.

"Okay." They sat in silence for a few minutes as she studied the walls. The expressive nature of her face fascinated him. He could tell by the tilt of her head whether what she was looking at intrigued or puzzled her.

"So why did you pick us?"

Hannibal had a healthy ego about his skills. It was hard not to have one, when people paid the amount of money that they did and waited for as long as they did to get his art on their body. Unfortunately, Jade had hit the nail on the head when she said that sometimes people forgot the purpose of tattoos.

To his disappointment, most of his non Dark Sons customers came in with little more than a general subject and wanting him to design something beautiful. He treasured those rare times when someone came in wanting to memorialize something, or some event. He loved taking their vision and giving it life.

Jade tilted her head. "What do you mean? Why did I pick you?"

"I mean, there's at least two other world class tattoo artists in the Denver area. And lots more in other places. You said back piece, so I'm guessing you were planning on spending thousands of dollars before you won our bet. When someone spends that kind of money I'm curious why they would pick me."

He was glad that she took a moment to really think about what he had asked. Her face grew soft, and a blush pinkened her cheeks. He was wondering if she was thinking about the other night.

"The first time I saw one of Ink's tattoos, I was at a Warrior competition. She was the mother of one of the younger competitors. Women rarely get elaborate pictures on their arms, so it fascinated me. It was this lovely angel with its wings wrapped around a small child." Jade got a faraway look in her eyes. "The child had a look of such joy and wonder on her face it made me want to smile. Then I saw the grief and sorrow etched into every line and shadow of the angel's face. I knew this woman suffered something that no mother should ever have to go through."

She cleared her throat before continuing. "It took me months to ask her about it when I saw her again."

Hannibal knew the tattoo she was talking about. It was one of the first they'd done when they had opened the shop.

They'd been struggling with money, but when that woman came in asking to do a memorial for her daughter who had recently died of cancer, neither of them were willing to charge her more than the cost of the supplies.

They'd learned through friends that this woman was struggling financially and emotionally. Having to deal with the expenses from the failed treatments. A single mother who still had a son to take care of. He must have been the one competing with Jade.

The woman knew she couldn't afford a tattoo but had been willing to sacrifice because she needed something of her daughter to hold on to. They'd both worked long hours sorting through photographs of the little girl to find exactly the right one to use as a template. Hannibal had designed the line-work while Ink did the shading and actual tattoo.

"She told me what you guys did for her. Not just the tattoo but the charity ride to help her with her bills and to make a donation to the Children's Cancer Fund in her name."

Hannibal shrugged, not sure what to say. Ink and he had grown up poor, helping out that woman had felt right.

"Anyway, I wanted to find out about the guy who created such a wonderful memorial. I've always been fascinated by tattoos, probably since I was a teenager. I read all the magazines and online blogs about tattoos and, of course, watched all the shows once cable started producing them, but that was the first time I saw one that both broke my heart and gave me hope. Ink wasn't easy to find." She gave him a glare like it was his fault she'd had trouble finding them.

"What's that look for?"

"You guys were absolutely awful at anything social media related until recently."

Hannibal laughed. "Yeah, that's when we hired Gia. She works the desk and does all that for us."

"Little Miss Sunshine at the front counter?"

Hannibal shook his head. "She's much better in print than in person. But honestly we keep her up there because it cuts down on the looky-loos. She's nicer once you get to know her."

"Is she now?" Jade's eyes narrowed.

Hannibal wondered if maybe his little athlete was jealous. It was tempting to tease her, but he didn't play those kinds of games.

"Yes. Her and her wife have been loyal customers for years."

Jade's shoulders relaxed. "She doesn't look old enough to have been getting tattoos for years."

"She's older than she looks."

"Anyway, I finally tracked down a blog of one of your regular customers. He shared pictures of both of your work pretty regularly. I have to admit, if he hadn't posted pictures of the different stages of the clockwork heart, you did for him, I would have sworn it was a computer generated graphic, not a tattoo. The shading you did to make it appear like it was carved right out of his chest was amazing."

"Gears has a blog?" He was surprised that the motor-head even knew what a blog was. "I'm so going to give him shit for that."

"I think it's his wife's. But she's definitely a fan of yours. After seeing a few more pieces of your work, and some of Ink's fantasy styled pieces, I knew the tattoo that I had in my head needed to be done by the two of you."

Hannibal traced his fingers along the vine and flower tattoos that swirled up her leg. Now that he had time to study it, no single artist had done this work. Some of the leaves and flowers looked years old. Some newer. Only from a distance did the styles and workmanship look the same.

"Is there a special meaning behind this?"

"Yeah." Chill bumps rose on her skin as he traced the vine from where it started near her ankle and followed it up to a rose that wrapped inside her calf. "The first time I won money at a Parkour tournament. I went out and got this. Each leaf represents a competition where I didn't win but feel I did well. Each thorn is a competition where I did badly. Each flower represents a win, a sponsorship or an event at which I know I did my absolute best. As I kept competing, I kept adding."

Now that he understood the symbolism behind the artwork, he studied it closer. Her leg was practically covered in vines intertwining with one another. There were a good amount of flowers, but it was easy to see that the thorns well outnumbered the leaves by at least five to one.

"You're pretty hard on yourself." He traced one particular jagged vine that seemed to be covered in tiny little thorns.

"I'm honest with myself. I know when I've given everything I can and when I let myself slack off."

The perfectionist drive was something he knew far too much about. Arguing with her wouldn't solve anything, so he moved on. "Do you have any other ink?"

He didn't think she did. They hadn't gotten her completely naked the other day, but there was little of her skin that had been covered. By the way she flushed and looked down, there must be something he'd missed.

"Come on, you can't turn shy on me now. Let me see."

She rolled her eyes. "Only if you promise not to laugh."

Hannibal had seen his share of bad tattoos. Ridiculous ones, embarrassing ones, and some just plain ugly. He tried to picture what she could have that would make her blush so prettily.

"I don't think I can promise that. I mean, if you have Elmer Fudd tattooed on your…" he paused, trying to think what part of her body he hadn't seen. It had to be some-where on her stomach or middle back. In the clothes she'd been wearing the other day, not much of her hadn't been exposed. So it was hidden somewhere. "On your stomach. I can't say I won't laugh."

"It's not Elmer Fudd, it's just… you know what? It's easier to show you." She lifted her shirt, confirming his suspi-cion that the tattoo was somewhere on her stomach.

She raised the fabric and lifted her breasts. He saw it and blinked. Laughter was not his first or even third response.

Curving in a sort of W on the rib cage under her breasts was a mixture of oddly faded colors with wavy uneven lines. Was it a pattern or a picture?

He leaned forward to get a closer look. The tattoo had to be at least six years old and was so unevenly faded it must have been a disaster from the beginning. He thought he could make out wings of some sort. Was that a person in the middle?

She dropped her shirt and crossed her arms. "It was supposed to be the goddess Isis. My mother loved her stories and legends. I was nineteen when she died and didn't have a lot of money. The guy I went to had a book full of beautiful art but I should have been suspicious at the price."

"You actually paid him for that?"

"Not after I saw it. It was partially my fault. I didn't double check that any of the work in the book was his own. And I didn't stop him because unfortunately I couldn't see over my boobs when he was working."

Hannibal wished her story wasn't a common one, but he had done plenty of cover up jobs on things that should have never been permanently placed on the body.

"Is that what you want? A cover up job?" With most of the color faded, it wouldn't be too difficult, but finding the right design and placement was always tricky.

"No. I mean someday I'll probably get it covered up, but even ugly as it is, it's still a memory of my mom."

"What did you have in mind then?"

For the next twenty minutes, she painted a picture with words. The more she talked, the more vivid the picture in his mind grew. A kaleidoscope of butterflies curving up from the swell of her hips. At the base of her spine, a cracked cocoon that had the Olympic rings broken and jagged.

The interviews he'd watched had told of her broken Olympic dreams, so the symbolism wasn't lost on him. She wanted the butterflies to start off towards the bottom as simple patterns with little color growing more intricate as they worked up her back. Until they did the final one on her shoulder in hyper-realistic 3D style.

He could picture the placement that would be needed to make it appear as if it was about to take wing and fly away.

It was the story of her life. About the broken dreams of a little girl who didn't give up and had found a new dream.

It was hard to imagine going through what she did so young. One month away from being part of the Olympics and favored to win a medal, she'd slipped during training. The bad landing resulted in multiple torn ligaments in her knee, knocking her out of competition.

She had been on the mend when her mother took ill. Between her mother's sickness and her own medical bills and injury, they weren't able to afford the training and physical therapy she would have needed to get back into Olympic shape.

Reading between the lines, it was easy to see that she'd given up her training in order to remove some of the stress from her mother, who was battling with cancer. The way the story was told, her friend Eric had helped her and her mother out and convinced her to try an unconventional way to regain her strength and flexibility.

The two of them had done Parkour in the backyard and competing in local competitions until they turned eighteen and set out on the road together. They'd thought her mother was in remission. A year later, her mother died within weeks of finding out that the cancer had moved to her brain. Hannibal was glad her mother hadn't suffered for long. Her father wasn't mentioned in any of the publicity pieces.

Jade had incorporated years of struggle and triumph into the image she wanted. As she continued to describe the unique elements she wanted hidden within the piece, he could see she was taking bits and pieces from her life and working them in. An Egyptian scarab, which he now knew represented her mother, and several specific patterns to be worked into the wings that probably represented other major events in her life.

Even the final butterfly was a testament to the fact that out of everything, not only had she been reborn, but she was ready to fly free. The words she used to describe the different butterflies showed she'd definitely studied their work and had planned which ones she wanted him to do without her ever saying his name.

"So what do you think?" Nerves were clear in her question.

"I think it's going to be gorgeous. Just like you."

"Do you think you guys can do it?"

"You painted a vivid picture with your words. It may take some time to make sure we have everything you want, but I can't wait to start sketching it out."

Joy was like a light in her eyes. Her excitement, something palpable in the air. He should start writing the minor details she'd mentioned, but with her sitting there almost breathless with excitement, he couldn't.

She was a temptation he couldn't and didn't want to

resist. Her joy for life radiated off of her. He couldn't wait another minute for a kiss.

Hannibal wrapped his hand around the back of her neck and pulled her towards him. She tasted like apples and cinnamon. What had she eaten? Mixed with her own flavor, he imagined this was what ambrosia tasted like.

Her body seemed to melt against him. Hannibal moved them until he splayed her out on the couch, his body hovering above hers. He grabbed her wrists and put them over her head, and held them there with one hand.

The skin of her neck was soft as he nibbled down the lovely column. "I can't wait to get you under my gun. Do you understand how much I love the idea that my ink is going to be on you forever?"

She moaned. "I want that too."

She pressed up against him. Her breasts rubbed against him like she was trying to get friction. Hannibal skated his other hand over her body, slowly following each line of her muscles and curves. He continued down until he reached the bottom of her skirt and slowly slid it upwards.

"Please, Hannibal."

He loved the aching edge in her voice. He wanted to memorize everything about her in this moment. The only thing that would make it more perfect was if Ink were here to hold her down for him.

Chapter 12

If you could read my mind, you'd either be traumatized, aroused, or both.

Jade

"**K**eep your hands above your head and don't move them." Hannibal's rough command rumbled across her skin, tightening things deep inside Jade.

There was something about his enormous form, hovering just over hers, that was incredibly sexy. He made her feel delicate, which was a new experience. While she had always been shorter than other people, her build and strength often had people describing her as stocky or sturdy.

Her hips and breasts had kept them from saying manly, but in her experience, men weren't attracted to women with better definition than they had. She wouldn't wish away any of her muscles for the sake of someone else's insecurity, but it had made dating complicated.

The fact that Hannibal was stronger than her made everything inside her quiver in anticipation. Hannibal slowly ran his hands up from her hips, leaving chill bumps in his wake. He pulled her shirt up, then off over her head and undid her bra.

He quickly tossed the fabric to the side. It took little time and soon all of her clothing was scattered across the room. She lay on the butter soft leather of the couch completely naked. He devoured her with his gaze like she was the finest meal.

"You're so fucking gorgeous. Can't wait to taste you."

Nerves flared and color rushed up her body. Jade had never enjoyed when her past partners had gone down on her. Embarrassment and their lack of enthusiasm killed her excitement.

From the hungry look in Hannibal's dark eyes, she didn't think that would be a problem this time. Jade's breath caught. He was so handsome with his strong jawline and close cropped hair. Watching his sexy mouth as he kissed his way down her body caused her body to clench in anticipation.

His fingers were cool against the heart of her core as he spread her pussy open. A jolt of pleasure rocked through her as his tongue flicked and hit her clit like a marksman. She arched up with a moan, wanting more.

He drove her higher with expert skill. His mouth better than some toys she had used in the past. Hannibal must have been reading her mind because he knew right where and how she needed him.

Jade dug her heels into the couch and tried to grind

down on him. She needed a little more to push her over the edge.

"God, that feels so good." Her voice was breathy with her growing desire.

Hannibal's finger was amazing as he worked it inside her opening. Her moan was embarrassingly loud as he slowly rubbed up and down along the inside of her core. It took him only a few strokes to find that spot deep inside her that made stars shoot across the backs of her eyes.

Jade gripped the arm of the couch behind her to fight back the urge to grab his head and start grinding against his face. Pleasure was building in a slow burn and she didn't want to race towards the finish line yet.

"Fuck, you taste so good." His dirty words threw fuel onto the fire he had lit inside her.

She clenched down as he slid a second finger inside her and started a beckoning motion. His tongue alternated circling and flicking her clit with fast, firm strokes.

"Oh God, Hannibal. What if someone hears us?"

"The room is soundproofed."

That was odd, but any thoughts or concern scattered as he sucked her clit into his mouth with such force her back arched in pleasure. Her hands came off of the arm she had been gripping and clutched onto his head. She ground herself against him as the orgasm exploded over her.

Hannibal made a tsking noise as he pulled back out of her grip. "That's not where your hands are supposed to be, naughty girl. And you were doing so good at following my orders."

She panted, trying to catch her breath. "Sorry. It just felt too good. Your mouth is a deadly weapon."

He chuckled, his eyes twinkling with an emotion that had her stomach fluttering. "Compliments won't get you out of trouble. Bad girls have to take their punishments."

The word punishment should have frightened her, but instead, excitement bubbled through her. "A spanking?"

The eagerness in her voice was embarrassing. The encounter the other night had taught her how much she enjoyed a bite of pain with her pleasure. She wouldn't mind doing that again at all.

"No, not a spanking." The mischief in his eyes made her shiver.

Hannibal stood up and strode to the back of the room. He opened one of the cabinets along the wall. Jade sat up, wondering what he had in there.

What would someone have lying around in a tattoo studio for punishment? She hadn't even considered what would be inside the cabinet when she had seen it earlier. It definitely wasn't the array of paddles and whips that were in there.

Her eyes grew wide as she took in the sight. On the inside of the door, laid out like a display case for a kinky sex shop, were cuffs, chains, and coils of rope. The shelves held two duffel bags and an assortment of packages that she thought she recognized as sex toys.

Maybe it should have bothered her that not only did the men she was fooling around with have these items, but they had them in their place of business. But strangely, the idea was erotic to her. Jade had only had a couple of lovers in her life. But all of them had been almost timid about sex.

She'd been afraid to let them know about her fantasies or even ask for what she wanted. Knowing that these men not only would fulfill her every kinky dream if she asked, but would know how to do it made her feel safe. Hannibal grabbed a set of the cuffs off the door and picked up two packages and unwrapped them.

Jade stood up to get a better view of what he was doing.

"No, no, naughty girl. You sit right there. You'll see what I have soon enough."

The stern tone in his voice had her sitting back down without a thought. She squirmed, a sense of awkwardness coloring her cheeks.

Here she was in his office completely naked and, like the last time, he was fully clothed. The dynamic of that was erotic, but she had daydreamed about what he would look like without a shirt.

None of the photos she had found of him showed his chest. He was always wearing a tight t-shirt or Henley, with his leather cut obstructing the view.

She wanted to see what was hidden underneath those clothes. He turned his back, blocking her view of what he was doing. A few seconds later, the scent of alcohol filled the room. Was he cleaning something?

When her nerves got to her, she couldn't resist talking. "Am I ever going to get to see you without a shirt on? Or maybe without your pants?" The second question was under her breath, but she thought he had heard her.

Hannibal's chuckle was menacing. "Oh my naughty little Jewel, all you ever had to do was ask."

He shrugged out of his leather vest, folded it, and placed it on the shelf next to him. Then, in a move sexy men everywhere have perfected, he reached behind him and pulled his Henley off in a single motion. Her mouth went dry at the site that was revealed.

Skin the color of brown sugar covered muscles that could win bodybuilding contests around the country. Blackwork tattoos sprawled from his shoulders and disappeared down into his pants. Most of them were so intricate she wanted to spend hours studying them up close.

Spirals of blacks and reds formed a skull with the angel wings and flames across his chest. Each feather looked like it could curl up and take flight right off of his chest. Two silver rings glinted from his nipples and she wanted to take them into her mouth and play with them.

She licked her lips at the thought. On his arm was a Ranger tattoo as well as the Dark Sons' name in Gothic letters in a banner above it.

"I love how you're looking at me. Like you want nothing more than to get your hands on me."

She still couldn't tell what Hannibal had in his hands other than the cuffs dangling by a short chain.

"I do want to get my hands on you. I want to trace every line and curve of your body with my tongue."

"Now, I think I can arrange that." Hannibal put something in his pocket and clipped the cuffs to a belt loop before striding over to her. Her body hummed in anticipation of getting her hands on him. She reached out and her fingers brushed over the V dip of muscles that disappeared into his pants. "But not tonight, *cher*. Not tonight."

Hannibal gripped her hands and pulled her up to her feet, spinning her around until her back met his front. Her thoughts swirled with the quick motion and her breath caught in her chest.

"Hannibal, what are you doing?"

He had her wrists pulled up behind her back. The pressure pulled her up to her toes.

"Ah, it's a pity we couldn't have had a sweet night exploring each other's bodies instead of me punishing you." His tone didn't sound like he was disappointed. "I think you've already forgotten all the lessons Ink taught you back at your office. When we're here like this–" His arm wrapped around her chest and pinned her close. "What do you call me?"

Memories of them in her office collided with the here

and now. The muscles in her thighs trembled and her pussy started dripping with excitement.

"I'm sorry. What are you doing, Sir?" His grip around her chest loosened, and soft leather closed around her wrists. The sound of Velcro punctuating the action as the restraints tightened around her wrists.

"That's better. Did you already forget that you're gonna get punished?"

She had forgotten. But really, was it her fault he was being so sexy and distracting? "Sorry, Sir. What's going to be my punishment?"

The pressure on her wrists released. In reflex, she tried to pull her hands forward. The cold chain bit into her back as the leather cuffs kept her hands where they were. The chain between her wrists was short, but not so tight that the position put an uncomfortable strain on her shoulders.

His body pressed up against hers. The skin of his torso was hot against her bare back. She groaned. The hard length of him pressed against her bound hands. It felt so big.

"Ink and I have different philosophies when it comes to punishments. Now, I don't mind turning a beautiful ass a lovely shade of red if I have to. But I prefer more creative punishments."

His hands stroked up her stomach and cupped under her breasts. The cool metal of a chain slid against her skin. She looked down. In his hand was what she could only guess was a set of nipple clamps.

Her clit pulsed in anticipation, her nipples contracting to tight points in excitement. She had never tried clamps because it always seemed wrong to try it in her solo explorations. That didn't mean they didn't feature in many of her late night fantasies.

Hannibal pinched her nipples. His fingers twisted and

rotated them, sending jolts of pleasure shooting through her and down to her clit

"Take a deep breath in." She followed his instruction that rumbled through her chest.

The tight pinch of the first clamp forced out a gasp as it bit down onto her nipple. An intense shock of pain morphed into a throbbing pleasure. She swore she could feel her heartbeat at the captured point.

"Oh God," she cried out as he put the second clamp on. She didn't know if she wanted to push into the pain or pull back from it. It was like the sparks of pleasure were overriding any clear thought in her brain. The metal chain hung like a weight between the two clamps. He gave the metal a gentle tug, and she screamed her pleasure as a lightning bolt of ecstasy shot straight through her nerves.

"I think you like that."

"Oh God, yes. So much."

"Hmm." He ran his tongue up her neck to her ear. "That makes me very happy. Close your eyes for me."

She did as he asked. The loss of her eyesight caused the sensations running through her body to increase. All she could do was feel.

She jumped when Hannibal traced around the edge of her nipples, causing the chain to bounce. Odd and wonderful sensations rushed through her as the muscles contracted. Her core twitched, aching to be filled.

"I like to punish with pleasure. Do you know what's gonna happen now?" He reached in between her legs, his fingers slipping between her folds. "I'm going to make you come so many times that you beg me to stop. Unfortunately for you, you will need to earn my mercy."

The idea of begging someone to stop making her come seemed unlikely, but she was curious. "How would I earn your mercy, Sir?"

His thumb ran over her bottom lip. "You're going to have to make me come with nothing but this."

Her groan slipped out of her lips as he pressed his thumb into her mouth. The thought of being able to taste him like that was exciting. She had given blow jobs before, but it had been more of a chore than something she looked forward to. He pressed down on her tongue and for a moment she pictured it was his cock and she sucked on it with everything she had.

"Good girl." He pulled his finger out of her mouth and she whimpered.

Something slipped slowly between her pussy lips and deep inside her and she flinched at the size. It was almost like an enormous egg spreading her open. Before she could decide if she liked the feeling, something brushed up over her front and across her clit. It felt like a bunch of small strands of silicone. Hannibal used efficient motions as he buckled her into stiff panties. He stepped away from her and she heard something rolling across the room. The urge to open her eyes was almost overwhelming.

"You can open your eyes now."

She turned to face Hannibal. He was standing in front of the tilted drawing table, a strange chair in front of him.

"What's that?"

His lips tipped up in a smile. "Already looking for more punishment?"

Her mind scrambled for a minute. "I'm sorry, what's that, Sir?" She couldn't help but smile. The dominance games were so new and she found she loved them. All she had to do was follow orders.

The simplicity of that was exactly what she needed. Even if she was about to receive a punishment. She looked down and saw that he had indeed put an interesting sort of panty on her. The silicone nubs still rubbed against her clit and the egg sat inside her. The panties were made of some sort of latex and held together on the sides with adjustable buckles.

"It's called a saddle chair. Many of us use it while tattooing. It helps with posture over long periods of sitting."

The chair was indeed on rollers but not shaped like anything she had ever seen before. The seat, instead of being flat, was curved and looked like the saddle someone named it after without a pommel or cantle in the back. She wasn't sure how that would be more comfortable than the round versions, but it was definitely an interesting concept.

"Only a few of us use them here. I have found that they are very useful for other things."

He reached forward, tugging lightly on the chain attached to the nipple clamps. Pleasure zinged through her and she stepped forward as he tugged. The panties were slick between her legs and the egg inside her made her gait awkward as it pressed on her insides as she moved.

He positioned her so she straddled the chair and had her sit down on it. The shape of the chair forced her legs apart and pressed the silicone up against her clit. Her own excitement was lubricating the strange tickler. Hannibal reached behind her and pulled a lever,

The seat dropped a couple of inches with a jerk. She moaned as the strange devices pressed into her pussy. Her face was now at the height of his waist. Hannibal used his foot to hit something on each of the wheels of the chair and she heard them click. The slight rolling of the chair stopped, and she assumed he had locked the wheels into place.

With her arms bound behind her back and legs forced open by the chair, she was off balance. Completely at his mercy. She should be scared, but the whole thing turned her on. She licked her lips, anticipating finally being able to see the cock that she had felt pressed against her.

He picked up a small box from the table and then tugged

at the chain attached to her nipples. Right as the pleasure started shooting through her, a slow vibration pulsed deep inside her, adding to her excitement. He pressed a button on the box and the panties vibrated.

The tiny fingers of silicone buzzed like fingers flicking through the lips of her pussy. It wouldn't take long for the sensations to push her over the edge. Between the aching in her nipples, the stimulation of her clit and the large round device humming inside her, it wouldn't be long.

Hannibal cupped her cheek with a gentle hand and tilted her face up. "One orgasm and I'll let you taste me. After your second orgasm. You can suck me. I know you like competition, so let's make it a race. I'm going to see how many orgasms I can force out of your body before you make me come. Do you understand?"

Jade's whole body heated. She'd never had over two orgasms in a night. And those had been at her own hand. Hannibal was so confident that not only was she going to have two, but that he was gonna force even more from her body. With the first one already barreling down on her, she didn't want to argue, but couldn't wait to see if he could live up to his claims.

He gave her breast a light tap, causing pain to spark in her nipples. "I asked you if you understood."

"Yes, Sir. I understand."

He slid a finger over buttons on what must be the remote for her toys. The egg inside her switched to a deep, pulsing vibration. He placed his hands on her shoulders and pressed her down into the seat. The movement forced the nubs harder against her clit. She moaned, enjoying both the increased contact, and the trapped feeling the movement caused.

The vibration in the panties increased and the slow orgasm that had been building ripped out of her in an almost painfully quick way. She screamed, unable to process the sensations that were pounding her. She tried to stand to get relief, but he held her in place for several more seconds.

Finally, the vibrations against her pussy slowed, and she panted in relief. Her hands ached from clenching on the back of the strange chair as she tried to keep her balance. Her clit was so sensitive it pulsed in time with her heartbeat.

Hannibal opened his jeans and the bulge became so much more evident. He lowered them and his boxers and she got her first glance at him. He was long and thick. So much bigger than any man she'd ever been with. She had to fight back a groan at the sight of the titanium ring on the tip of his dick.

Hannibal stepped forward, bringing the gorgeous cock closer. "What are the rules?"

It was hard to think with that temptation in front of her, but she remembered what he had said. "After the first orgasm, I can taste it. After the second I can suck it. Then we race, Sir."

Jade leaned forward and tried to keep her balance. She wanted to use her tongue to play with the piercing that so fascinated her, but it was hard with her hands behind her back. Using her grip on the chair, she could run her tongue up the length of him. His scent hit her, a wonderful mix of spicy cologne and man. The taste of his pre-cum was perfect on her tongue, called to a primal part of her.

She placed small kisses up his length. Her panties kicked into a medium gear and she moaned against his length. She licked and kissed as she ground herself down on the seat. Not because she was desperate to come, but because she wanted to finally take him into her mouth. The egg inside her switched to an odd pulsing rhythm alternating between short and long pulses.

The silicone nubs continued to pulse at the frustrating

gentle speed, causing her orgasm to build with agonizing slowness. Hannibal took the chain on her nipple clamps and pulled slowly upward. She licked and kissed for all she was worth as the pain grew. Her breasts were lifted, pulled by the chain, the weight of them held up by the clamps on her nipples. She fought back a scream as pleasure and pain shot down to her core.

It was amazing and wrong, painful and right all at the same time. She ground down on the seat in a frantic dance, chasing her orgasm. She must look like someone riding a horse at a show as she tried to both push pressure down and relieve the pressure on her nipples.

Her breath came quick as she tried to focus. She shouldn't stop her ministrations to his body, but she wanted her own release. The skin of his cock was velvet against her hungry lips. She began flicking around the crown of his head with her tongue and tried to make him feel a fraction of the longing she did.

Focusing on the tip around the piercing, she couldn't wait to find out how it would feel inside her body. Could she get something that intimate pierced? The idea fascinated and terrified her. Hannibal let go of the chain and her breasts bounced. Her body shattered into its second orgasm.

She wanted to clutch onto him, feel his skin under her hands as she broke apart. Instead, she dug her nails into the leather of the chair behind her on the seat. Not waiting for instruction, she swallowed him down into her mouth. The zing of the metal against her tongue an interesting sensation.

He was so big. She didn't know how much of his length she could swallow, but she was going to do her damnedest to make this the best blow job he had ever gotten. With tongue and lips, Jade explored every texture and curve. She pulled back and sucked hard, then bobbed her head back down until her throat strained around him and she choked.

Her panties kicked into high gear and her body clenched as a third small orgasm hit her. She barely remembered not to bite down. Her nipples throbbed with the beat of her heart and her clit screamed at the abuse, so sensitive that tears were forming in her eyes. How was pleasure unpleasant?

She hummed around his length, gasping for air every time she pulled back. The super sensitive nerve bundle between her legs sending pulses of pleasure that were driving her insane. Hannibal started moving his hips along with her motions. His pants filled the room as much as hers.

"Fuck Jade, your mouth is magic. Yeah, just like that." He gripped her head in his hands, running his fingers through her hair. He held her still, fucking her mouth with shallow thrusts.

She pushed forward, trying to take in as much of him as she was able. He hit the back of her throat, and she gagged but didn't care. Jade tried to force her throat to relax. The rub of his piercing against the inside of her mouth only adding to the intense sensations.

"*Ça c'est bon, Cher.* That feels so good." His sexy voice speaking French ratcheted up her excitement.

She pushed herself back down on him. Trying to remember what she'd read about how to push past the gag reflex and take him all in. She loosened up her throat and tried to ignore the tiny orgasms racing through her body.

Already, she'd gone past the limit she'd ever achieved before and the thought that there might be another bigger one in her future made her legs tremble. He took one hand out of her hair and hit a button that changed the game completely.

The egg inside her started a heavy rhythm that slowly

sped up and down and dropped the intensity of the nubs against her clit to a low buzz. Her clenching pussy must have moved the egg because it was now pressed directly against her G-spot. The pulsing rhythm echoed through her body and into every nerve.

Hannibal steadied her head as he slowly fed his length into her, pushing past and down into her throat. A wave of pleasure overrode her brain. Her air was cut off, and she didn't care because another orgasm was building up from the base of her spine. She gasped as he pulled out and then pushed back in.

Her breath cut off, the sensations inside her, the movements of the chain tugging at her nipples, all of it at once. There was nothing left for her to do but feel.

Hannibal was talking to her, saying dirty, sexy, wonderful things, and she didn't care because all she could do was live in the sensations. Her body trembled as he pushed in and out. A tidal wave was looming, and she knew it would destroy her.

Agony and ecstasy crashed together as Hannibal pulled the clamps off of her nipples with a quick jerk. Lightning and fire exploded in her body and he fucked her mouth with a frantic pace that matched her own. She screamed her orgasm around his cock, her eyesight wavered.

Hannibal's shout barely registered before his release splashed over the back of her tongue, and another brutal orgasm shook her and threatened to steal her sanity. She couldn't remember how many there had been at this point. Jade whimpered. She didn't think she could survive another.

The vibrations stopped, though her body still hummed like an over tight string. The last taste of him slid across her tongue as he pulled out of her mouth. Everything was blurry and distant as she floated outside of herself in a blissful state of satisfaction.

She was flying through the air, weightless. Or was he carrying her? It didn't matter. Her arms dropped and she couldn't remember how to make them work. They were on the couch. That was nice. She cuddled up against a warm chest that she hoped was Hannibal's.

Ring.

The strange sound was under her head. Jade didn't want to move, but it came again.

Ring.

It was a phone. Strong hands moved her, and she smiled up at Hannibal. He winked at her and pulled a phone out from somewhere. She scowled at him. Why was he answering a phone call now?

"Hey Brother, what's up?"

She pouted. "Who are you talking to?" Her words were slurred and slow. She didn't really care, so she closed her eyes and put her head against Hannibal's chest.

"It's Ink, *Mon cœur.*"

Hannibal's voice sounded even better, rumbling through his chest into her ear. "Oh, say hi for me." Jade snuggled down, wanting to float through the wonderful sensations running through her body.

"All right, I've got some things to finish up here, then I'll be home."

His words splashed cold water onto the blissful cuddling session they were having. That was right. She needed to get up and go. She had to go to her home, and he had to go to his. She wasn't ready to move yet, but she would have to.

"How are you feeling?" Hannibal asked.

"Good, amazing, wonderful, and all those other words."

He chuckled. "That's good to hear."

Jade sat up, enjoying the ache of her body. The twinges of pain helped to clear her head. He wasn't inviting her to stay longer. She should go.

There were a whole host of problems that she had to deal with back at her own home. Responsibilities she should take care of, the gym to run, everything like that. It was tempting to sit here and lose herself in this man's arms forever. It was perfect.

Well, not perfect. Perfect would be if Ink were here to rub her feet. But he wasn't, and it was time to go before she overstayed her welcome.

Chapter 13

Your best friend will always pick you up after you fall… after they finish laughing.

Ink

There is no sound so satisfying as the crack of the whip echoing in the evening air. Ink gripped the familiar leather handle of his favorite six-foot, eight-plait bullwhip and forced his body to settle. Accuracy was his goal tonight. Hitting a small target every time. He narrowed his focus down to the clothespins that were arranged on lines around him.

Ink inhaled slowly. Exercise like this had become almost a ritual to him. The weekly practice was a large part of his life for almost a decade now. He took one last mental run through of what he had planned, then moved.

He exploded into action, moving through the targets. The clothespins flew backward one by one. Left hand. Right hand. Left hand. Right hand. Each crack in a steady rhythm like precision gun shots.

Ink had been ten-years-old the first time he picked up a whip and had several scars to prove it. By the time he had been sixteen, he'd been winning cracking competitions. It was one of the few ways he had been able to make his father proud. Even if that joy had been lessened when the bastard stole every cent he ever won.

In the end, it didn't matter because he was never more alive or aware than when he was throwing out the leather and making it do exactly what he wanted. As soon as the last of the fifty clothespins lay flat on the ground, his unwelcomed thoughts flooded back into his mind.

He had waited to call Hannibal until he knew his Brother's last client should have been gone. Hearing Jade's voice in the background had hit him hard. The tornado of emotions spinning with unwelcomed negative emotions. Not jealousy, exactly. More shock that not only had his Brother arranged to meet Jade without him, but that he hadn't told him about it.

Though why that was a problem was a mystery. They had both been with women without the other. Checking in before doing so would have never occurred to him in the past. The uncertain feelings the argument had caused were having more repercussions than he thought.

The two of them had argued before. Hell, no friendship that had lasted over a decade could be perfectly peaceful. But never once had they let their communication break down so badly. And never to the point of almost silence for three days.

It was his fault. Ink stepped away from the practice targets into a cleared portion of the backyard. They owned five acres and their house was set square in the middle of it to ensure their privacy. The house was surrounded by trees, but they'd cleared out a half-acre of it to give them a decent sized yard. It had the added benefit of creating an area for Ink's practice with whips.

They didn't have any neighbors close enough to complain when he turned up the music to a level that it vibrated in his bones. The angry beat soaked into and through Ink and he let fly with his whips. There was freedom to be found in focusing on nothing but the rhythm and timing of the cracks of his whips. His playlist was an old friend and time seemed to flow by him as one song flowed into the next. His muscles burned and sweat dripped down his neck and over his chest, drying in the night breeze.

Movement near the house caught his attention and he finally let himself stop. He shut off the music and wrapped his whips around his neck. Avoidance at this point would be nothing but cowardice. He turned to face Hannibal. His Brother leaned against the back of their large house in one of the few shadows.

It was almost impossible to read his expression, but his Brother seemed relaxed. Was that because he'd let out his frustration on Jade's willing body? Hannibal stood with his arms crossed as if he had been watching him for a while.

The silence of the night stretched out between them like a heavy weight. The music and the crack of his whips always chased off many of the nighttime critters that would have made sound. Rather than rushing in with his anger at the forefront, the exercise had let him find his patience. He took his time coiling up his whips and supplies, putting them away while he gathered his thoughts.

What was there to say? Regardless of their interactions with Jade, they needed to fix their friendship first. By the time he was done cleaning up, Hannibal was sitting in one of the chairs on the back porch. A second bottle of beer like an offering on the table next to him.

Ink settled down into the chair, taking the beer and

tipping it up to his lips. The cool lager tasted even better after his long workout.

"I had a pleasant surprise at my last appointment tonight." Hannibal broke the silence.

"Is that so?" What was he supposed to say? Ink was smart enough not to lash out, but only barely.

His Brother had done nothing wrong. Even though it felt like a betrayal. Hannibal wouldn't do anything to be purposefully hurtful to a stranger, so he trusted he wouldn't do it to a friend.

"Seems our little Jewel forgot to mention she already had an appointment with me this week. Whoever took her info misspelled her name, and I thought there was a guy coming in for a consult."

Ink's shoulders relaxed, and he took another sip of his beer. "I guess that was a pleasant surprise."

Hannibal chuckled. "You could say that, and not only for the reasons you were thinking." He leaned forward and rested his arms on his knees. "We need to sort our shit out, Brother."

"Yep." Problem was, Ink didn't have any idea of where to start. The things he'd learned about Jade's life tonight made him both want to get closer to protect her and stay further away. The visceral reaction he had at hearing her voice in the background tonight was a good indicator that walking away wasn't an option.

Hannibal put his beer down a little too hard on the table. "Are you still in?"

Ink crossed his arms and glared at Hannibal. "Being in or out isn't the question. The problem is that you went and changed what being in means without even a conversation."

"Yes, I did. And fuck! I know I should have cleared it with you first. But Brother, we are in our thirties. I don't know about you, but the revolving door of women whose faces I barely remember the next day, is growing old."

Ink couldn't argue with the sentiment, only the execution. He'd been feeling the same way too, even if he hadn't put it into words. When you're in your twenties, the idea of a different woman every night seems like a version of paradise. But the truth was, eventually, it became as boring as spending time with your own hand.

"So what? That means we grab the first woman we meet, settle down, buy a dog, convert our dungeon into a nursery?"

He deserved the look that Hannibal gave him. One filled with anger and indignation. "Are you saying you don't feel something for Jade? That she doesn't feel like fire and the two of us are fucking moths?"

That was a perfect description of his emotions. The need to get close to her. Watch her. Study her and enjoy the warmth of being near her. But he knew that only ended in getting burned.

"Oh, I feel it. But I'm not a puppy chasing my first steer. You throw yourself into these situations with no thought of the consequences. You know nothing about that woman."

"And that's where you're wrong. She's not the only one who can cyber-stalk a person."

Hannibal ran down the details of everything he had found about the woman and damn him if every little piece he learned didn't make him want to find out more. So many questions answered, but so many more revealed.

"Yeah, but she's got troubles."

"You mean that piece of shit, partner? We walked in on him, threatening her. Not exactly scared of a skinny little pretty boy."

"That's just the tip of the bull's horn. Highdive pulled me aside today."

Hannibal sat back in his chair with a raised eyebrow and took a sip of his beer. "He got an opinion on who we're sleeping with now?"

"Seems that Jade's troubles run deeper than her partner trying to steal some extra cash from the safe. He's got debts. And not the kind that harasses you with phone calls to collect. Not only that, but he used their business as collateral."

"Shit. Did he tell you who the debts were with or how much?"

"The amount he mentioned was over a hundred grand, but he didn't mention who it was with." He should have asked, but he'd been too focused on being right about not getting in too deep with the woman. There were a lot of people in the moneylending business. Everything from small town jerks all the way up to the Italians.

"Hell, I don't think Jade knows about that."

"You think she would have told you about her illegal debt at your consultation today? How in depth did you get with her?"

"Is that jealousy in your voice?"

Ink rolled his eyes. But Hannibal was probably correct.

Hannibal sighed. "I didn't think to tell you she was there. It felt right, and I went with it."

Ink didn't want to sit around discussing feelings like they were some kind of woman's coffee club. However, it wasn't good to let this stuff fester. He sighed. "Yes, I think it is jealousy. It's your fault with this exclusivity thing." He ran his hand through his hair. "Damn, I haven't considered that kind of commitment in a long damn time. Before you put it out there with Jade, I wouldn't have given two thoughts to who you, she, or anyone, messed around with while I wasn't there. Now I don't know where I stand. How any of this works."

"If this is gonna work, I mean really work. We are all

going to have to have individual relationships. There's going to be times where it's going to be her and me alone or you and her. The strength of those relationships is what will make the three of us work in the long term." Nothing Hannibal said was new to him. They'd seen other polyamorous relationships and how they worked. But since the two of them never got serious with anyone, he hadn't really considered what that would mean in his own life.

The idea of Hannibal spending alone time with Jade didn't really bother him. He trusted his friend with everything. The man was more likely to cut off his own arm than betray him. Ink couldn't believe it, but it was the thought of spending time alone with Jade himself which made him nervous.

"You're right." That didn't mean he had any idea what to do about it. Sure, he'd fucked women alone before, but he hadn't dated a woman solo since high school. Other than Didi, he hadn't been in anything one would call a relationship since joining the military.

"So you're willing to try? Not just some half-assed attempt, where you leave all the emotional shit to me and only show up for the fun parts. I mean really try."

Hannibal's words rocked him back for a moment. He knew, after the first few women they'd hooked up with, he'd left the emotional work to his Brother, not wanting to listen to yet another woman reject them as nothing more than a fun time. But had he only been around for the fun stuff? He thought back over the last ten years and realized that his accusation was nothing but the unvarnished truth. Sure, he'd been there to help draw the women in. But he had avoided anything outside of the physical.

Jade was already different. She haunted his thoughts with her challenging spirit and honest responses. He found himself wondering what she was doing. Dreamed up fantasies of what he wanted to do with her next. The last few hours worrying about her and the mess that her partner was dragging her into were proof of that. It would have never worried him if another person was in that kind of trouble.

He wouldn't lie and pretend that he was only willing to put out the effort to make Hannibal happy. Jade was worth the risk. He wanted to learn where this could go. At some point over the last few days, he'd realized that he wanted more than 'the fun stuff'.

Was he the reason they'd never had a relationship after the first few times they tried when they got out of the military? Did they draw in women who were only looking for a good time because that was all he'd been willing to risk? He didn't want that to happen with Jade. If this thing with her fell apart, it wouldn't be because he didn't put in the effort.

"Yeah, I'm all in. I've got the day off tomorrow. Maybe I'll swing by and surprise our little Jewel."

Hannibal's laugh boomed through the backyard.

"You fucker. You know I'm stuck in appointments all day tomorrow. You want alone time with her."

Ink smiled around his beer as he took a sip. "Maybe."

Hannibal shook his head. "Wait until I tell you about the tattoo our girl wants. It's going to be fucking amazing."

Chapter 14

I hate the word surprise unless it is followed by the word party or vacation.

Jade

J ade threw her car into park. All the pleasant feelings Hannibal had raised in her body were gone. On her way home, with the clock reading almost one a.m., she'd received a notification that someone had disabled the alarm at her gym. It could only be Eric trying again to take something from the gym. She should have changed the code at the same time she changed the combination to the safe.

The giant luxury blacked out SUV that was parked in front of the gym wasn't Eric's usual style, but she had no doubt it was him inside. What the hell did he hope to accomplish? Even if he could figure out the combination to the safe, he knew that they did deposits every night. So the only money there would be a little over $100 and change for the register.

Eric couldn't even access the computer since he'd broken the monitor in his fit the other day. She'd been forced to use her laptop, which was in her bag in the trunk, until she got time to buy a replacement. So focused on her anger and what she planned to tell Eric, she didn't even notice there was more than one person in the office before it was too late.

"What the hell are you doing in here?" Jade stared around the room in disbelief.

A large man covered in black work tattoos held Eric pinned to the wall by his throat. A second man in a tailored suit looked at them with cold eyes. Logic would dictate that the large man currently doing violent things to her partner was the scarier of the two men, but something about the man in the suit had all her fight-or-flight instincts firing.

He had wide Slavic features that made him appear cold and brutal. His dark hair cut close to his head and even in the expensive suit, Jade could see he had the same black-work tattoos that marked him as a member of the Bratva, or Russian Mafia. He turned his icy blue-eyed gaze onto her, and Jade's throat went dry.

"You must be his woman. I believe he said your name was Jade." The man's Russian accent was thick, confirming her fears about his background.

"I'm not his woman." Jade tried to hide her fear under bluster.

The man tilted his head, as if considering. "His business partner then."

"Yes, he owns a small part of my business." Why had he brought these men to the gym in the middle of the night?

"Your partner here is behind on paying back some money. He brought us here promising to be able to make payment."

Jade glared at Eric, her anger spiking her pulse even

more than the fear. The safe on the floor next to them was open and obviously empty. How had they gotten in without the combination?

"I'm not sure why he would do that." What was she supposed to say?

The man tossed down two small packages of wrapped money. She recognized them as the starter cash that had been in the safe.

"That doesn't even begin to cover what he was supposed to give us." He gestured at the wrapped ones and fives.

"Where's the money, Jade? You have to give it to them." Eric's voice was strained since the big man still had his hand wrapped around his throat.

"Eric, who are these guys?"

"I'm sorry, that was rude of me. I'm Andrey Petrov and that is my associate Maxim. Do you have the money your partner owes us?"

Jade didn't like the way he kept emphasizing the word partner. It made it seem like this man held her responsible for Eric's actions and debts.

"I told you I needed the money. You said you'd get it for me." Eric's whine grated against her nerves.

Indignation overrode sense, and she snapped at him, "No, Eric. I told you if you told me what you needed the money for, then I would buy out some more of your shares."

"It seems Eric here likes to lie to both of us." She knew her words were unwise, but her shock and anger seemed to have taken control of her mouth. It was like the guy was trying to build some sort of camaraderie between the two of them. While she was pissed as hell at Eric, it didn't mean she wanted anything to do with these two men.

"Just give him the money, Jade and I'll explain everything."

Jade wanted to roll her eyes and she probably would have if the situation wasn't so tense. "I don't have that kind of money lying around. We've never kept a lot of cash in the safe."

Eric tried to move, but Maxim held him in place. "What about the money from today? Give that to them. I can get them the rest tomorrow after you give it to me."

"Did you ever pay attention to anything that went on here?" The urge to shake her friend even as he was held against the wall was almost overwhelming. "The deposit tonight wasn't even two hundred dollars. We don't do most of our business in cash. People use credit cards. I'm pretty sure you wouldn't have been dragged to an out of the way business in the middle of the night if a couple hundred dollars would have made them happy."

"It seems your lovely partner is smarter than you are, Eric."

Eric tried to shove away the big man holding him, his outrage clear on his face. He was obviously more pissed about being called dumb than afraid of what they were going to do to him. "Fuck you!"

The man's punch to his stomach sounded so painful that Jade flinched and her adrenaline spiked. If she didn't de-escalate things quickly, they would both end up badly injured or even possibly dead. Her brain scrambled to find a way out of the situation Eric's recklessness had gotten them into.

They'd been in trouble before and she wished this situation was a surprise. In the beginning, they lived in their car more than an apartment because he couldn't be trusted to pay the bills. When they started making more money, she had made sure she was the one responsible for paying for things.

Which looking back meant she covered all the expenses out of her portion of any winnings they got. She'd honestly thought him buying into the business had been his way of repaying her for all the years that she'd bailed him out.

It was impossible now to believe that fiction. He probably didn't even think of things that way. Never even considered the consequences his actions might have on other people. Earlier, he had said he needed ten-thousand-dollars. Which probably meant he needed more.

She'd never borrowed money from a loan shark, but she'd seen enough movies to guess that the interest had probably hiked the amount up and above what he even realized he owed. A second punch had Eric coughing in pain.

"Please stop." She tried to hide the concern and fear in her voice. Jade focused on the man who was obviously in charge. "How do we resolve this without him getting hurt anymore? There's no money here, other than what you guys already took. And even when the banks open up, it will take time for me to transfer money around to pull together the money. There's paperwork, and a contract needed to buy him out of the business."

"I told you I'm not selling any more to you."

Jade glared at the idiot. "Are you fucking kidding me? Got a man's hand wrapped around your throat. We're in an office in the middle of the night like a bad action flick. You owe these men money for God knows why. I'm offering you a lifeline and you want to toss back at me?"

Eric seemed to finally process the situation. His huffy attitude wilted under her harsh words. "Fine. You're right. Just set up the deal, then it is settled."

Andrey Petrov nodded. "I will give you two days to get together the money to pay off his debt, in exchange for him handing over his portion of the business."

"I didn't say I was paying off his debt. I said I was going to buy his shares out in the business."

Petrov stepped forward and Jade's body froze like a deer

caught in headlights. He tapped her cheek with a roughened palm in a disturbingly gentle gesture. "I repeat. You have two days to pay his debt."

Her body trembled. She wished she trusted Eric enough to believe that he would go from the bank straight to pay off his debt. But unfortunately, it was too easy to picture him taking off with the money and leaving her alone to handle the debt for him. Her mind bounced between the different options she had.

The original thought had been to give him the $30,000 she had saved, leaving him with a small portion of the business still in his name. With everything that had happened, she couldn't stomach being in business with him any longer. She needed a clean break.

There was an account that held three months' operating expenses for the gym. It was the intended collateral for the expansion loan. She could dip into that to round out the money she had in her personal savings. With that, she would have the full fifty-thousand-dollars, but no safety net. It would be worth it if it would save Eric.

But how to make sure that he paid off his debt with that money right away and not decide to fly off to some small country for a couple of months?

"Have a man at the Cross Street bank at three o'clock on Friday so I can watch Eric hand over the money."

Eric glared at her, and Petrov chuckled. "I can do that."

"Good, then we'll take care of everything then."

The Russian gave her face a light tap, making her stomach flip. He looked back at Eric. "You have an excellent woman here. Shame you threw away your partnership like that."

Eric's eyes narrowed, and the expression on his face turned ugly. "She's never been mine. Her stupid obsession with tattoos, and her celebrity crushes were always more important to her than me. I was always there for her. She was never there for me. I don't owe her shit."

Where was all this hatred coming from? She wished there was some way to turn back time so she could figure it out. Tension she didn't understand vibrated in the air.

"Is that right? Are you not loyal to your friends?" The barely veiled amusement in the Russian's voice grated on her nerves.

"No, he's the only one who doesn't care who he betrays. To him, not being willing to fuck him was the same as not caring for him."

She had known that he wanted more from her than friendship, but thought they had settled that years ago. From the anger and vicious jealousy about her celebrity crush, it was obvious she had been wrong. How had their friendship dissolved into this?

The smile on the man's face seemed completely out of place, as if he never used those muscles. "I don't care who you fuck as long as I get my money. I hope you don't betray me, because I will burn down everything you care about."

He gave a jerk of his head towards the door. And Maxim let Eric go. The two Russian men strolled out of her office as if they had simply concluded a normal business meeting. She waited until she knew they were out of earshot.

"I can't believe you borrowed money from them."

"There she is, the judgmental, oh, so perfect Jade." Eric straightened his clothes. "Too good for her friends. Too good for TV. She never makes mistakes like us mere mortals."

"Is that what you think of me? You think I look down on you? Christ, you were my best friend. Hell, my only friend."

Eric's snort was loud. "That's what you said to the cameras, but the second they were off, you had nothing but criticism. You have always tried to control me through money. Blew me off at every chance. You abandoned me for this backwater life."

"Getting on to you about paying the rent, and making sure we had enough money to buy the plane tickets in time, wasn't trying to control you. It was making sure we could continue to live the life you wanted. I didn't love life in the spotlight, you did. Life isn't about parties and the adoration of fans, Eric. If I hadn't stepped back from the competition circuit, we would have been pushed out of the light soon, anyway. That's how that business worked. Someone younger and with a more interesting story would have taken the spotlight and the sponsors. I thought you understood that, that I was trying to set up something lasting for the both of us."

"Maybe, but this isn't what I wanted. And none of that had to do with why I was never good enough for you."

She took three steps forward and slammed her hands down on the desk. How dare he come at her when she had just bailed his ass out of a fire so big it could have cost him his life. "Not wanting to sleep with you didn't mean you weren't good enough. We've known each other since we were twelve-years- old. You're like a brother to me. I'm sorry if you felt otherwise, but I didn't. Before these last few months, I would have done anything for you, except sleep with you."

"Yeah, well. Looks like you're throwing away your brother now. Just like your father threw you away."

His words rocked her back, and her pulse pounded against her throat. "Get out." Rage was like ice in her voice.

"I'm sorry, Jade." Eric backpedaled, but it was too late.

"I said get out. And you're right. Once those papers are signed and I watch you give the money to that Russian jerk, we're done. Don't call. Don't text. Nothing."

"Fine." Eric stormed out of the office and slammed the door behind him. The sound hit her like a blow to the chest.

She was clinging onto sanity by a thread as she tried to save his ass and he dared compare her to that man? She couldn't stop the tears that poured down her face.

How the hell was she going to fix this mess without destroying everything she had built?

Chapter 15

This may be my safe space, but I never promised it was yours.

Ink

His plan to get to Leap early and try to catch her before she opened had failed. He had gotten distracted for hours watching some of the videos of Jade that Hannibal had suggested. Watching her in her element was addicting. He had even found some of her competing in gymnastics back when she was young.

The woman was a fascinating mix of determination and humor. In her interviews, she'd shown a self-deprecating sense of humor about herself and what she did. The way she was always supporting and encouraging everyone around had engaged him. But the recent ones of her doing Parkour stunts and teaching some of the basic moves showed how passionate she was about the sport.

Some of the things she did in tricks were nuttier than a five-pound fruitcake. The long distances she leaped. Free running wasn't something he had ever watched, but it was mesmerizing. Going from building to building couldn't be safe, and he had wanted to shake her by the shoulders, and tell her to rein it in. But almost every video caught the pure joy on her face as she seemed to fly through the sky.

It was like he blinked and instead of being morning, it was already past three in the afternoon. Ink had forced himself to stop and get some food before heading over. It was late afternoon when Ink finally pulled into the parking lot at Leap. He had hoped to catch her at a slow time, but from the look of the parking lot, he was going to be out of luck. Over twenty cars were in the lot.

He parked his bike near the back and headed in. Unlike the previous time he had been here, there was a young woman sitting at the desk in the entryway wearing one of the gym's polos.

Her smile faltered slightly as she looked him up and down. "Are you here for the open gym?"

Her tone clearly said she didn't believe he could possibly be there to work out. He looked down at himself and smiled. They probably didn't get many people coming into the place wearing cowboy boots, jeans, a black Henley and a motorcycle cut.

"No, ma'am. I'm here to see Jade." Ink gave her the smile he knew fooled people into believing he was an innocent country boy.

"Oh." Her smile returned. "Does she know you're coming?"

"No." He gave her a wink. "I was hoping I could surprise her."

The woman's cheeks flushed. She looked over at the clock on the wall. The time read 5:55. Ink knew the gym didn't close until nine. Maybe he should have waited to catch her near the end of the shift.

"She's scheduled to do a free run demonstration in about five minutes. You could go in and watch if you want."

"Is she teaching more classes tonight? I could come back later. I don't want to interrupt."

"No, she usually does a demo at the beginning of the open gym, but there are no private lessons scheduled. We have almost the full staff here tonight, so she should be able to break away after she does her thing."

She probably shouldn't be sharing that much information with a stranger, but he was grateful for the intel. "Thank you, kindly."

Maybe he could convince her to step away and talk for a bit.

"Have you ever seen her free run? It's an impressive sight. She's one of the best there is."

"I've seen videos, but I've never seen her do it in person."

"You should definitely go in then." He nodded and gave her a grateful smile.

It wasn't hard to figure out where Jade was doing her run. A group of about thirty people were milling around an interesting multi-level structure. He tried to be as unobtrusive as possible and stood near the edge of the crowd.

Jade's smile was strained as she talked to some of the younger students. She seemed worn down with stress and something more than working a long day. Ink had seen the same fake smile on people too many times to believe it. Something was wrong with their little Jewel. Was it the people here causing her stress?

He watched as she interacted naturally with the surrounding people, looking for a clue. All of them were vying for her attention, but no single person stood out.

It didn't take long before the crowd was backing away. Jade set herself up at the start of what looked like the entrance of the giant wooden structure. What was the purpose of all the outcroppings, bars, and holes?

Several of the spectators held up phones and started recording. The countdown clock on the wall started a countdown from ten. When it reached one, it was like Jade had been shot forward from a cannon.

She bounced upward, back and forth between two completely sheer walls until reaching the top of what had to be a fifteen foot climb, gripped the top of the structure and swung herself with a flip over the top. She ran forward and did some sort of side cartwheel onto a lower ledge. Ink lost sight of her for a minute as she slid through a small hole.

Then she was flying across the back, swinging from a set of bars he hadn't noticed. People were moving, spreading out around the structure. It was hard to describe or even process the different movements as she moved so quickly.

She was in constant motion. Her feet never slowing or stopping. She hurled her body in, up, and through the structure. Each movement was designed not only to get her from A to B, but to do so in a way that had him catching his breath in awe.

There was no way he could do half of what she did. And he didn't even think he would have imagined trying a quarter of the tricks that she executed. It was an acrobatic dance that had her moving back and forth, up and down.

Loud beeping rang through the room. The clock showed it had been almost two minutes since she had begun. Jade had to be in superior shape to maintain that level of activity for that amount of time.

As the clock hit one minute and fifty-eight seconds, she leapfrogged up to the top of the structure, which had to be almost thirty feet off of the ground, and threw herself somersaulting off the edge. Ink's breath caught in fear.

Terror of what a fall from that height might do, racing through his mind.

The crowd roared as the final tone sounded. Ink weaved through the crowd, desperate to make sure Jade was okay.

A laugh burst out of him. He'd forgotten about the foam pits scattered under the different dangerous obstacles. People were whistling, cheering, and calling her name. Ink added his voice to theirs.

He moved closer to the edge of the foam pit and saw her slowly making her way towards the edge. Her breath was fast, but not particularly strained. Sweat barely beaded on her skin. Once again, he was amazed by this dynamic woman. She'd overcome things in her life that would have turned others into defeated wrecks. Even today, when she was obviously worn down and stressed, she created joy for others. He needed her in his life.

Jade's eyes caught Ink's for a brief moment and lit up with excitement. She was a temptation that would easily turn into addiction. It was no wonder Hannibal was already obsessed.

The moment passed, and her expression dimmed. The smile was still there but now held the rehearsed cheer reserved for customer service, not genuine joy. When she was close enough, he offered her a hand out of the pit. She grabbed it and he pulled her up next to him. Ink pressed his body against hers.

The surrounding crowd interrupted and pulled her away with questions and comments on the different tricks she had done. Her eyes tracked him as he moved away and settled himself out of the way against a wall. He could be patient.

This was her business, and he had to respect that. Just like she would have to respect, if she came to visit him unexpectedly at his shop, that he might have to finish up some things before giving her his full attention.

It took about five minutes before she broke away from her admiring fans. The crowd dispersed throughout the gym. Some stayed in the free run area she'd used. Others moved over to the obstacles and the mountain climbing area.

It was an interesting mix of people. The ages ranged from late teens to someone who looked like they were in their late 40s. He counted five other people wearing the gym's polo, and he guessed they were her staff.

"This is a surprise." Her smile was tight. Did she not want him here?

She had appeared to be happy to see him, but now he was questioning himself. "This is a pretty impressive setup you've got here."

"You saw it the other night."

"Yes, but I was a bit distracted," he teased. "How you work the crowd is impressive. You can tell by the way your staff moves between the areas making sure everybody is being safe that they are well trained."

She looked back over her shoulder, studying the room, and her smile grew real again. "It took a while. But my staff is great. All of them aren't only good at what they do. They also love it."

That sense of exhaustion seeped back into her body, and her shoulders slumped. What was weighing her down so badly that she couldn't let go of it for more than a moment?

"What's wrong, darlin? You look like you've had a hard day."

"Is that a polite way of saying I look like shit?" Her joke fell flat.

Ink ran his gaze up and down her body, letting her see his admiration and desire in his eyes. "No. Still looking as sweet as stolen honey. Doesn't mean I can't worry."

A blush filled her cheeks. "I had a bad night that lasted far too long and bled into morning. Then I had to spend all day setting things in place to clean up the mess. Honestly, I really need to relax."

Ink stepped closer and cupped her cheek. He ran his thumb along her cheek with a gentle sweep. "The pleasant woman at the front desk said you're fully staffed tonight. How about you cut out early and let me take you for a ride?"

She gave a small shake of her head, but then seemed to reconsider. "You know what? That sounds like an amazing idea." Mischief lit her eyes. "Is that an offer to ride on the back of your bike or something else?"

Ink chuckled, loving how even when stressed she didn't lose her playful spirit. "It sure is." He teased back, leaving the choice of how to interpret his answer up to her. He would be happy to help her relax in any way she wanted.

Jade leaned into his touch. "Well, I've never actually been on the back of a bike."

"Now that is a right shame."

She hesitated for a moment, then stepped back. "Give me a minute to set everything up and get changed. I'll meet you outside."

The feeling of Jade behind him on the bike was surprisingly comfortable. In the past, he rarely let anyone ride with him. If someone they were with needed a ride, he left that to Hannibal.

The way she wrapped around him was wonderfully tight without being restrictive. He was glad she had agreed to go for a ride. Bringing her back to Hannibal and his house hadn't been a plan, so much as an impulse. He wanted her to see the place they had created for themselves.

Like her gym, their house was important to the two of

them. More so than even the shop since they had designed it from the ground up. The purchase of the land had been the first thing he did once they knew they were staying.

A few years ago, something had settled inside his soul. The success of the business and the amount of money in his account hadn't been as satisfying as the first time he slept in the house that they owned. He glanced back to catch Jade's reaction as they pulled up the driveway. He couldn't help but chuckle at the shock on her face. He pulled up near the walkway and parked.

"Wow, this place is nice."

He helped her off the bike as she turned her head trying to take everything in. "Not what you were expecting, darlin?"

"I don't know. After the long drive through the woods. I think I was kind of expecting more of a serial killer shack than a suburbia mini-mansion."

Ink laughed. He loved the honesty that seemed to always come from Jade. "Just because we don't have neighbors doesn't mean that we don't want a nice house."

"We?" She turned back to him with a smile. "You and Hannibal share this house?"

"Yes. We weren't kidding when we said we share everything."

"It must be nice to have someone you're that close to." Ink could see sadness swimming in the back of her eyes and wondered if she was thinking about that asshole of a business partner. "You guys said you'd been together since the military. How long is that?"

Ink paused and considered. "I met Hannibal in my second year and we served almost five years together. We've been out for ten years. So for almost fifteen years we've been friends."

"That's almost as long as Eric and I have been friends. But we met in middle school."

"Are you implying I'm old?"

She smiled at him. "Not at all." Ink enjoyed the heat that filled her gaze. "Do I get to see the inside?"

"I think that can be arranged."

He offered her his arm and escorted her into their house. Nerves played havoc with his stomach. The overwhelming desire for her to like the place was ridiculous. They designed it to make them happy, not some random woman. Not that she was a random woman.

He shouldn't have worried. Her expressive face lit up with delight as she looked around the living room. She wandered through the space, studying the unique pieces of artwork that they had displayed on the walls.

"Most of these are your work." She looked at him over her shoulder.

"They are."

Jade had stopped in front of one of his favorites, the black and white drawing unusual for him. He rarely worked in charcoal, but it had turned out wonderfully. In the middle of a dark forest, a woman in a flowing dress was tied with her hands above her head, her back facing the viewer. In the foreground, a blurred shadowy figure held something coiled in his hand. If you knew he was the artist, it wouldn't be a hard guess to say that something was a whip.

Ink loved doing tattoos, but artwork like this had been his passion since he first picked up a pencil. He still spent hours every week working on pieces designed solely for himself. His work was kept in a special storage unit he rented, only putting their favorites up on the walls. Hannibal occasionally tried to convince him to do a gallery show or try to sell some of them. But money wasn't why he drew.

As they both looked over the drawing, Ink realized that

the tied up woman bore a surface level resemblance to Jade. The strong well-defined muscles and the long curling hair, which was amusing because he hadn't based this particular picture on anyone.

Ink pictured their little Jewel tied up like that in their backyard and his cock grew painfully stiff. The trust and hunger that would be in her eyes, the way her body would shiver in both fear and anticipation. He wanted her not only willing but eager to feel his whip.

"Is that a whip in his hand?"

"It is. People usually guess a length of rope."

Jade shook her head and nodded over to a shelf nearby where he had one of his showier whips coiled up on display. "I saw that, so maybe my brain was already going there. Is it yours?"

"The picture or the whip?" Ink teased.

"I have no doubt the picture is yours. Only you could not have a single face in the picture but still display such emotion."

"You're right. They're both mine." Ink studied her expression. Was she afraid?

"Are you any good with it?" Jade's tone was curious, and he wished he could see inside her head.

"I try to practice every day. It relaxes me."

She gave a nervous laugh. "Hard to imagine a whip, as relaxing. But then again, I leap over buildings and obstacles to relax, so I guess I can't really judge. I saw a whip cracking contest once. Some of the people there were pretty good."

"I haven't been in a contest since I was a teenager. They are a lot more common in Texas than they are here."

"I can imagine." She bit her lip as if trying to hold back a question, but Ink was patient and after only a minute, she spoke. "Have you ever used a whip on a person?"

"Would that scare you?"

"A little."

He stepped forward, closing in the distance between them. He cupped her cheek in his hand. Jade trembled against his hand. Some would consider him an asshole, but he didn't care. He loved the fact she was scared. Loved knowing she was forcing herself not to move away. Facing uncomfortable thoughts for him.

She was so brave. He ran his hand down her neck slowly and stroked his thumb up and down her pulse point. "It's one of my favorite things." Her breath quickened, and he tightened his grip on her neck slightly. "Don't be afraid, little Jewel. I promise I know exactly what I'm doing. It's probably nothing like what you're imagining."

"That's good." Her voice was breathy, and her pulse raced under his thumb. "I've watched videos." Her nipples stood out against her blouse like little beacons of temptation. The combination of her fear and obvious arousal was intoxicating. "I've been thinking about you and Hannibal, and what we did, a lot. I've never felt like that before. It was overwhelming."

"I'm glad you think about me. I've definitely been thinking about you."

"I can't get you out of my mind. Overwhelming or not. I want to feel that intensity again."

Ink leaned in and let his breath brush over her ear. "If you think that was intense, you're going to love what we can do to your body. That was only a tiny taste. If you really give yourself over to us, we'll show you what it's like to fly."

"Why do you want to do those things to me? What do you get out of it? I mean, the books I've read all talk about a submissive enjoying it because they get to relax. Hand over control and exist in the moment. I'm going to be honest, that sounds unbelievable and wonderful at the same time. But it doesn't seem fair to put all the stress on someone else, or I guess in our case someones else."

Ink raised his head and looked into her eyes. He saw a desperation there that called to a dark part of himself. He tried to put into words what he knew and liked about BDSM on an instinctual level.

"Being the dominant means using all your skills, focus, and attention to bring out the best in your submissive. Whether that means giving them pleasure or making their life better in other ways. They give me their trust and I enjoy being the one who they look to. During a scene, I let go of all the petty worries of the day and focus on that one person. Reading their breath." He slid his hands down from her neck, down the front of her chest until his hands circled around her breasts, lightly brushing over her tight nipples. "Being aware of the signs that your body gives off. When to be gentle and when to push you past what you think you can handle."

Her eyes softened, and he saw the hunger he expected in their depths, but also pain. "I know I shouldn't, but I want that so badly. I want to let go of the day I've had. Forget everything except now. Can you really do that for me?"

It was tempting to say yes. Drag her to the back of the house where Hannibal and he had their private dungeon set up. But her tone held an edge of brittleness which told him something bad had happened. More than the jerk breaking into the office trying to get some extra cash. He wouldn't play with her if she was as likely to break as to fly. She was in trouble and he wanted to know about it before they went any further.

"What's going on, darlin'? You said your night was stressful and your day even more so. But from what Hannibal told me you both had a good time last night."

She shook her head, and he was sad to see some of the

lust drunk look leave her eyes. "I really don't want to talk about it."

"Does it have to do with Eric?" Ink didn't even like saying the guy's name. The thought that the asshole was going to drag her down with him made his anger rise.

"Yes. Let's just say things came to a head. I need to buy him out now, instead of on the timetable I originally had planned. So I spent most of the day talking to the banks and moving money around to make that happen."

"He's giving you more problems?" Ink didn't want to say too much and risk giving away how much he already knew. She wasn't likely to appreciate finding out that the Dark Sons had had her investigated. That they knew all too much about her private business.

"Yes, he said some things last night that were cruel." She took a deep breath. "No one can hurt you like someone who has known you most of your life. It doesn't matter, because, like I said, tomorrow I'm going to be buying him out. The contract's being drawn up now and the money's all been moved to the local bank. It's hard knowing that when I give him the check and have him sign the contract tomorrow, it's probably the end of our fifteen-year friendship."

"Do you want one of us to go with you tomorrow?" His offer surprised him, but he hated the idea of her having to face the man alone.

"Thank you, but no. This is something I need to do by myself. We'll be somewhere public, so it's not like he can do anything. I swear I'm okay. I honestly just want to forget everything for a little while."

Ink hoped it would be that easy, but he couldn't say more. Respecting her wishes would be hard. He didn't want to steal that sense of strength that was at the core of her being. But she raised an instinctive need to protect and make her life easier.

If what she needed was to forget and lose herself and sensations, then he could do that for her. He glanced at the clock on the wall by the TV. Hannibal would be home soon, if his Brother didn't linger at work. Maybe he could set up something that would help all of them.

"Are you willing to give yourself over to me? Trust me and Hannibal to take away all your worries?"

She looked around as if she expected his Brother to appear out of thin air. He couldn't help but laugh. "He'll be home soon and I promise you, I won't be done doing even half the things I want to do to your body by the time he gets here."

"Oh." The word was more a gasp than anything else. "Yes. I think I'd like that."

Ink wrapped his hand into the back of her hair and pulled back. Her body arched, and he continued the movement until she was off balance. Her pupils were wide as she looked up into his eyes.

"No thinking. Just feel. I've got you. Just let go." Her breath hitched, but she was still tense, not trusting him to keep her from falling.

"Yes, Sir."

He used the hand not in her hair to pinch down on her nipple until her gasp turned into a whine. "Little Jewel, in this house, when we're like this, you call me Master."

Jade hesitated, and he twisted her nipple. Her groan was loud, but she finally relaxed into his hold. "Yes, Master."

He scooped her up over his shoulder and chuckled at her little squeak. As Ink strolled through the house, she seemed too shocked to even struggle. He pulled out his phone and sent Hannibal a text. If their little Jewel needed to forget, he was going to make sure that by the end of the night, she didn't even remember her own name.

Chapter 16

Anticipation is half the fun… or so my Dom tells me.

Hannibal

Hannibal strode into the playroom, his dick already painfully hard. The ride home from the shop had been a complete failure of self-control. He had broken every speed law and a good amount of other traffic laws. It was all Ink's fault, of course. He had been cleaning up some paperwork at the office when his Brother's text had come in, triggering the mad rush home.

Ink: *Going to tie up our little Jewel, Join us, if you can.*

Images of what the kinky fucker was doing to their woman had his cock pressing painfully against his zipper. If he was too slow, he knew he'd come home to her, passed out, and be forced to wait until round two. Ink had answered none of his texts about waiting.

The sight in the room almost took his breath away. Jade stood in the center of the room. Her arms were chained above her, giving him a perfect view of her naked body. A spreader bar stretched her legs apart, making sure every inch of her was visible. The marks on her skin were only a light pink—Ink had been going gentle on her.

The only things she wore were a blindfold and a set of noise canceling headphones. She wouldn't know he was here until he touched her. Her moans were an interesting mix of frustration and pleasure.

Ink was using a matched set of floggers on her back that he recognized as their softest deer skin. Most subs considered a session with those as nothing more than a light massage. It was surprising to see his Brother, who usually went in for the harsher tools, going so light on her.

"Were those her choice or yours?" Hannibal knew Ink had noticed him the moment he walked in, though the man never stopped the gentle Florentine motion of the floggers.

"I wanted to be sure she was warmed up for us. Nice and relaxed before I really got started. Plus, our girl is a masochist. This is almost a torture for her." Ink's smile said he was enjoying her frustration.

The steady thuds against her skin were perfectly in time with the low music playing in the room. "Poor girl. Are you piping in the music to the headphones?"

"Of course. It's a lot louder in the headset. I wanted to be sure she couldn't hear us talk."

"Something I need to know?" Hannibal was concerned. Ink rarely took the time to talk when there was a naked, willing woman in front of him. What could have gone wrong in the less than twenty-four hours since he had seen her?

"She had another encounter with that partner of hers, I think, after she left you. Had her wound tighter than a grandfather clock. Says she has it under control."

"You don't think she does?" It was tempting to remove Eric from the equation. If he put Jade in danger, he wouldn't hesitate to make that happen.

"Possibly. We'll have to keep a close watch. She wants to relax, to forget about him and all her worries for a night. I told her we might be able to help her out with that."

"Sounds like fun." Hannibal strode over to a shelf and grabbed one of his favorite toys. He shrugged out of his cut and shirt, then took off his boots and socks. He positioned himself just far enough away from Jade that she wouldn't brush up against him as she wiggled under Ink's tender blows.

He slipped his hands into the vampire gloves. They were a wonderful invention designed to heighten sensation through a combination of textures. Soft fur on one side, supple leather on the other, and dull metal tips at the ends of every finger. Ink moved his strokes down her thighs.

She arched her ass back chasing the leather tails, the motion also causing her lovely breasts to press forward as if begging for touch. Hannibal couldn't resist any longer. Using the soft fur side of the glove, he brushed his hands down the front of her chest.

She jerked back, startled, and had to catch her balance on the chains holding her up. "Hannibal." She sighed, her quick mind obviously realizing what was going on. His name was a moan filled with hunger and desire as she leaned into his touch.

As he ran the soft fabric over the tips of her breasts. He alternated between teasing brushes of the fur and the friction of the leather against her nipples. Her moans vibrated straight through him.

Ink stepped back for a moment and switched out to heavier floggers while Hannibal distracted her by playing with her nipples. She was so gorgeous, the way she arched forward against her chains, trying to get more pressure. A beautiful sight. The spreader bar kept her balance precarious. So, she couldn't do much more than arch and wiggle.

He lowered his mouth down and took one of her nipples into his mouth, gently sucking it in and teasing the tip with his tongue. She squirmed, her thighs clenching as if trying to close her legs to get pressure on her needy little clit. Ink chose that moment to land the first blow with the harder leather against her ass.

Her startled scream had both men chuckling. Ink continued his rhythm and soon she was trying to push out her ass at the same time she pushed her chest forward into Hannibal's mouth.

"Oh God, yes. Please!"

Hannibal stood up. He took the headphones from her ears, leaning in to nibble her ear. "What a lovely surprise. I come home and find you all needy, and wet. Is that honey for me?"

"Yes, Hannibal. I want you so much. Please Master Ink, can I come now? Please." Her words were desperate and fast. His Brother must have been edging her from the moment he sent the text.

"That was not very polite of you." Hannibal ran the metal tips of the glove over the sides of her breasts. He took the tips of each nipple between the metal, pushing down until she squirmed and gave a small squeak. "You call him Master, and I don't even get a Sir. I don't think you deserve to come."

Ink chuckled and brought a hard blow down onto her shoulders. They both stepped back, letting her swing and try to catch her balance.

"Sorry, Master Hannibal."

He used one hand to steady her and tilted her head back. "Are you?"

Ink brought the flogger up between her legs and landed a blow onto her tender pussy. Her groan was adorable. Hannibal continued switching between the soft fur and the scratching pinching of the tips of the gloves, while Ink worked a steady rhythm, moving up and down her body from behind with the floggers.

Her body had broken out into a sweat that beaded her skin with moisture. She squirmed at every touch, hard or soft. Her moans were a sweet counterpoint to the music that flowed through the room. It was hard to ignore his own painfully stiff cock. But if they were going to make their girl fly again, he needed to find his patience.

When her breaths started coming in pants and her eyes glazed, Hannibal nodded to Ink. They both stepped forward and pressed her between them. Holding her immobile with the bulk of their bodies.

Hannibal licked her neck and enjoyed the salty taste of her skin. He worked his way down her body with his mouth. Her pussy flushed and her obvious excitement dripping onto her thighs was a welcome sight.

Hannibal spread Jade open, enjoying her earthy smell as he slipped his tongue into her folds. He loved the taste of her against his tongue, the way she unselfconsciously ground against his face, trying to get the friction she needed to orgasm. The chains above her rattled as she jerked against them.

Ink dropped down on the other side of her and was nipping at her very red ass with his teeth. Hannibal flattened his tongue and put slow, deliberate pressure on her swollen clit. It wouldn't be enough to push her over the edge that they wanted her hovering on.

"Please, Masters, please. I have to come, please. I have to!"

Hannibal chuckled at the wonderful desperation in her voice. Through her legs, he saw Ink pulling out a butt plug from his pocket. They were going to make sure she was ready for what they wanted tonight. His Brother loved claiming a woman's ass and was always prepared to make sure she enjoyed it as well.

Hannibal stood and tossed the gloves to the side. Leaning in, he ran a hot breath over her neck. "You want to come for us?"

"Yes."

"Maybe we'll be nice and let you come. If you're good."

"I'll be good. I swear."

"Have you ever taken two men at the same time, little Jewel?" Hannibal asked.

Her body tensed. "No."

Ink leaned in and whispered in her other ear. "Has anyone ever claimed that gorgeous ass of yours?"

"No."

Hannibal nipped the spot right behind her ear, and she bucked. "Then we'll have to get you ready. Are you okay with that?" He tweaked her nipple. Then began rolling her tight peaks between his fingers.

"I think so." Her voice held hesitation.

Behind her, he saw Ink teasing the crack of her ass with his fingers. Her body seemed torn, whether to push back against him or to pull away.

"That isn't a question you can answer with maybe, little Jewel." Hannibal ran his hand down and through her damp folds and slowly started circling her clit. His Brother would be circling and teasing the sensitive flesh around her ass.

She drew in a deep breath. "Yes, I want to try. But you'll stop if... if it's too much?"

Ink purred. "Of course we will. Red stops everything. Always. Where are you right now?"

"Scared, but green."

Hannibal positioned himself so he could watch Ink as he played with his favorite part of a woman. They matched their rhythm as one rimmed her ass, the other circled her clit in slowly quickening circles.

Her breathing was their sole focus. She panted and groaned as they did their best to keep her right on the edge of orgasm. Ink spread lube around the sensitive flesh. Her body finally relaxed into the motions, and Ink slipped a finger inside of her before she could tense.

She thrashed and Hannibal picked up speed on her clit until she pushed back and Ink slipped a second finger in. Her moans were the sounds of sweet victory. Hannibal used his other hand to tweak at her nipples.

Soon she was thrusting back against Ink, finger fucking herself on his hand. Ink pulled his hand back. Smirking when she cried out in disappointment. He replaced his fingers with the butt plug that was only slightly thinner than his own cock. She didn't hesitate and pushed back onto the metal like she had done it a thousand times before.

"Oh my God that feels so good."

Ink nodded at him, and he increased the speed and pressure he put on her clit. Ink fucked her with the plug while she ground herself down on Hannibal's hand. It was time, and they both knew it.

His Brother started a brutal rhythm with the plug, drawing it in and out of her in time with her bucking hips. She gripped the chains above her head as a flush rolled up her body and she started twitching as the orgasm overtook her.

Ink pushed the plug in deep one last time, leaving it inside her as she came apart. It was beautiful. The way she tossed her head back and screamed her pleasure to the ceiling satisfying something deep inside him.

Hannibal pulled a condom out of his back pocket and quickly stripped out of his jeans while Ink held her through the thrashing. He slipped the condom on in record speed. He quickly unhooked her ankles from the bar, then her cuffs from the chains above her head. Hannibal picked her up and looped her bound arms around the back of his neck while Ink stripped out of his own clothes.

She felt almost as light as a feather as he maneuvered her over his cock. Her eyes focused, and he gave her a knowing smile. She moaned as he felt himself at her entrance. He slipped his arms under her leg and slowly slid her onto his cock.

God, she was tight. Warm and perfect wrapped around his cock. "You feel amazing, beautiful."

He used his arms to work her up and down his length in slow curls. "Oh God, Hannibal, I feel so full. You're so big and ahh—"

"Wait until you have us both in you. Do you want that Jade? You want both of us fucking you at the same time?"

"Yes. Please. I don't know how I'll survive it, but I want you both."

Ink slipped up behind her. Hannibal could feel him working the butt plug slowly in and out of her. "I can't wait to be the first one inside that ass, darlin'. I'm going to make sure you are feeling me for days."

Hannibal had to focus on anything but the liquid heat that was their woman, or he would not last until Ink worked his way inside. Finally, his Brother stopped playing and pulled the plug out and he positioned himself behind her.

Ink pressed against her back and Hannibal stilled as he slowly slid inside Jade. Her groan was erotic as hell and she clenched, causing them both to echo her sounds. It took all his willpower to hold them motionless. Her fingers clawed at his back while she fought to relax.

There weren't enough words in the dictionary to describe the sensation of her tightening around him as Ink's length rubbed his through the thin barrier of her body. He knew she would be feeling the stretch now with them both almost fully seated inside her.

"So much. Feels So Good." Her hands clawed at his back as she tried to find purchase.

Finally, Ink settled fully inside her. Hannibal held them still for just a moment. And then his control was at an end. He lifted her up and down in quick, short motions over their cocks. She screamed her pleasure.

This was the moment he fantasized about during the night. Three bodies totally in sync with one another, nothing but their own natural rhythms driving them. He controlled the beat in the most primal of dances. He thrust forward as he raised her up and down. The two men were completely in sync as they filled her and pushed her and made her beg and scream.

It didn't take long before her pussy fluttered around him heralding her orgasm.

"I'm close." He growled, knowing that he wouldn't be able to hold back much longer. That once Jade lost herself in another orgasm, she would drag him right over that cliff with her.

"Me too," Ink growled from behind. His Brother's hands slipped around the front of her body and Hannibal watched as his Brother gripped her nipples between his fingers and twisted them in quick, sharp motions. On the third twist, she exploded.

Hannibal slammed home again and again as her body contracted around his. Pressure built in his spine and he lost the smooth rhythm as his orgasm raced out of him. He emptied himself into the condom with a roar. Ink's cry followed his as the three of them lost themselves in the pleasure.

They stood like that for a moment, catching their breath. Ink step back, stumbling a little as he slid out of her body.

Jade was limp in his arms, her head on his shoulder. Her breath was warm against his neck.

Hannibal walked her over to the bed they had set off in one corner of the large room and laid her down. He took a moment to wrap her in a warm blanket before moving off to the attached bathroom to take care of the condom. He passed Ink on his way in, the man had already done his cleanup.

When he got back to the bed, his Brother was already spooned up behind their little Jewel and was running a slow hand up and down her side. Hannibal crawled in on the other side, knowing it would be at least a few minutes before any of them were ready for round two.

Chapter 17

Some people are like clouds, when they disappear it is a beautiful day.

Jade

Jade felt like she'd competed in a brutal Spartan Race last night. Her muscles ached in the wonderful way that only exhaustion and hard work could achieve. Tiny bruises peppered her body in more embarrassing locations than she cared to admit. But she was happy.

Ink had fulfilled his promise to make her forget all of her problems for a single night. Breakfast had been surprisingly natural and lighthearted. Hannibal had cooked a hearty breakfast that was so good she'd stuffed herself to the point of bursting.

The ride back to her car had been silent because she wasn't sure how to say goodbye to the fantasy that had been staying with them. She didn't want to appear desperate or clingy, but given the choice, she would have stayed with them all day. His passionate kiss goodbye had settled her a little.

Unfortunately, all dreams end and it had been time to get back to her life.

Sitting in her car in front of the bank, she tried to psych herself up. She was ready to take control of her life and her business. The new contract that would sever all ties to Eric sat in a folder next to her on the seat. This was it. It was time.

She'd called to confirm that the bank could issue the cashier's check for $50,000. Once he signed the paper and she handed over the check, the business would be all hers. Jade's nerves jangled in fear at the thought that she would be without a financial safety net for the first time since they opened.

Her stomach clenched. If anything expensive happened after she signed, there wouldn't be any money for months to do anything about it. She'd briefly talked with the loan officer she had been working with on the expansion ideas. He assured her he would consider approving the expansion loan earlier than planned. If he did, the money would be enough to cover both the expansion and replenish her funds. But without the three months of operating costs in the bank as collateral, it would be a tougher sell, and the interest rate wouldn't be as good.

Depending on what they decided, she might have to wait until she saved the money back up. That would take almost a year. Some faceless people in the back office of a bank would decide her fate.

Fifteen minutes later, she was sitting alone in the lobby of that bank, completely unsurprised that Eric was late for their appointment. Maxim, the very large Russian from the other night, was sitting quietly on the other side of the room. She didn't like the smug, knowing look on the man's face. Ten minutes after they should have signed the papers, Eric finally came through the door.

Of course, he didn't look the least bit apologetic. His hands were fidgety. And he gave her an angry glare. "Let's get this over with."

Frustration and a deep sense of loss were a cold lump in her throat. Even now, he didn't seem to care. He wasn't grateful that, once again, she was bailing him out of his problems. Her friend of fifteen years didn't seem sad that their business partnership was ending.

He was acting petulantly. Probably because he wouldn't have the free paycheck coming into his bank account every month. Jade tried to extend an olive branch, as they went through signing the papers with the bored-looking Bank employee.

"You know if you ever need a job or work, there'll always be a teacher slot available for you at Leap."

"You'd love that, wouldn't you? Have me as your employee so you can gloat over how much better you are doing than me. There's no way in hell I'll ever step foot inside that place again. And if you don't think I'm going to tell everyone how heartless you are, you're sadly mistaken." Eric's words were like a slap.

It wasn't the fact that he could affect her reputation and business with his lies. She'd already had to deal with that whenever he got in a mood and lashed out. Did he really believe that she didn't want him to succeed? "I don't know when you changed, Eric. I miss the old you."

His hands clenched on the desk. They signed the last of the paperwork.

"I hope someday you realize I never wanted to hurt you."

"Whatever, Bitch."

"Why do you have to be so cruel?"

The Russian man, who up to this point had stayed silent, snorted. "He's cruel because he hasn't gotten his fix today."

Jade sat back in shock.

"Shut up, errand boy. You don't know what you're talking about." Eric's defensive words caused her to take a closer look at him.

How had she not noticed how much weight he'd lost over the last few months? His skin was sallow and perspiration dotted his hairline. His jittery muscles, the vicious mood-swings. It all made sense now. She leaned forward and touched his hand.

"Oh my God, Eric. We can get you help."

"Don't need help, Jade. What I needed was a friend. Instead, you tossed me away so you could own the business by yourself. Don't act like you care about me."

"I do. I just couldn't keep letting you walk all over me. What you were doing was going to drive our business into the ground." Jade shook her head. "Forget the business. I'm worried about you. I'm sure we can find you an excellent program, help you get your life back under control."

"I don't have a problem. And I definitely don't need your brand of help." He pushed the signed contracts her way and snatched up the check that the notary had put down on the table. He tossed the check at the Russian and stormed out of the room.

The smug smile on the Russian's face as he looked down at the money was annoying. He slid the check into an inside pocket of his coat and gave her a nod that sent chills down her spine. She bit her tongue as he left the room, not wanting to draw his attention back to her.

How could she have missed the signs Eric had slid so far? His gambling didn't surprise her. He'd always been drawn to games of chance. Loving the thrill of pitting himself against people in every way possible, but it never once occurred to her he would do drugs. They were athletes. While they might abuse their bodies physically, and indulge in a little bit too much drink, they were only too aware of what that garbage could do to a body.

She gathered up the papers and organized them back into the envelope to send over to her lawyer as soon as she got a chance. A strange thought hit her. Why had Eric given the Russian the whole cashier's check? Was that why he was happy, because they were getting more than they were owed?

She'd assumed he would have the bank split the money into two separate checks. One to pay off his debt, and one for himself. Was it possible he really owed the Russians $50,000?

Her phone beeped with a text. She looked down and saw it was from an unfamiliar number.

???: *Hey girl, this is Cami. The girls and I wanted to invite you to the Clubhouse tonight for a party. It gets a little wild, but your men will be there. I think you'd have fun.*

Jade stared down at the words with a smile. This was the first time in years anyone had invited her out simply to have some fun. There were several things she had to do this afternoon, and she needed to teach a class this evening at the gym. But that would be over by seven. She saved Cami's contact info to her phone while she thought it over.

This was supposed to be a clean start to her life. What better way to kick it off than going to a party with some new friends? She was going to swing by her lawyer's office. Then go to her doctor's office. She'd gotten tested the day after she met Hannibal and Ink. Had it really only been five days? The results were back, and all that was left was to pick up the paperwork. She wasn't ready to give up condoms yet, but it never hurt to be prepared.

If she didn't go. She would probably spend the night worrying about Eric and everything that had gone wrong.

Jade: *Hey Cami. Sounds fun. How wild are we talking?*

Cami: *Wonderful. And it depends on how late you stay. No one will bug you. But none of us are shy about showing our affections. If you get what I mean. Imagine strip club meets frat party.*

Jade hesitated for a moment, wondering if she was being invited to an orgy of some sort. Would it matter if she was? She had never been afraid to try new things. As long as they did not expect her to do anything with anyone but Hannibal or Ink, it might be an interesting experience.

After the discussion about exclusivity they'd had, she didn't think they would want to invite others to join them. She also trusted them enough to believe that if she was uncomfortable, they wouldn't mind her leaving. She gathered up her nerve.

Jade: *Sounds good. Send me the address and time I should be there.*

Cami: *Perfect. Why don't you come early and you can hang out with us for a little before the party starts?*

Jade: *Will do.*

Cami: *See you then!*

Jade slid her phone into her pocket and gathered up all her belongings. This was a good thing. Tonight she would find out if she could fit into Hannibal and Ink's world.

Chapter 18

If my job sucked any harder than it does now, I'd orgasm.

Ink

Ink settled down in the chair next to Hannibal, impatient to get this meeting over with. Usually he didn't mind Church. It was an opportunity for the Brothers to socialize and catch up on the business of the Club. Knowing that Jade would arrive soon changed the game. He wanted to see her again, but he didn't want her out there alone.

Last night had been a frenzy of bodies. She took everything they'd given her and fed that energy back to them. They'd barely slept. The extra caffeine he'd needed to wake up this morning was well worth it.

He wanted to find out what had happened in her meeting with Eric. Make sure that everything had gone well. But he didn't want to seem like he was hovering and pester her with texts. It was out of character for him. He wasn't the type to worry.

When he wasn't worrying about her problems, he was imagining ideas he had for her tattoo. Ever since Hannibal had shared what she wanted, his imagination was in over-drive. The two of them had spent all day sketching and pulling together the unique elements she'd requested. It was still rough, but both of them thought it was going to be one of their best pieces of work.

Hannibal had balked at his idea of adding swirling watercolors throughout the background, thinking it would be too much coverage. Until Ink had shown him a mockup of what he'd in mind. The spirals of color would fade in and out in a weaving pattern, dancing between the butterflies. The pattern would add an extra sense of movement to the picture. Ink couldn't wait to see if she liked it.

The Old Ladies inviting her here tonight had been a pleasant surprise. Those women were as tight-knit as the Brothers. He hoped their acceptance of Jade would help their little Jewel feel secure. Give her the support she needed to understand their world.

Last night had soothed some of his darkest concerns, but it was a hard reality that it took a special woman to be willing to hook up with a member of a motorcycle club. If she was uncomfortable hanging out on what was usually their wildest night of the week, it would be good to learn now, rather than after more emotions got involved.

Ink snorted at himself and looked over at his brother. It had been Hannibal pushing them forward at lightning speed, but after the last couple of days, he understood why his brother had wanted to push. Now that he'd gotten over his initial reservations, he had to admit that the idea of claiming a woman as their own was a siren call. He just hoped they wouldn't end up crashed on the rocks.

Hannibal looked over at him. "Do you know why Hawk moved Church to today instead of Sunday?"

Ink shook his head. "No, I've heard there's been some trouble with the Russians but nothing more concrete than that."

The room was filled with every Brother who could attend the last minute meeting. Everyone was involved in their own side conversations, but no one appeared tense. The officers entered the room, closing the door with a loud thunk.

"Okay, settle down." Hawk knocked his knuckles on the long table. Their President was a man in his mid-50s, but you wouldn't guess it if it weren't for the gray in his hair and beard. The man had a presence strong enough to wrangle the over fifty Brothers with just a look.

His VP Sharp sat to his right, dark hair and scruffy look that sometimes led people to the mistake of underestimating the man. To his left was Highdive the Sergeant at Arms, a brutal man who was also one of Ink's closest friends.

The men sitting at either end of the table were a contrast of the range of types of men who made up the Dark Sons. Tek, the Secretary and resident computer guru, was the image of corporate America, with clean cut looks, blond hair and blue eyes, if he wasn't wearing a cut no one would have guessed he was in an MC. Dozer their Treasurer would be recognized as a biker no matter what he wore. Ink had heard the ladies say he looked like a grizzly, muscular Santa Claus.

Hawk banged the gavel down on the table. "Listen up. We have two things to settle tonight before we can get the fuck out of here and out to the party. Let's get the first one done quickly. Since Max is no longer with us, we need to elect someone as Road Captain."

Hawk's words sounded cold and a few people muttered. Many of the Brothers thought Max had died a few weeks ago. Taken prisoner by the Russians when he'd gone against orders and attacked them, thinking they had his woman. The official story was that he, his woman and one of the top men in the Bratva had died during the encounter.

Ink and Hannibal had been there that night and knew the truth. Max and his woman had faked their deaths to hold off the upcoming war. They were currently down in Texas with the National Chapter until things settled.

The move was supposed to be temporary, but with the Russians as well as several government law enforcement agencies after both of them, there was no telling when they'd be able to come back. Or if they would find a new home elsewhere. The Club had held a memorial for him to make sure that the fake story was believed.

Normally, all the Brothers would have been trusted with the information. However, it had become unfortunately clear that the Russians had some way to find out what was going on inside the Dark Sons. The Officers have kept the information need to know only.

Grinder stood. "I nominate Dragon. He's got the level head we need in the position." He sat down and there was murmuring through the Brothers.

They had patched Dragon into the Club about a year ago. Everyone respected the tall as fuck Native American man, but officer positions usually went to people who had been in the Club longer.

The truth was the Road Captain's job wasn't one many people sought after. It meant a lot of traveling and having to attend almost every run. Dragon and his Old Lady Tari were trying for another baby. So he wasn't sure if the Brother would want the position. However, he would be stuck with it if no one else was nominated. You couldn't decline.

Ink looked over at the Brothers present. Yes, it was important that the man in the position had an even temper, but it was more than that. Each position was about the security of the Club. The Treasurer looked after the financial concerns, the Secretary made sure everyone knew what was going on, and the Sergeant at Arms maintained physical security. The Road Captain was at the heart of the Club, making sure they stayed bonded and no arguments spiraled it out of control. He had to understand what was inside everyone's minds and try to cut off problems before they started.

That was why it was better to have someone with a longer history in the position. The more he thought about it, the more he realized Grinder was the perfect candidate.

He had been with the chapter since they formed, didn't have an Old Lady and was still young enough to enjoy the long runs necessary to hold the position. Grinder was friends with everyone, even if he was one of the wilder Brothers. But with the rest of the Officers being more conservative, it would be good to have something different in the leadership.

Ink stood. "I nominate Grinder. He's not tied down with an Old Lady and still remembers how to have fun on a ride." Chuckles filled the room. "As long as Sharp can spare him from the garage. He's got a flexible work schedule. Plus, he's been a patched member longer than Dragon, knows us better."

"Thanks." Grinder didn't seem like he was really grateful, but he was the right choice.

"All right, we got two candidates. Anyone else have a name they want to put forward?" Hawk paused long enough that it was clear no one else was going to speak up. "Let's make this simple. All in favor of Grinder being our next Road Captain, raise your hand."

About three quarters of the room raised their hands, including Dragon, making his lack of desire for the position clear. Once people saw his hand was up, pretty much everyone in the room raised their hand.

Grinder swore under his breath, and Ink couldn't help but chuckle. The man had probably guessed that without another candidate put forward, he would be drafted into the position, so he'd offered up Dragon.

"All right, that's done. Get your ass up here to the last empty seat at the Officer's table." Hawk's smile was teasing. Grinder joined them to the good-natured ribbing of everyone he passed.

The Club wasn't a democracy, though they did occasionally hold votes. Every one of them accepted that if Hawk decided he didn't like the outcome of something, he could and would overturn any decision. That was what made the role of the Officers so important. They could advise him and help take care of the day-to-day functions of the Club without getting dragged down by red tape.

They spent the next forty-five minutes going over the usual business and Ink couldn't help but check the clock every time they brought a new mind numbing subject up.

"Now for the real reason we had to move this damn meeting up." All chatter stopped. Hawk looked at Tek. "Share with us what you found."

Tek leaned back in his chair as if relaxing, but Ink could see the tension in his shoulders. "We've never had the best relationship with the local Bratva, but as you all know, last month that tentative peace went to shit. Both sides made mistakes that ended badly."

Almost every one of them growled at his retelling.

"The fact that the explosion that claimed Max also took out one of their deep undercover agents and a lot of their guys has the entire family pulling any support they had once given us. They haven't declared war yet. But we believe it will not be long before that happens. So far I've only found nuisance feints. Cyber-attacks on some of our businesses which we can't prove were them. Petty harassment of our people that skirt right on the line of acceptable. So far, we haven't been able to trace any of it back directly to them."

Hawk leaned forward, putting his hands on the table in front of him. "Normally, that would be enough for us to rip up our treaties. Unfortunately, their harassment seems to be focused here in Denver. Petrov and I have a long history and not a good one. National is aware of the problem and wants to hold off on war as long as possible. Give them time to build up resources and information. That means we need to be extra vigilant about everything. Protect our families and keep them tight. Make sure they don't become easy targets. Check in on our businesses on a more regular basis to make sure they haven't gotten a foothold so we won't get blindsided."

"We're supposed to believe Petrov won't escalate?" someone shouted.

"He will. But I believe he will wait for an excuse. He likes to pretend that everything is someone else's fault. So starting now, everyone has to take extra shifts for the Club. If you've got family, let them know. Sharp will send out the rotations and the extra responsibilities that we're going to want each one of you to pick up. Clear your schedules as much as possible. And don't go anywhere unprepared."

Highdive stood up and his gaze swept over the room. Every one of them felt the seriousness of the situation by the fury contained within his eyes. He gave everyone in the room a moment and made sure that all eyes were on him before he spoke.

"We are not to provoke them. However, I don't want a single one of you fuckers hesitating for even a second. If you think they're coming at you then, fuck the consequences, you act. This is going to be war. I know it. You all know it."

It was as if ice ran down Ink's spine at the blunt words.

Highdive continued, "Those Russians are not going to know what hit them when they're stupid enough to step their foot over that line. If you have any contacts, you should be working them. Share anything you find immediately with Tek. You have even a prickle at the back of your neck and want backup, I want you contacting me. Being a Dark Son means you are never alone. Asking for backup is what we do. I want no lone wolves on this shit."

His gaze swept the room.

"Dark Sons for life!" Hawk shouted out the words in a tone that would have made a drill sergeant proud.

The Brother's responses echoed through the room. "Dark Sons for life!"

Chapter 19

Never believe the words 'This is a great idea' after the second shot of tequila.

Jade

The Dark Son's compound was intimidating. Jade's pulse had raced when she pulled up to the gated entrance and a rough-looking man in a Dark Son's cut had approached her car. Only after she had given her name had he opened the gate and waved her in with a smile.

She pulled into the dirt lot and parked her car next to one of the few other non-motorcycles there. Over fifty motorcycles were lined up in front of the main warehouse style building in an impressive display. She had never realized how many different styles and models of motorcycles there could be. Some had shining chrome reflecting the early evening light as if they were showroom models, and others wore dust and a dull grit, as if they had been ridden long and hard.

She was early, the clock on her dash showing 7:45.

Should she wait a few minutes before trying to go into the building? Jade hated being late, but being too early could be almost as rude.

She looked around, trying to stall for time. The large fenced in property held several buildings. A wide, well-maintained dirt road ran around them and deeper into the property. Just how big was this place?

"Jade!"

Jade turned back to face the enormous building. Val stood waving at her from the entrance. An amused smile tipped up her lips as she took in the woman's outfit.

The two of them were dressed very similarly in tight jeans and a scoop necked black shirt. Jade thought her own outfit was a little bit more sensible since she was wearing a pair of Doc Marten boots. The leggy redhead had on a pair of thigh high-heeled boots that made her even taller. Val was also wearing a Dark Son's leather cut and had rhinestones across the front of her shirt that said, 'Biker Babes Ride Hard!' in sparkling letters.

Should she have dressed a little more feminine? She had considered a skirt and heels, but her nerves had gotten the best of her. Jade had finally opted for comfort over sexiness. She knew she couldn't compete with what some of these women would be wearing.

If that meant her men weren't as interested in her as the eye candy, it was better to know that now. She would never be one of those women who took hours to get ready. Primping and fussing weren't in her nature.

Jade forced a big smile, determined to fake comfort in the strange surroundings. "Hey, Val."

The taller woman pulled her in for a hug, the height difference only making it slightly awkward. "I am happier than a Coon dog on a hunt that you showed up here tonight, girl. We've seen your playground. Why don't you come in and see ours?"

Jade followed her inside and had to admit that the size and fun feeling of the room they entered impressed her. She had expected it to be small, crowded, dark, and maybe dirty. Maybe she had been in a few too many roadside bars while traveling on the Parkour circuit.

Other than a few women whom she recognized from their lessons, there weren't many people in the large room. With all the motorcycles outside, she expected this place to be packed.

The Clubhouse was a large open room with a long cherry wood bar off to the right. Seating areas were scattered around, ranging from bar style tables to comfy looking leather couches. Towards the back of the room, she saw several pool tables and dart boards. Off to the sides were a couple of hallways that probably led deeper into the building.

Pixie, Tari, and Cami sat at the bar, along with an Asian woman she didn't recognize. The four of them were throwing back shots. An amused and vaguely familiar man stood behind the bar, his arms crossed.

As Jade got closer, she could see the name Decaf was embroidered on his vest.

"Come on, join us for the next round." Pixie waved her over. "What's your poison?"

The woman was a bundle of sunshine, no matter what she was doing. Jade's muscles relaxed. "Tequila." She loved the taste of it even without salt or lemon and the way the sharp alcohol mellowed all her nerves.

Tari laughed and slapped the bar. "A woman after my own heart. Tequilas, Decaf!"

Jade hopped up onto a bar stool. The man behind the

bar lined up new shot glasses for them. "Where are the guys?"

The room they were in seemed hollow, with only the few of them in it.

"Oh, they're in the b-back. Doing 'Club Business'." Cami threw her hands up in the air and did air quotes around the last two words.

Jade did a quick double take as she took in the outfit the purple-haired woman was wearing. "Should I ask why you're wearing a Dallas cheerleader's outfit?"

It wasn't out of the realm of possibility that this woman was a cheerleader, but she was a little curvy and not quite as tall as the women Jade often saw on TV. Cami did a perfect imitation of a ditz giggle and tossed her hair over her shoulder in an exaggerated style.

"One." She held up a dramatic finger, and Jade wondered how much the girl had already had to drink. "Cheerleaders get all the hot guys. Two." She held up a second finger. "M-Most of the men here can't stand the Dallas team. So it'll likely get me in t-trouble."

Jade couldn't help the laugh that burst out of her. "And that's a good thing?"

Pixie grabbed a shot off of the bar and spun around. "Oh, that's the best thing." She held her shot up into the air. "To trouble!"

All the women grabbed their own shots, so Jade followed their lead. They all clicked them together.

"To trouble." Jade threw back her shot with the rest of the women, glad that she had come.

The Asian woman held out her hand after they were done. "Hi, I'm Anna. I haven't been able to break away to join you all yet, but I've heard the lessons you've been giving are a lot of fun."

"Oh, they are." Val laughed, the sound musical. "As my

aching muscles will tell you, they are definitely a real workout."

She winked and Jade smiled, remembering the first lesson where her men had challenged that Parkour wasn't a real workout. Had that only been a little under a week ago?

"So what? We wait out here until the men get done with their business?" Jade hoped her question didn't sound like a complaint.

"The joys of being an Old Lady." Pixie swooned back exaggeratedly.

Jade took in the leather vests all the women were wearing. She had figured like the men, the cut was part of the uniform. "So what, you're their wives? Is that what Old Lady means?"

"Not necessarily." Val smiled. "At least not in a legal sense."

Pixie smiled. "I'm living in sin."

"Actually, I think Tari and I are the only ones of us that are actually married," Val said.

Cami shook her head. "Nope. Tek and I are married."

Pixie's look of shock was comical. "What do you mean, you and Tek are married? How could you not have invited us!"

Cami smirked. "Well, since I don't think Tek kn-knows either, it would have been awkward to have a party."

Confusion and disbelief warred for supremacy in her emotions. Jade took comfort in that all the women seemed to be feeling the same thing. "How exactly are you married and he doesn't know about it?"

Cami waved her hand as if it was no consequence. "I hacked into the office of r-records and filed our paperwork a few months ago."

Tari let out a deep laugh. "That's priceless. Dragon and I got married last December. Mostly because Mama Rios insisted. I think her exact quote was, 'The leather vest is very pretty, *mija*. But I want to watch you walk down the aisle and hear you say the words before God'."

These women were strange and fun. Jade liked how they didn't seem to care what their relationships would look like to the outside world. They had a love for life that was wonderful. "Well, if it's not a wedding, that makes you an Old Lady. What is it?"

Pixie got a smile on her face that turned her innocent looks into something dirty. "Well, your man, or men," the woman winked at her, "have to claim you before at least five brothers. And then you show your devotion right back."

The way the woman said the word *claim* made it obvious that she wasn't talking about words. Jade's cheeks flushed and her eyes widened as varied dirty images played through her mind. She cleared her throat.

"So, you just…" She wasn't sure how to put it into words. Her stuttering was amusing the women, if the looks on their faces were any indication.

"Let our men fuck us in front of a bunch of their Brothers?" Pixie blinked fake innocent eyes at her.

"Yes?" Jade coughed as she spoke the word.

Val chuckled. "Yes, darlin'. That's what we mean."

Anna rolled her eyes. "Not all of us. Stop teasing the poor girl. I'm not quite the exhibitionist these other women are. The rules are exactly what she said. They just have to claim you. Then you have to promise to be loyal, for life, in front of witnesses."

Cami giggled. "But it's so m-much more fun the other way."

Jade tried to picture it. The image of how Hannibal had held her up fucking her from the front while Ink filled her from behind leapt to the front of her thoughts. It had been such an intense, overwhelming experience.

She didn't consider herself a shy person. But being that open and vulnerable in front of a crowd wasn't appealing. Jade shook her head, trying to throw off the thoughts. It was early days yet, and not something she needed to be thinking about now.

Cami bumped her shoulder. "I warned you, things get w-wild around here."

"That you did."

"Not as wild as some of the stunts you pull on your YouTube channel." Pixie's comment was a welcomed change of subject. "You should see some things she can do. She's like a cross between Spider Man, Wonder Woman, and a Cirque du Soleil Acrobat."

Anna's expression showed that it impressed her. But Jade blushed and tried to wave it away.

"Don't you be modest with us," Val scolded. "We've all seen your videos. You run across buildings and dive over gaps for fun. I do believe you're crazy, talented but crazy."

Many people thought the same thing when they saw her stunts. "Lots of practice over much safer obstacles. I know what I can and can't do. Honestly, it's not the running across the top of buildings that is dangerous."

"What is the dangerous part?" Cami asked.

"It's scaling the buildings. Running across the rooftops, while fun, there's very little chance that I'm going to do more than twist an ankle or take a bump and bruise if I land wrong. But free climbing, whether it was on a mountain or the side of a building, has more risk. It's the drop that'll get you every time."

Her attempt to lighten the mood with her last joke had failed. Pixie looked shocked. "What's the tallest building you've ever scaled without gear?"

She thought about it. A few years ago, when she'd been younger and dumber in an attempt to get some extra followers to her YouTube channel, she had agreed to something that still gave her chills occasionally. "Eight stories. It was an apartment building, downtown." She'd almost fallen six stories up, but had managed to barely catch herself. The video had gone viral, but she'd never tried something with that level of danger without safety equipment again.

"Could you climb to the r-roof of this building?" Cami asked.

Jade pictured what she'd seen of the outside of this building. It wouldn't be hard. The front at least had a slight overhang she could use to lever herself up. Lots of windows on the second story with windowsills. With two stories, she only needed two or three pull up points.

There was also a pipe running down near the corner of the building. If it was thick enough and well secured, it would be a lot easier to shimmy up that.

"Yeah. That wouldn't be much of a challenge."

"Oh, I want to see this," Anna said.

"You want me to climb to the roof of this building, right now?" She shook her head. She wasn't in the right clothes, though she'd climbed in these boots before. "I'm just here to relax."

Cami hopped off her stool, her little cheerleader skirt flaring out around her. "How about this?" She had a twinkle in her eye that made Jade nervous. "If you prove you can c-climb to the roof of this building right now, I'll pay for all of us to do six more m-months of your private lessons and give you the contact number for my Old Man's friend, Kane. He runs a mercenary company out of Denver. I've been thinking about suggesting your p-place to him anyway. Those guys train and do drills all the time, at different locations. Your gym would pr-probably be the perfect setup for something like that."

Jade's heart fluttered. Cami had inadvertently stumbled

on one of her dreams for the place. Drawing in people from the military and law enforcement for training could easily double, if not triple, her customer base. Once she had her outdoor area expanded, she could create areas that would be good not only for climbing, but for things like paintball, or military style training exercises.

"Oh, I know that look." Val smiled. "I think that says you're on."

Chapter 20

Good friends are like condoms. They protect you when things get hard.

Hannibal

Hannibal didn't bother to stop to give Grinder some good-natured ribbing about his unwanted promotion. He'd received a text twenty minutes ago when Jade arrived, and the urge to see her was itching under his skin. After everything they had discussed, he needed to see with his own eyes that she was okay.

Maybe now wasn't a good time to foster a deeper relationship with her. It might put a target on her back. The problem was he didn't think she would believe they only wanted to pause things, not call them off completely.

The risk of losing the spark developing between them wasn't something he was willing to chance. The main area was almost completely empty of people. Where were the Old Ladies? Surely, Jade would be with them.

Decaf waved him over from behind the bar where he was

stationed. "That woman of yours is insane. You might want to get outside and stop her before she breaks her neck."

Hannibal raised an eyebrow. "What do you mean?"

"I mean, her and the women went outside. Cami bet her she couldn't scale up the building to the roof and I think she really intends to do it."

"She what?" Ink's angry voice was behind him.

Not bothering to continue the conversation, Hannibal headed straight for the front door. The Clubhouse was only two stories. But why would someone want to climb it when there were perfectly good stairs?

Hannibal took a deep breath, trying to calm the fear that was bubbling up inside him. He had seen videos of his woman doing much crazier stunts than climbing up the side of a building. The structures at her gym were almost three stories tall, but there was padding and mats there.

He hit the gravel at a pace close to a jog barely in time to see motion off to the left. There she was. Her brown hair flying behind her as she ran full tilt at the building.

The Old Ladies' cheers were loud and full of enthusiasm. Jade hit the building and ran up the wall at full speed. Her hands caught on a pipe about ten feet off the ground and she pulled herself up and somehow managed to balance. His heart paused its beating as she leapt sideways onto another metal pipe that ran from the second story up to the roof.

She shimmied up so fast it was like there was a rope pulling her upwards. Less than a second later, she gripped the edge of the building and pulled herself up onto the top. His breath escaped in a relief as she turned around to face her cheering audience. The little bow she did with her hands extended out to the side was adorable.

"What the hell do you think you're doing?" Ink's voice bellowed, and everyone's attention turned to them.

Jade stood balanced on the edge of the building looking

down, and her expression was not amused. Ink's temper was always faster to ignite than his own. Jade crossed her arms and cocked her hip in a pose that told everyone she wasn't happy with the tone of voice Ink was using with her.

"Just having some fun while you guys were busy," Jade shouted down.

Hannibal stepped up behind Ink and kept his voice low. "She does this kind of thing every day, Brother. Don't let yourself get rattled."

His own thoughts and emotions were in turmoil, but lashing out at Jade wouldn't help. Something about seeing her do the crazy stunts in person had every protective instinct kicking into gear. Yelling at her would only start a fight.

This woman who fascinated them didn't live a quiet life. She did crazy stunts and tricks for a living and taught others how to do them too. Jade's YouTube channel had hundreds of thousands of followers. Asking her to stop would be like asking them to give up tattooing.

"That's different. There are mats and safety gear." Ink tilted his chin and raised his voice. "Step back from the edge before you break your fool neck."

Hannibal groaned as Jade's eyebrow rose in disbelief. She leaned forward and looked over the edge of the building and back around to the other edges of the roof. The mischievous smile she gave was the only warning they got.

In a move that was sure to give him nightmares for months to come, she took a step to the right, turned around, and stepped back off the edge of the roof. The Old Ladies screamed and Hannibal's throat closed as she fell straight downward. He could picture her legs snapping as she hit the ground.

Jade's hands caught first on the top of a window, then on the bottom sill in a maneuver that slowed her momentum.

Then she dropped past the final story and gracefully onto to the ground.

Ink's growl mirrored his own as the two of them strode forward. She was safe, that was what was important, but that move had been nothing more than a taunt. And there was no way they would ignore it.

The Old Ladies were laughing and cheering at her antics. It didn't help to diffuse their moods.

Jade smirked as the two of them invaded her space. "All safe and sound on the ground. It's good to see you guys. Is your Club business over?"

Hannibal didn't know if he wanted to laugh or pull her over his knee. Ink's response was to grab her by the back of the neck and pull her in for a passionate kiss.

The heat between them was electric. Hannibal's cock grew stiff as Ink used the kiss to claim and punish her all in one stroke. When they finally broke away, she was panting.

Hannibal grabbed her before she could recover and turned her face toward him. "My turn."

He lifted her up, so she had to wrap her legs around him as he plundered her mouth with a kiss. Hannibal put all the emotions her little stunt had caused into the embrace. Fear, excitement, and frustration. He wanted her to know exactly what she had put him through.

She tasted like tequila and he wanted to strip her clothes off right there and claim her against the wall. But this wasn't the time or the place. He had spent the day worrying about her and the business dealings she had with her friend, Eric. Then, the news about the probable war with the Russians had put his emotions on hyper-drive.

He needed to calm down before going any further. They had a plan for the evening. See how their little Jewel reacted to Club parties. Introduce her to their Dark Sons Brothers.

None of that would be accomplished if Ink and he gave

in to the urge to strip her bare and take her up to one of their favorite rooms. He broke the kiss with a sigh and let her lower herself to the ground.

"That was amazing." Pixie bounced over to them, breaking the heat of the moment.

Jade stepped back, and Hannibal enjoyed the dreamy smile on her face. She seemed to shake herself back into the moment.

She looked over at Pixie. "I guess you guys are stuck with me for another six months then."

Cami joined in on the laughter. "You know we would have kept c-coming anyway. Somehow you make exercising fun. And I'm not giving up until I can do the S-Salmon Ladder."

Hannibal shook his head and made a gesture towards the door. "How about we take this back inside where at least all your trouble making will be contained."

The comment was directed at Cami, but it was Jade who huffed and rolled her eyes. She hooked her arms with the other women before storming inside.

It was Friday night at the Clubhouse, and while it wasn't one of the wildest nights, they'd ever seen it was definitely filled with raucous fun. Sharp, Dozer, and Dragon had left an hour ago, taking their women with them. Having new babies had definitely changed his Brothers, and he didn't think it was for the worse.

He had been slowly relaxing, as their little Jewel didn't seem to have an adverse reaction to some of the more wild antics of the surrounding people. It was a simple truth once the alcohol started flowing, the more sexual things got. Half the women dancing around were barely dressed and many of his Brothers were taking advantage of the easily accessible pussy.

Cami and Jade seemed oblivious to it all and were playing a game of pool at one of the back corner tables. Tek, Ink, and he were amused by their smack talk. Cami was apparently some sort of pool shark, using strange mathematics to sink impossible shots while taunting Jade.

It was impressive that the woman could even play since every time she leaned over it was obvious that earlier in the night Tek and she had had some fun. The woman's thighs and what he could see of her ass under the short cheerleader skirt were bright red. Hannibal recognized the stripes and light bruising that indicated an intense spanking.

"I crushed you again!" Cami threw her arms up in victory and spun around, her skirt flaring.

The woman was a big bag of crazy, wrapped up in a curvy cute package. Hannibal didn't know how his strait-laced brother put up with it. Until the two of them had gotten together, everyone had believed that Tek was as vanilla as they came. The last long months had proven, underneath the buttoned up exterior, the guy was one kinky fucker.

When his woman got alcohol into her and finally relaxed, she lost all traces of the stutter that plagued her when she was nervous. Cami had also blossomed in other ways, really coming into her own. Now it was as if she had lost all inhibitions and skipped down any path that her wild mind came up with.

Jade shook her head. "Have you ever heard of being a gracious winner?"

Hannibal couldn't tell if she wasn't really upset. Cami, who had apparently had a few too many, didn't seem concerned. She crawled up onto the pool table and stood glaring down at Jade. She put a dramatic hand to her chest.

"I do not need to be a gracious winner because I'm the amazinist, bestest pool player in the world. I'm the best cheerleader." She did the drunken little high kick. Her gaze caught on Tek and she smirked. "I'm the best hacker and secret-finder around."

Jade bowed down before Cami. "I shall not question your abilities. Anyone who can hack into the courthouse and falsify documents is much too scary to go up against." Her tone was teasing, and Hannibal wondered what stories the women had been sharing.

Tek walked over to the table and held his hands up to his woman, who leaped into his arms. Cami peppered kisses around his face, giggling the entire time.

Hannibal moved up behind Jade and wrapped his arms around her waist. She tilted her face up and he gave her a light kiss on the lips.

Tek set Cami down on the edge of the pool table. He looked down at her with a raised eyebrow. "Have you been doing something I should know about, little criminal?"

Cami's eyes went wide, and she gave a desperate glance in Jade's direction.

"Nooo." The word was drawn out and so obviously a lie.

Jade snorted. Ink stepped up next to them. "Do you know what she's trying to hide from him, Jewel?"

Jade gave his Brother a playful smile. "Nooo." She extended the word the same way Cami had.

The ideas running through Hannibal's mind were dirty and kinky. Would their woman be up for playing a game? His pants felt uncomfortably tight as his cock filled at the possibilities.

He pressed his hard length up against the back of Jade's luscious ass. Hannibal cleared his throat and gave Tek a smile. "I think we have two little liars here. What do you say we see which one of them will give us the truth first?"

Tek smiled as he lifted Cami off the table and turned her around.

"I'll never break. No matter how much you torture me." There was laughter in Cami's voice, and Hannibal knew she was in for the game.

"Is that so?" Tek spun her around, so she faced Jade over the pool table and pushed her chest down, flipping up her skirt.

Hannibal leaned down and whispered into Jade's ear. "Safe words apply, little Jewel. You could always just tell us what you know then we wouldn't have to break you."

He ran a hand over her ass, and he gave it a smack, chuckling at her gasp.

Ink ran his hands over her ass as well. "You have the best ideas. Do you want the honors or shall I?" He gave her a second spank.

Did he want to get his hands on her ass or did he want to watch as both women were tortured. The thought of watching their expressions as they tried to hold back against the sensual assault was too tempting.

"She's all yours."

Chapter 21

Three may keep a secret, if two of them are dead ~Benjamin Franklin

Jade

J ade couldn't believe this was happening. The idea of playing a game like this excited her beyond reason. They were in a room full of people. Sure, they were in the back corner, but was she okay with people seeing her get spanked?

Because it was obvious that was going to happen. Honestly, the hedonistic vibe that filled the party had infected her with its wild delight. She'd seen everything from make-out sessions to full on sex happening all over the large room. Not all the activities were limited to only two people.

She thought it would bother her to watch others in intimate situations. Like she was invading their privacy. But everyone was so open and obviously enjoying themselves. Not only didn't it bother her, but instead it intrigued her.

Hannibal had reminded her she would have her safe words, and she believed him. She trusted both he and Ink would stop if she asked. Screw it. Why worry about what should bother her.

She stared first at Ink, then Hannibal giving them her best fake glare. "You'll never break me. I'll never give up her secrets."

Both men chuckled. The deep, rich sound vibrated through her like the bass wave of a dance song. Her nipples tightened painfully against her bra.

Hannibal turned her to face him. His hands paused at the front button of her jeans, as if giving her a second to protest. But she lifted her chin in defiance. He undid the front of her pants and she felt Ink's hands on her hips. They pulled down her jeans with a swift motion.

Cool air hit her ass, and she was glad she had worn the black lacy thong tonight. Ink's rough hands rubbed down her ass. She gasped as a sharp pain glanced across her right butt cheek as his teeth nipped at the skin there. Hannibal turned her and used a tight grip on the back of her neck to force her chest down on the pool table.

Cami mirrored her position on the other side of the green velvet, her beautiful purple hair in disarray. Her eyes shimmering with lust and a hint of playful mischief. Jade mouthed the word 'sorry' to her friend.

She hadn't realized her teasing comment might get her new friend in trouble. Cami winked at her, and she knew they were good.

"Last chance, little Jewel." Ink's words vibrated up her spine as his hands brushed over the skin of her ass. "Tell us what the little thief is hiding and you won't pay the price."

Her insides clenched, and she could feel moisture forming between her pussy lips. "I'll never tell!"

And she hoped she wouldn't be the one to break first. While it was hilarious that Cami had filed a marriage certificate without telling her Old Man, it really wasn't her place to spill the secret.

Jade jumped at the loud smack and Cami's yelp. Her friend's pupils dilated, and she panted. Heat and sting bloomed across her own ass as Ink copied Tek's action.

Soon, the fire of pleasure and pain mixed inside her and started the wild dance that she loved. Music pumped in the background, the sounds of partying and drinking blended in with the sounds of Cami and her spanking. Each strike warmed her body in a delicious way. The blows paused and both Hannibal and Ink's hands rubbed down her heated cheeks.

One of them pushed aside the thin fabric of her G-string and ran his fingers through the dampness, which was soaking through the fabric.

"Are you going to tell us what we want to know?" Ink gripped her hair, forcing her head to rise off the table. "I really hope not. I hope you both hold out a whole lot longer. Do you have any idea how much I enjoy watching your skin flush under my hand? The sounds of your moaning and the way you push back goes straight to my dick."

She could feel his length pressing up against her. "I'll never tell." Her voice was breathy, and her whole body ached with need. The game was fun, but confusing. How could they think she would want to talk when everything they were doing only excited her more?

Cami groaned from across the table. She saw Tek behind her doing something that had the woman squirming. As her friend's breath caught, she knew Cami was seconds away from orgasm and it pushed her closer to the edge as well.

Jade had never paid attention to the woman in porn before, preferring instead to focus on the man. But there was something overwhelmingly erotic about a woman only a few feet away from her panting and close to climax that had her clenching her own legs tight, trying to get some friction.

A short smack to her ass sent lightning flickering through her. Ink returned to his assault on her body. Jade licked her lips. Her breath matched that of Cami's as she inched closer and closer to the edge of release.

Her friend gave a scream of frustration as Tek stepped away from her and back up into a standing position.

"Bastard," Cami whined.

"You get to come when you tell me what you're hiding, little thief."

"Fuck you," she gritted out between clenched teeth.

Tek chuckled and ran his hand over her curvy ass. "I love you too."

Her breath calmed. To Jade's surprise, instead of returning to spanking her, he squatted down. His head disappeared from view.

It wasn't hard to imagine what he was doing as Cami's cries of pleasure returned. Tek seemed to know his woman well because she soon began thrashing.

Jade pushed back into Ink's blows, her excitement rising as she pictured Tek tonguing Cami. She spread her own legs wide, hoping either Hannibal or Ink would pick up on the invitation to play with her needy clit. The little bundle of nerves was throbbing in time with her pulse.

"None of that, precious. If you want something, you don't tease, you ask us for it."

Pain lashed across her ass, and she bucked off the table with a scream. What had he hit her with? She looked over her shoulder as the fire melted into an intense pleasure throbbing right into her core.

Ink had taken off his belt and held it doubled over in his fist. Her thighs trembled at the thought of another blow. So intense, yet the rush after the pain ebbed was like nothing she could imagine.

Jade dropped her head down, needing to know if a second strike would be as wonderful. She pushed back her ass with a moan. "Please."

Another lance of fire as she now heard the snap of leather.

Cami gave another scream of frustration as again her pain morphed into a wild pleasure. Tek stood again, wetness covering his smiling mouth.

Cami tossed her head and shouted, "Goddammit, Tek. I need to come."

Jade's mind was a scramble of signals as a third lash hit her right under the swell of her ass, causing her to rise up on her tiptoes. She arched back and her nipples brushed against the table, the sensation pushing her so close to orgasm she wanted to growl in frustration.

"Please make me come. Touch my clit. I'm so close."

Hannibal nipped her ear. "What do you call us when we're like this? How do you ask nicely?"

Another lash came down on her, this one crisscrossing one of the original blows. Her thoughts shattered. Pain and pleasure were no longer separate. It was all sensation.

"Please, Masters, please touch my clit. Make me come hard."

A hand was almost instantly inside her panties, rubbing circles around the sensitive bundle of nerves. Her breath caught as a wonderful wave of sensation built inside her. She panted, trying to keep on top of it, letting it build higher before falling off the edge.

She clenched her hands on the table and knew she couldn't hold off much longer. All the touch stopped, her body clenched painfully at the loss. She punched her fists down on the table in frustration.

"No!"

Both her and Cami's cries were almost simultaneous. Jade had a lot of respect for the woman across from her. Frustration and anger built in her as the orgasm that had been so close slipped away from her. This was true torture. How had she held out three times?

She didn't want to give away her friend's secret, but this ache hurt. It was uncomfortable to realize she didn't know if between the two of them she really was the stronger. If Hannibal and Ink pushed her to that edge one more time, she would be willing to tell them anything.

A light touch across her ass where welts had to be forming quickly reignited her passion. Maybe if she hid her reactions, she could trick them into an orgasm. Her two men were warm against her hips as they both played with her.

Strike. Caress. They began a rhythm that drew her in and destroyed all higher thought. Ink would deliver a blow from the belt across her ass. Then Hannibal's hand would spend several seconds building up the pleasure within her, thrusting inside her with his fingers and rubbing against that spot that sent warm waves through her whole body. After the third repetition of this, she could feel her orgasm blossoming so close to the edge she would do anything to make sure this time she would come.

Cami shrieked in frustration. "Fine, fine I'll tell. Just let me come."

"Tell me first," Tek's voice growled, "and I'll fuck you so hard you won't be able to walk."

He did something behind her that had Cami moaning and bucking back against him.

"Fine. I hacked into the courthouse two months ago, and I filed a marriage license in our names. Your legal name is now Joseph Turner."

Jade would have laughed at the completely shocked look

on Tek's face if Hannibal hadn't chosen that moment to drop down to his knees and start licking her clit. Powerful thrusts of his fingers had her spiraling into a blinding orgasm.

She bucked against him, Hannibal's hands gripping her ass, chasing her pleasure with pain and forcing the orgasm higher. Jade came gushing against him and screaming out his and Ink's name. Her legs quivered as he pulled her off the table.

Thankfully, Ink stepped up to her front, keeping her from falling over. Over his shoulder, she barely saw Tek had Cami pinned against the back wall. His cock thrusting into her in a brutal rhythm.

Ink ran a gentle hand down the side of her cheek. "Guess you held out longer than Cami. What now, little Jewel?"

She stood with her pants down around her ankles and Hannibal's large body behind her Ink's in front of her. So many dirty, wicked thoughts rushed through her mind until she settled on one.

"Is there a bed somewhere around here, so I can ride one of you while the other fucks me from behind?"

Both men chuckled. Hannibal bit the back of her neck. "I think we can find something that'll do."

Chapter 22

The "earth" without "art" is just "eh".

Ink

Ink ran his hand down the smooth skin of Jade's back, marveling at how her skin almost glowed copper in the dim light of the room. Last night had been a revelation in so many ways. His emotions had run through the entire spectrum, from terror over her safety to ecstasy in her arms. She belonged between Hannibal and him. Even when he had been angry at her for climbing up the side of the Clubhouse, never once did he wish she wasn't theirs.

She had taken everything she had seen at the party in stride, and even seemed to enjoy the game that they played over the pool table. She had ridden them almost to exhaustion in one of the bedrooms upstairs at the Clubhouse and then caved in to their demands that she come back with them to their house. Where they started all over again and she kept up with them when they woke her at least three times during the night to satisfy their needs.

Waking up the last time to her mouth wrapped around his cock while Hannibal fucked her from behind had been unreal. For the first time since he was a teenager, he had barely lasted long enough for her to get her own pleasure. Her talented mouth pulled him straight out of dreams and into orgasm.

It was tempting to wake her up once again. But both she and Hannibal lay in the exhausted sprawl of people who needed sleep. So he slid out of the bed and decided to finish up his work on the art for her back. For the last couple of days, they had spent every spare moment working on the image they wanted to put on her back.

Hannibal had finished up his portion yesterday before they'd left for the Clubhouse, and he was almost done. He slid on a pair of black joggers and headed out to the drawing table they had in the back room. The sunroom was the perfect place for both Hannibal and him when they wanted to do their artwork.

He wanted this to be something that captured her essence. He pictured her joy as she scrambled up the building and remembered the sound of her laughter as she teased with the Old Ladies. Ink drew swirling bright pastel colors across the page. Her joy that could barely be confined within the tight black lines of wings.

His fantasy stylized butterflies danced and ducked in an arching pattern, weaving their way in between Hannibal's hyper-realistic ones. Co-creating artwork was a very specific talent. The elements needed to meld together to create a unique whole.

Hannibal and he had worked together before and found that creating an overlay of Hannibal's finished work was the best way to complete the design. They printed it out on a clear sheet of plastic which Ink could periodically place down over his own work to make sure that everything fit and flowed seamlessly together.

Once the piece was completely done, they would size it to her back and create the stencils that they would use for placement. They would photograph the original and use it for the final piece as a reference as they inked it onto her skin.

It'd been a long time since he had lost himself in work like this. He let the emotions and the stories flow into the beautiful picture that she had inspired. Time lost meaning for him as he worked the colors to create the perfect balance. He used his thumb to smudge the last bit of color in place and took the overlay and placed it on top of his own drawing with a smile.

"My God, that's beautiful. I don't know what to say." Jade's voice startled him and he wanted to curse his own inattention.

Only here in their house, with the high-tech alarm system and all the security measures they had put into place, did he ever let his attention slip. Even then, not usually when anyone but he and Hannibal were in the house. How, in less than a week, had he come to trust this woman so much that he let his guard down so far that she could sneak up on him?

He shook off his dark thoughts. "Do you like it?"

"Love isn't even a strong enough word. I adore it."

Hannibal strode into the room behind Jade and leaned down to give her a kiss on the cheek. His dark skin a beautiful contrast against the golden light of hers. Ink stood and claimed his own kiss from her soft lips. She was wearing one of their t-shirts. The neck gaped open, giving him a tempting view down her shirt.

"I can't wait to get started. In my mind I couldn't have pictured something that amazing."

Ink gave her a playful slap on her ass. "We've still got a lot more work to do to get the stencil created. Your gym is closed on Monday. If you come in, then we should be able to get started."

She cocked her head. "I thought you guys were closed on Monday too."

"We are, but that's the beauty of being the owner. We can open the shop up whenever we want," Hannibal teased. "All right, I'm gonna start breakfast for us."

Ink looked over at the clock. "Don't you mean lunch?"

"Nope. Because I wouldn't know what to make for lunch. But I can do a mean breakfast."

That was nothing but the truth. Hannibal was usually the one that cooked both breakfast and dinner if they weren't in the mood to order out. The man's mama taught him how to cook, and Ink never complained when he was willing to do the cooking. It was an interestingly domestic scene as they all puttered around the kitchen, gathering together things and setting up plates on the breakfast bar.

Ink studied Jade as she sat laughing with Hannibal, eating the hearty breakfast that he had laid out for them. Her smile was addictive. She brought joy wherever she went. If there was a way to make sure she remained happy, he would burn down the world to make sure she stayed that way.

Unfortunately, there wasn't a way to make that a reality. Ink hadn't had any good examples of what a healthy relationship looked like when he was young. His father had been a drunken, abusive asshole. And his mother, an abrasive woman who stepped out on his father more times than he could count. The heartless woman hadn't cared one bit that her son knew what she was doing.

Sometimes he missed Texas. The warm weather and people who were satisfied with a simpler life. But he never missed his family. Jade leaned over and rubbed her thumb between his eyebrows.

"What are you thinking about that makes you all frowny?"

He chuckled, completely shocked that he could be falling for a woman who used a word like frowny. Ink shook his head in amazement. "I'm thinking about my family."

"Oh, are you guys close?"

Hannibal snorted.

"No. I haven't seen them in over fifteen years. I'll be happiest if I never see them again. How about you?"

Jade leaned forward and grabbed a glass of orange juice and took a sip. "I was really close to my mom. She died a while back from cancer."

Hannibal ran a hand over her back. "I'm sorry. What about your dad? I never read anything about him."

She shrugged. "He was a smooth talker who told my mom he was estranged from his wife. She believed him. The truth was, he would float between his wife and my mom. Whenever things would get hard with me and my mom, he'd take off. Go back to his wife. Whenever things got tough there, he'd leave her and come back to us. Somehow, he convinced my mom to take him back every time. He was the ultimate fair-weather man. When mom got sick the first time, it was too much for him. That was the last I ever saw of him." She shrugged as if it didn't matter, but Ink could tell how much it hurt her.

"He was an asshole who didn't deserve you." Hannibal's anger was obvious, and Ink wondered if they would be hunting the missing man down.

"Maybe. He didn't like things messy or complicated. And there's nothing more complicated or messy than going through chemotherapy. What I never understood was why Mom kept taking him back. I mean, sure, I've got a couple of pleasant memories of him as a kid. But if I'm with someone, I want him to be with me good times or bad. Loyalty is something I need. That's what made this thing with Eric so hard. He accused me of being like my dad. Like I was bailing out on him because things got hard."

"I thought the two of you weren't together?" Ink didn't like the burst of jealousy that roiled under his skin.

"We were never lovers. But one of the reasons I cared about him so much, and put up with all of his immature bullshit, was because he had been there for me when Mom got sick. He was there for me when I got hurt. He had been a steady friend through all the hard times. But the last three years have been too much. I tried to help him. I tried to be there for him. But at some point, he just stopped giving a shit and was sucking me dry."

"You don't have to justify anything to us where that snake is concerned," Ink said.

"I feel like I do. A couple months ago, I told him I couldn't take it anymore. He blew it off at first, laughing. I guess now he finally understands. If he would wake up and take responsibility for his actions, I would be willing to give him another chance." She snorted. "Guess I'm like my mom except I don't have romantic feelings or a child with him."

Ink rubbed her back, afraid to ask but needing to know. "Did everything go well yesterday?"

She shrugged. "As well as it could have. He signed the papers." She shrugged again. "I tried to make him see why I was doing things this way, but he wasn't receptive. I don't know if I'll ever see him again."

Ink pushed her hair away from her face and tucked it behind her ear. "There's being loyal to someone and then there's being someone's a victim. Sounds like he didn't want a friend because you don't steal from a friend or take advantage of a friend."

"My head knows that, but it will take a while for the rest

of me to catch up. Honestly, no matter how awful it sounds, what I'm really feeling is relief."

Ink squeezed her knee. "I can't imagine what you're going through. If Hannibal turned on me I don't know what I'd do."

Hannibal laughed and shook his head.

"Yeah, I can't see that. Can I ask you a personal question?" Jade smiled as a little of the darkness left her eyes.

"Of course, *cher,*" Hannibal said.

"I get where Ink got his nickname, but where does Hannibal come from? Are you secretly a serial killer?"

Ink burst out laughing at the shocked expression on his Brother's face.

"If I was, that wouldn't be a very smart question."

She giggled. "No, seriously. I've always wondered."

Ink also thought she was trying to distract herself from the topic of her old friend. He crossed his arms. "He'll tell you it's because to be with him is like riding an elephant across the alps. But I know the actual story."

"Please tell me he doesn't actually use that line."

Hannibal grumbled and crossed his arms. "Only once, and he's never let me live it down."

"So what's the real story?"

Ink smirked. "He was a sniper in the Rangers. Sometimes that means setting up on a perch in inconvenient places, for very long periods of time."

"Okay."

"So one time he was balanced up on a roof for almost two days. He must have fallen asleep because a car pulled up to the back of the building and blew its horn. He ended up tumbling down the roof into a pile of snow and ended up having to run out of the village before a mob of angry locals got him. Our C.O. luckily thought it was hilarious and said he startled and ran like Hannibal's elephants from Roman trumpets at the Battle of Zama. He's just lucky we didn't call him Zama."

Jade giggled, and Ink was glad they were able to lighten the mood. He was afraid things with her ex-friend weren't over, but there was no use in dwelling.

"If you tell anyone that story I'll deny it."

"My lips are sealed."

Ink smiled at them both. "So what are your plans for today, darlin'?"

"I've got a class to teach in about two hours, and a pile of paperwork I've been avoiding. Why?"

"How about you join us back at the Clubhouse once you're done work for the night? You could spend the night here."

The look Hannibal gave him was filled with happiness and joy. Ink wanted to roll his eyes. Jade was the only woman they had ever spent the night with at their house. Both times had been more a matter of exhaustion than forward planning. Inviting Jade to spend the night on purpose was a big step for him.

"Maybe if you're a very good girl. You can get Ink to show you some of his whip work." Hannibal winked at Jade.

The shiver that ran across her skin had his cock coming to attention. "I don't know about that. Is he any good with the whip?"

"Oh yes, darlin'. I'm very good with my whip."

Chapter 23

I didn't have a welcome mat at my door for you because I'm not a liar.

Jade

J ade stepped out of the car sore, tired, and floating on cloud nine. The tattoo Hannibal and Ink had designed was going to be spectacular. It was more than she had ever dreamed possible.

The relationship between the three of them was advancing at a speed that left her breathless. It had been less than a week, yet it felt like she had known them forever. Her thoughts and daydreams were full of images of the three of them and their possible future together.

A relationship between three people wasn't traditional. Before she met Hannibal and Ink, she wouldn't have even considered it. But it seemed to work for them.

The things they did to her body should be illegal, or at least classified as a dangerous addiction. If they didn't work out, not only would it shatter her heart, but no man would ever match them in the bedroom. The phrase 'ruined for other men' had taken on a new meaning.

Her gym had been the center of her life for years. All of her time and energy had gone into making it a success. It was all hers now. It would succeed or fail based on the decisions she alone made. It was finally at a place that it didn't require her attention every moment of every day.

She was making new friends. Not just the Old Ladies, but the Brothers she had met last night. All the people she had met at the Clubhouse had been wonderful and open. It was hard not to want to be a part of the Dark Sons' family, because that's what they were.

It was amusing to realize she was waxing poetic about a motorcycle club. She wasn't blinded by the rose tinted glasses she wore. The Dark Sons weren't Boy Scouts. Even she understood everything they did couldn't be legal. Or why would they call themselves outlaws?

Despite that, she liked them. Even Hawk, the gruff and kinda scary man who was their President, hadn't set off her danger sense. Unlike the men who had come with Eric the other day.

She walked through the doors of her gym and tried to force her head down out of the clouds. Christina scrambled out from behind the front counter on a quick path to intercept her. The look of anxiety and worry on her face was concerning.

"What's wrong?"

"There are three men waiting for you in your office."

Jade was confused. "Why did you let someone in my office?"

She glanced over towards the stairs to the office. "I didn't let them in. They just kinda pushed by and went in themselves."

Terror prickled up her spine. "Can you describe them?"

"Yeah, two muscle-heads. The kind that look like they eat barbells for breakfast. Lots of black tattoos. The third guy has dark hair and odd, washed-out blue eyes. He's wearing a suit but doesn't look like a corporate paper-pusher."

"Did they give you their names?" The description matched Eric's Russian contacts, but she was praying she was wrong.

"No. They actually didn't say anything. They walked by me and went straight up to your office. They ignored me when I tried to stop them. John tried to get them to come out of your office. But even he was freaked out by them." She looked guilty, but if the men were who she thought they were it was probably better they hadn't pushed. "So we figured we'd wait for you to get here."

"All right. You did the right thing. I'll handle it."

"Do you know them?"

"I think so, unfortunately. They're people Eric knows." Jade didn't want to air all of her dirty laundry, but the woman deserved at least a partial explanation.

Christina's shoulders relaxed. "Oh, God. What has he done now?" The tone in her voice said Eric had lost more than only her respect.

"I don't know, but they shouldn't be here. I bought the business off of Eric yesterday so his problems aren't mine anymore."

"That's awesome. I'm so happy for you. And honestly glad to not have to listen to him anymore. Okay, good luck with them." Christina gave her a hug.

Dealing with the men up in her office would probably take some time. Her class was supposed to start in ten minutes.

"Is there anyone free right now who might be able to teach the beginner tumbling class?"

"Yeah. Linda is training on the wall right now, but I'm

sure she'd be willing to pick up an extra shift. She's been saving for that vacation to Thailand."

"All right, do me a favor and see if she'll cover my class for me. I'm gonna deal with the guys upstairs."

"Will do." Her employee gave an uneasy glance in the direction of Jade's office. "Good luck."

Her fears were realized when she opened her office door. Andrey Petrov sat behind her desk as if it was his office instead of hers. Two new goons stood against the walls, somehow managing to loom even though there was no one else in the room.

Why would he show up with more muscle when their dealings were done?

"Mr. Petrov, what are you doing here?"

He glanced up at her from her chair, a smug smile on his face. He stood and spread his arms wide. "Ah, my lovely Jade. It is good to see you."

Razors of ice skittered across her nerves. This jovial act was disturbing. "I didn't think to ever see you again."

"Yes, well. We have unfinished business. I'm here to collect the rest of my money."

Jade jerked back. "What do you mean? Your man collected your money yesterday. I watched him take the check."

"Yes, he did. But Eric owed us $107,000, and the check was only $50,000. Which means you still owe me $57,000 dollars."

Jade's knees buckled, but she caught herself before falling. How could Eric have owed these people so much money? Fear trembled through her, but she clenched her fists and found her courage.

"Well, that sounds like you have a problem with Eric. Not me. I gave him all the money I owed him from the business.

If that wasn't enough to cover the debt. You need to bring that up with him."

The Russian man made a tsking sound that grated on her nerves. "You are mistaken. We sat here in this office and you promised me I would get my money. As I see it, his debt is now yours."

"That's ridiculous. It took everything I had to buy him out of the business. There isn't any more money."

Her thoughts scrambled for ideas as the man walked around her desk and approached her. Even if she was willing to give this man his money, she couldn't. Even if she got approved for the expansion loan, it would be weeks before she would have access to the funds.

If she used that money to pay this guy back, then it would put her plans back years. That was if she didn't go out of business in the meantime. Paying the loan back and the business expenses without the increased income from the planned upgrades would be near impossible.

How could Eric not have warned her that this was the situation? Why has he only been asking her for $10,000? She grabbed desperately at any possible solution.

"I thought he only owed you $10,000."

"No. That was the amount of his weekly payments. He was several weeks behind. I'll be kind and offer you the same terms if you can't pay for everything immediately. But I would need the first installment today plus ten more installments."

"That's ridiculous. You said he only owed you $57,000 more." She didn't understand why she was arguing about this. It wasn't her debt.

"Interest is a very tricky thing." His chuckle was cruel.

Jade shook her head. How the hell had Eric borrowed money from someone who would charge interest rates like that and threaten his life if he couldn't pay? She straightened her spine.

"I'm sorry Eric misled you. But that's not my problem. He's no longer even a partial owner of this business. So I've got nothing to do with it anymore."

Petrov moved so fast that she barely registered it. He held her against the wall by the throat. Breathing was hard. A blow landed on her stomach and knocked what air she had out of her lungs.

"I think that you don't understand. I own you now. Unless you can hand me $57,000, you are mine. You will do anything I say whenever I say it."

Jade clawed at his hand in panic. Her gaze searching the room for something or someone who could help. No magical savior appeared.

The two thugs the man had brought with him looked on with amused smiles. Guns she hadn't noticed when she came into the room were now painfully obvious. Anger was like a bonfire inside her.

She choked out words. "So what? You'll kill me if I don't follow orders like your lapdogs?"

Frustrated tears leaked out of the corner of her eyes as she struggled to breathe against his grip. He let her go with a disdainful laugh. His eyes were ice as he looked down at her.

"No. That wouldn't work for you. I've found other motivations are more effective."

She rubbed at her throat. "Then what?"

"You obviously don't value your own life. I've seen the stunts and nonsense you risk your life doing. But I would guess you care about your staff, your students. The children out there." He made a gesture towards the door. "From this moment on, every act of defiance will get one of them hurt. You won't know which one. You won't know how long it'll take before I act, but you'll know that every disrespectful word out of your mouth will cause one of them pain."

Jade's heart ached. She might not have developed close friendships with her staff, but they were the closest thing she'd had. The kids in her classes were innocent. Could she live with herself if one of them got hurt?

She studied the face of the man staring down at her with cold eyes and black-work tattoos poking out from the edge of his collar. The soulless men who traveled with him didn't even seem to care that their boss was threatening kids. It wasn't a bluff.

If she spoke disrespectfully to Petrov, he would probably march right out there to prove he was a man of his word. From the other side of the door, the sounds of children playing were loud. Probably from her tumbling class. It felt like the creak of a coffin closing on her freedom.

She needed time to figure out what she was going to do. And that would take playing this evil son of a bitch's game.

"What do you want me to do, Sir? I don't have $10,000. There isn't any way I can get it today."

He condescendingly tapped her cheek twice and stepped back. He chuckled. "See how much nicer it is when you behave. We will get along beautifully."

He strode back around her desk and sat himself in her chair, and motioned for her to take one of the opposite chairs. She held the word she wanted to say behind her teeth and did her best to appear to be respectful as she sat.

"You were at the Dark Sons' compound last night."

"How do you know that?"

"That is of little matter. Which one of the Brothers are you sleeping with? They've been a lot pickier this last year about who they let in for their parties. So you had to have an invitation."

What did he want from the Dark Sons?

"I wasn't invited there by a guy. The Old Ladies come here for classes. One of them invited me." It was the truth, and she didn't want to share that she might have a more personal connection.

"You left their compound but didn't go home last night."

Terror and protectiveness churned her stomach. How could he possibly know that? His information wasn't complete, but she didn't want to guess at how much he did know.

She stuck as close to the truth as she could without putting Hannibal and Ink in danger. It was a risk, but she had to try.

"I had some drinks and hooked up with some guy. I don't know if he was a Brother or not. I don't remember his name."

He didn't appear to be happy, but he also didn't look like he didn't believe her. It took all her self-restraint not to sag in relief.

"Do you think you can get back into the compound tonight?"

Not sure how to walk this tightrope between not betraying her new friends or endangering her staff and students, she stumbled over her words. "Possibly, I think so."

"Good." He pulled up a plastic baggie that was filled with small metallic black dots. "Do you know what these are?"

She shook her head.

"These are listening devices. You will plant these around the Clubhouse tonight. And I'll allow you to put off payment for a week. That should give you enough time to find the money to pay me."

"Why do you want to bug the Dark Sons' Clubhouse? It's basically a wild party, nothing else."

His chuckle made her blood run cold. "That is none of

your business. Do this, and no one gets hurt. Don't do this. And tomorrow someone you know will be in the hospital. Am I making myself clear?"

She nodded her head and looked down at her hands, unable to talk, for fear what would come out of her mouth would end up getting someone hurt regardless of what she did or didn't do tonight. The Russian man tapped the desk twice with his knuckles and stood.

She sat in her seat, clutching her hands into fists as the three men left her office. When the door finally closed behind them, she looked up at her desk and the plastic bag. It looked so innocent but held something that would ruin her life.

How could she do this? She didn't think the Dark Sons would react well if they found out she had betrayed them. Would their anger be any less violent than the men who had threatened her?

Hannibal and Ink deserved better than her. Could she betray the men she was growing to care so deeply for? She clenched her jaw against a scream of frustration that wanted to escape from her throat.

Tonight, she was going to be in an absolutely impossible situation.

Chapter 24

Don't break someone's heart, they only have one of them. Break their bones - they have 206.

Ink

Saturday night at the Dark Sons' Clubhouse was always a fun time. But for once, Ink wasn't interested in the beautiful women who flocked to the place looking for a ride on the wild side. Instead, he sat enjoying a drink with Highdive.

It was difficult to do anything but count down the minutes until Jade arrived. He'd expected her earlier, but she must have had to close up at work. It was almost eleven. If she was coming, then she should be here soon.

He glanced over at the door.

"You've got it bad." Highdive chuckled.

"What do you mean?" Ink looked around and saw Hannibal was at a table in the back with Smoke, Dragon, and Grinder. He glanced back at the front door before returning his attention to his drinking partner.

"You've looked at the front door at least fifty times in the last hour."

Had he? Ink didn't think it had been that often, but he was excited to get started on their plans for the evening. Their Jade had responded so perfectly last night that he couldn't wait to see how she reacted to his whips. It was as if she'd been created specifically for them.

If she enjoyed the kiss of his whip against her skin, it would be the ultimate sign. He snorted at himself. When had he become some sort of hippie looking for signs from the universe?

"Hannibal and I have plans for tonight."

Highdive shook his head. "Let me guess. With the woman I warned you off from?"

"Yeah. But she bought out her partner yesterday. So his problems shouldn't blow back on her anymore."

His Brother took a swallow of scotch. "Swear to God, all of my Brothers are made into absolute morons by pussy."

Ink laughed over his own drink. "Someday, Brother. A woman's gonna take you out too." He took a swallow and enjoyed the alcohol as it burned down his throat. That's what she'd done. Took him down, barreled right through all of his worries and concerns.

"Not going to happen. Some woman tries to take me down, I'm just going to tie her up and lock her away."

"I'm sure you believe that. It doesn't matter if you're a Shibari Master, she'll find a way to have you tied up."

"Fuck you." They laughed. "Guess that means you're going to be putting your patch on her back soon."

Ink only hesitated for a moment before giving a brief nod. How fast things had changed for him. If he'd been asked that even twenty-four hours ago, he wouldn't have believed it was even a possibility. Last night changed everything. He didn't want to picture the future without her.

If everything went well tonight, he would have to talk with Hannibal about speaking with Hawk. It was tempting to talk to him now so he could let everyone know Jade belonged to them. She still had to agree to it, but that was a formality. No Dark Son gave up once they had their sights set on a goal.

"You're a crazy fucker, but you're my Brother." Highdive clapped a hand on his shoulder. "Looks like your woman's arrived, so I'll make myself scarce." Highdive tossed back the last of his drink and walked away.

Ink looked up and saw Jade back-lit in the doorway to the Clubhouse. He smiled. It looked like she had been in a rush to see them, too. She hadn't taken the time to go home and change. Her hair was still up in the tight ponytail she wore for work. Her Leap polo shirt hid the amazing definition of her arms and the abs. The tight leggings she still wore were a bonus, though, because they hugged her ass in a way that made him want to stare at it for hours.

No makeup, probably still sweaty from work, and she was still the most gorgeous woman in the room. Ink stood and walked towards her. She didn't look relaxed or happy to be there. Stress was written into every line of her body. Work must not have gone well.

He had plenty of ideas on how he could help her relax. Was she freaking out over the idea of him introducing her to the whip tonight? If he couldn't get her in the right headspace, there was no way he was going to use it on her.

Maybe it would be better just to show her some of his practice drills instead, to demonstrate he knew what he was doing. No matter how much he enjoyed pushing limits and watching a woman tremble in anticipation and worry, he didn't want her to truly fear him.

"Hey darlin', it's good to see you." He scooped her up into a hug and almost immediately regretted it. She was stiff as a board in his arms. Instead of curling into him like she usually did, she arched away. He put her down and kissed her cheek. "Bad night?"

"Yeah, you could say that." She didn't look at him. "Anyway, could I get a drink?" She was looking around the room as if nervous.

"Sure." He put his hand at the small of her back and registered her small flinch. He guided her towards the bar and puzzled over her strange reactions. If this was anyone but Jade, he would back away from the don't touch me vibe she was throwing off.

She ordered a tequila. The instant the prospect set it down, she threw it back and gestured for another. He chuckled and filled it up a second time. She tossed that one back as well before turning around and putting her back to the bar. Not even a smile or thank you for the drink.

"Tell me what's wrong, darlin'."

"It's nothing I can talk about." Ink tried to step in front of her but she moved to the side, avoiding him. "You know what, I have to use the ladies' room." She slid away from him before he could even respond.

He watched, stunned, as she practically sprinted to the bathroom. With the way she had reacted to his touches, he'd wondered if she was hurt. But the quick gliding way she worked her way through the crowd put that theory to rest. Had he done something to piss her off?

"Hey. Where's she going?" Hannibal's smooth Louisiana voice asked. "Did you say something to piss her off already?"

Ink snorted at how in sync their thoughts were. He knew his Brother was teasing him, but the words hit hard. She hadn't given him the chance to say anything, but he was pretty sure she was avoiding him for some reason. He shook his head, completely confused by the cold reactions he'd gotten from their usually warm woman. "No, I'm not sure what's going on."

Hannibal sighed. "I know you don't believe in settling down with one woman, but please don't chase this one away. I really think she could be something special."

Ink didn't only think she could be something special, he knew it. "It's not that." He ran a hand through his hair. "I agree with you. I told Highdive we were considering putting our patch on her back."

The smile that quirked up Hannibal's lips filtered all the way into his eyes. "You mean that?"

"Yeah. But from her attitude tonight, I don't think it's me you have to worry about."

Doubt wormed its way into Ink's confidence. If she was worried about what they planned to do later, then she needed to talk to them, not throw an attitude. He hadn't thought she was the type of person to use bitchiness to hide fear, but what if he was wrong?

"What do you mean?"

"I mean that right now I feel like I'm a stranger who put unwanted moves on a woman who ran away as fast as she could."

"I think you're overreacting. Maybe she had a hard day at work."

Ink had considered that, but something was setting off his warning bells and they wouldn't settle. They watched her come out of the bathroom and instead of heading towards them, she slipped off towards the back and the pool tables.

Ink elbowed Hannibal and lifted his chin in the direction Jade had gone. "Overreacting? Then why instead of coming back to us, is she headed deeper into the party?"

Hannibal shrugged. "Maybe she's looking for me. I mean, I am the more handsome of the two of us."

Ink shook his head and laughed, but his heart wasn't in

it. They both knew that women usually preferred his country boy good looks over Hannibal's more intimidating physique. That their outsides didn't match what was inside was often commented on.

"I reckon we ought to find out."

Jade was watching a pool game in the back between a few of their Brothers. She was running her hand along the side of the table as the men took their shots. She didn't seem to flirt with them. In fact, she looked like she wanted to be anywhere but where she was. What was she doing?

Ink hung back. He wanted to see how she would react to Hannibal. His big friend didn't bother with subtlety and walked around the pool tables and scooped her up. At first she had the same stiff manner as she'd had when Ink had done the same thing, but Hannibal gripped the back of her head and claimed her mouth with a kiss.

Her body relaxed, the stress flowing out like a wave. The urge to join them was too overwhelming to resist. He slid up behind them. As soon as Hannibal let her lips go, Ink spun her into his own arms and claimed her mouth with his.

She tasted like tequila and sweet scotch which was Hannibal's favorite drink. For a few seconds, she was warm and willing in his arms. Her groan, a welcomed sound in his mouth. Here was the woman he was growing to care for so much.

She pushed against him sharply and struggled out of this grip. It horrified Ink to see tears trailing down her cheeks as she stumbled away from him. Was it him that she was reject-ing? Did she only want Hannibal?

"I can't," she sobbed. "I can't do this."

Hannibal stepped up next to Ink with a look of concern on his face. "What are you talking about, *cher*? What can't you do?"

Fear shot down his spine and stabbed into his heart. She shook her head and wiped tears from her cheeks. "I can't do this." Her voice raised in almost a shout. She looked around frantically. "I can't do you two. I can't do this Club. The motorcycles, the Old Ladies. I can't do any of it. Tell Val I'll refund her money, but I don't want them coming around my gym anymore. Don't ever contact me again."

Her words twisted like an ice dagger in his chest. It took all of his will not to reach out for her. He wanted to grab her and force her to tell him what he had done wrong. But he had his pride. It was obvious she had made her decision and he wouldn't go begging for affection. He had spent his entire childhood chasing the unobtainable love of his parents. He wouldn't ever lower himself to that point again.

She turned and fled towards the front of the Clubhouse. The Brothers who had been close enough to hear her words, stared at the two of them with a mixture of puzzlement and concern. He couldn't say or do anything. It took everything, every piece of strength, every ounce of self-control that he had, not to chase after her. To not let everyone see how much she was destroying him.

Hannibal's face was a mask of shock and concern. "Let's go get her. Something's wrong. This isn't right."

"Let her go, Brother."

Hannibal's look of disbelief was almost comical. How did that man still have hope after they'd been shot down so many times? And why had he let the man's stupid optimism cause him to let down his guards once again?

"If you're not coming, then I'm going alone."

"I don't go where I'm not wanted."

Hannibal growled at him but took off towards the door. Ink had to grip the edge of the table and fight the urge to punch a hole in a wall somewhere. He never went where he wasn't wanted. And dammit, that usually meant he was alone. It looked like he had been a fool again.

Maybe now Hannibal would finally give up on the stupid hope of finding a forever woman for them.

Chapter 25

Pretty words aren't always true, and the truth is often an ugly bitch.

Hannibal

Hannibal couldn't believe what a complete and utter ass Ink was being. But that was a problem for later. Nothing made sense about Jade's actions. The woman who had spent the last couple days with them wouldn't bail with no explanation.

Her words, 'I can't do this' had been filled with anguish and emotion that spoke of something deeper than deciding not to want to be with a man. If it was only their relationship, she wouldn't have cut off the Old Ladies as well. They had seemed to be growing closer last night without any tension at all.

He intended to get to the bottom of things, then shake some sense into his Brother. He stormed his way through the center of the Clubhouse. The smart people quickly got out of his way. He bowled aside the others without a thought.

Jade was at the door of her car by the time he hit the

parking lot. She was fumbling with her keys, and seemed unable to get her door open.

"Jade, wait."

She turned towards him. Her face was a complete wreck. Tears spilled from her eyes and ran down her cheeks in almost a constant stream. He had been right. Their woman was in trouble and instead of asking for help, she was running away.

"Just go away, Hannibal, believe me it's for the best."

"What's for the best? You running out of here without an explanation? Letting you destroy the man who is closer to me than a brother. Letting you rip the heart out of my chest. How is that for the best?"

"Don't say that. We've only known each other for a couple of days. Not even a week. You guys know nothing about me."

"That's bullshit. Not counting all the things I learned when I looked you up. I know what you taste like when you fall apart in my arms. I know what you smell like when you want us like we want you. I know what you feel like wrapped around my cock. I know what you dream about. I know what in your has life meaning and symbols that represent them. I know your hopes, your dreams. Some of your fears. Don't fucking tell me I don't know anything about you."

"You don't!" Her denial was a scream. She fumbled with the keys in her hand and the sound of the car finally unlocking was unwelcome. She ripped open the door and Hannibal grabbed her shoulder, not letting her get in.

"No. If you want to leave, I'll have to live with that, but you don't get to go until you give me the real reason."

She shoved at his chest with her little hands. It surprised Hannibal when she backed him up a step.

"Why? Because I'm nothing. I have nothing. I am noth-ing. You and he deserve so much more. He deserves someone who's actually loyal. Not someone who caves when times get tough."

Hannibal took a step back as shock punched him in the stomach. He tried to understand the words that were coming out of this bright, beautiful woman's mouth.

"Did you cheat on us today?" That was the only way he could think that she would believe herself disloyal. His fists clenched at the idea. He would destroy anyone who had touched her.

She shook her head, her shoulders slumped. "No, I wouldn't do that. There's no other man I want to be with other than the two of you. But I can't."

"Why?" His shout was so loud that he knew everyone who was outside was now staring at them. He didn't care.

"I can't tell you." She tried to turn away, and he pulled her back around, the tears in her eyes ripping at him, but he wouldn't back down.

"You're not nothing. You are everything to me. The woman I thought might be our forever girl. Why would you throw that all away?"

"Because of this." A strangled sob ripped out of her throat as she lifted her shirt and pulled something from her waistband and tossed it at him. Hannibal caught the bag on reflex, not understanding. He looked down, trying to make sense of what he saw.

He wasn't sure what he would have guessed would be in a bag Jade threw at him, but high-tech listening devices wouldn't have made the top one-hundred list. How had she gotten something like this?

The Russians. It was the only thing that made sense. The building conflict between them would mean they would do anything to get the upper hand. Horror tightened his throat. "Have you been working for the Russians all along? Did you seduce us to get into the Club?" The look of shock and disbelief on her face was too real to be faked, and something inside him relaxed. "It doesn't matter. Come inside and we'll figure this out." He needed to talk to Hawk or Highdive. Tek would need the information as well and see what he could get off the devices. He turned to look at the Clubhouse, pulling together a plan in his mind. "We need to go in and talk to Hawk."

The sound of her car door slamming shut and her car revving to life startled him out of his circling thoughts. Jade peeled out and onto the grass. She swung her car around at high speed. Before he could even react, she was racing through the gate and pulling out onto the road.

"I'm sorry, Brother," Highdive's voice next to him was like a splash of cold water shaking him out of his paralysis.

She had left them and was probably heading straight into danger. And there was shit he could do about it right now. He needed to get this thing settled. Let Ink know what had happened. Remove any threat to the Dark Sons.

"We need to shut this party down and send away all the civilians."

The look his friend gave him was priceless. "Your girl dumps you and you want me to shut the party down?"

Hannibal held up the bag of listening devices and waited while his friend squinted at them in the dark. It only took seconds for recognition to be clear on his face. "No, I think my girl might have bugged the place and we need to do a sweep to find out."

Highdive's face went stone cold, and he snatched the bag. He stormed back towards the Clubhouse. "We're on lockdown," he bellowed so everyone outside could hear him. "Get the civilians off the property."

Soon the music turned off and the same announcement was being made inside. He took a deep breath and headed back inside to help sort the chaos that always happened when they had to clear the civilians out in a hurry.

Ink grabbed his arm as soon as he walked into the room. "What the fuck is going on?" The curse coming out of his mouth was almost as much of a shock as the pure fury in his face.

"Not positive, but somehow, the Russians got to Jade. She was sent here to plant listening devices."

"So much for trust." The disgust in his voice was painful. He could see how much his Brother was hurting. "We fucking fell for her act. That's it. I'm done." Ink stormed away and Hannibal gave him his space because he knew it would be a while before his Brother was ready to listen to anything that didn't feed his rage.

Hannibal hoped she hadn't gone through with planting any of them. But that hope was shattered when they found three bugs. One at the bar where she had been standing, one in the ladies' room, and one on the pool table.

He needed to have another conversation with her. Even if she had told him about the listening devices in the end, she had betrayed the Club by planting them. Why hadn't she come to them for help before acting? Would any of his Brothers be able to forgive her if she finally came to her senses and talked to them?

More importantly, he wasn't sure if Ink would ever forgive her.

Chapter 26

What's the opposite of thank you? I'm pretty sure the phrase still ends in the word you.

Jade

Time slipped away as sobs wracked Jade's body. She'd pulled the car into a secluded spot the minute she was sure no one followed her. It felt like her emotions were ripping her into bloody shreds from the inside out. She screamed all the hurt and frustration into the evening sky.

What was she going to do? Eric had well and truly destroyed her life, every single bit of it. Everything that had meant anything to her would soon be in shambles. If the Russians acted on their threats, and she had no doubt they would, she couldn't live with the guilt of her staff and students getting hurt. Her only option would be to shut the place down and pray that would keep them safe.

Instead of choosing that path from the beginning, she

had stupidly thought she could plant the devices and make the bigger decisions later. But she didn't count on how it would feel to betray Hannibal and Ink. So she had blown up any chance she had ever had at a relationship with them by confessing and placing a target on herself and others.

She deserved whatever was going to come next. She had thought none of it through and acted on pure emotion. But even if she had gone through with planting the devices, what would Petrov have asked of her the next week and the one after that?

She didn't even have money in the bank to run. She'd emptied both her personal and business accounts in order to get Eric his stupid money. The money that he didn't even have the respect to tell her wouldn't be enough to solve his problems.

He may have been her best friend since childhood. But this well and truly cleared any debt she might have felt for the kindness that he had shown her as a child. Was that the point? He would only be happy if she were as miserable as he was.

Her phone rang, and she saw Hannibal's number across the screen. She closed her eyes and hit ignore. There was already a stream of texts from him she couldn't bring herself to read. She put her phone on silent. The temptation to answer would be too great if she kept hearing her phone ring.

Jade needed to be the one to fix this. She wasn't sure how she was going to do it, but even if the men never spoke to her again, she needed to make sure everyone would be safe. She dialed Eric, hoping to get more information, but it rang straight through to voicemail.

His phone was either off or he was purposefully ignoring her call. Rage replaced the sadness and hopelessness paralyzing her. Even if he wasn't able to fix this, he needed to know just how much he'd ruined her life. She would have the satisfaction of telling him to his face that he was right. She hated him.

Finding him wouldn't be hard. Years of chasing after him to get him home and sober before a competition meant they had always needed to know where the other one was. She pulled up an app she hadn't used in years.

She waited while the 'find a friend' app loaded. He was her only contact in the thing, so the map automatically settled on his location. Eric was in a part of downtown Denver she'd never been to. Probably living it up at some club without a care in the world about how much he had destroyed her life.

Her anger simmered as she drove the half hour to find him. The missed calls from Hannibal kept going up. Would he eventually give up on her? He should. Could he want the opportunity to tell her off? She would let him once she settled things with Eric. He deserved to take whatever revenge he wanted.

When she was close, she used the map to see if there were any bars or clubs near his location. His phone was showing in a building on Logan street near 16th street. The area strangely lacked anything that fit her ex-friend's lifestyle.

She pulled into a parking spot about a block away. The area was pretty rundown. Last week, she wouldn't have believed that Eric would be found dead anywhere near here. Maybe he had a hookup somewhere in one of the apartments. If that were the case, it would be hard to find him.

She wasn't willing to give up yet. She pulled on a black hoodie. The almost deserted street held closed shops and rundown apartments. That was all that was visible other than the spire of a church a block away looming over the neighborhood.

She followed the GPS, trying to get as close as possible before deciding what to do next. It directed her down an alley. Fear had her shoving her phone in the pocket of her hoodie and looking around. She crept down the alley. This had to be one of the dumbest things she'd ever done. It was after midnight, in the bad part of the city, and she was a female alone without even the comfort of mace.

If she survived her stupidity, she would try to have more sense in the future. The indistinct sounds of voices echoed back to her. She couldn't understand the words but knew they were coming from further down.

She moved into the many shadows between the two buildings. Barely any light from the street made its way down to her. Her survival instincts finally kicked in and told her it would be better if the men didn't know she was here. Unfortunately, her sense didn't override her curiosity, so she inched forward until she was up against a dumpster pressed up against the side of a building and leaned out.

At the end of the alley, a small parking lot was situated, lit by dim floodlights. It sat behind the buildings, hidden away from sight. Two cars were parked in the lot, one with its trunk open. Two men stood speaking Russian. They held bottles of bleach and chuckled. A tarp was laid out on the ground, Eric's bloody, beaten body sprawled in the center. His lifeless eyes stared off into the distance, a bullet hole gaping in his forehead. She gasped before she could think better of it.

The men stopped speaking and squinted down the alleyway towards where she was hidden. She pulled her head back, the quick movement unfortunately causing the dumpster to move and create more noise. The echo of footsteps moved towards her and her heart raced.

She looked down the alleyway behind her. The distance to the street was too long for her to run without getting caught. The men would be on her in seconds. She spun and lifted herself up to the top of the dumpster. One man cried out as he saw her.

She leaped up, grabbing the edge of the roof of the building and heard the unmistakable sound of gunfire.

Chapter 27

Everything you ever wanted is on the other side of fear, so take that fucker out quick.

Ink

I t felt like everything inside Ink had gone cold. His Brothers talked around him and none of it was able to pierce the fog he was in. He answered questions on auto pilot, giving what little information he had on the woman who had torn out his heart.

Not only had Jade rejected them and walked away with no explanation, but then it turned out she'd betrayed them. Planting listening devices for their enemies. The knowledge of that should've enraged him, but where that heat should have been was just the nothingness of ice.

His quick temper and lack of patience were at the core of who he was. It was why he'd been paired with Hannibal in the Rangers so they could balance each other out. Anger would be much easier to handle than this numbness. Was he going to let his issues from childhood turn him into a waste of space?

There were too many unanswered questions. He should be desperate for the answers. Instead, it had been Hannibal attempting to call her every few seconds for the last fifteen minutes. Not that she bothered to pick up. If they weren't important enough for her to give an explanation to, he would have to find the answers other ways.

Most of the Brothers believed she'd been under the Russian's thumb from the beginning. Her friend Eric's troubles were now common knowledge. The popular theory was that she'd been their puppet for months and when Petrov found out she had a connection to them, he ordered her to spy.

Hannibal didn't agree and believed she didn't know anything about it until today. His Brother's instincts were usually solid. His gut screamed at him to agree with him, but it was hard to trust in anything at the moment.

Her innocent act would have to have been flawless to take both of them in. Ink took a deep breath and tried to think clearly. He wasn't a sucker. She couldn't have fooled him that deeply. Did it matter? Even if their moments together had been real, when it had counted, she'd failed. Rather than turning to them for help, she'd betrayed them and bailed.

The officers had gone off to confer and came back a few minutes later. They'd announced that she needed to be brought back to the Clubhouse for questioning. She wouldn't have the option to refuse. Tek was tracing her phone to get a location.

His Dark Son Brothers were nothing if not efficient in a crisis. Already the entire Clubhouse had been swept for bugs. The three listening devices they'd found matched the make and style of the ones Jade had tossed at Hannibal.

That was the thing that didn't make sense to Ink. If the

Russians had something on her to make her betray them, why hadn't she completed the task? Giving the bag to Hannibal guaranteed she would be found out. Was that part of the plan?

Hannibal sat next to him with a grunt. "I'm worried about her."

"Why? Because she's not answering your phone calls or texts?" The bitterness in his voice was cutting. His Brother didn't deserve the attitude, but Ink didn't care. He had every right to be bitter. It'd been Hannibal's pushing that made him vulnerable to her in the first place.

"That's part of it. But you didn't see her before she pulled away. She was too emotional to be driving."

He was worried about her safety? "Why the fuck do you care if she was too emotional to drive?" The 'after she betrayed us and our Brothers' hung unsaid in the air between them.

"Because she might be on the side of the road in a ditch somewhere. Hurt and alone. Doesn't the idea of that bother you?"

Ink ground his teeth. The image of her bleeding in a wrecked car flickered through his thoughts. He clenched his fists and tried to ignore the fear that rose to challenge the numbness that had settled over his heart. She shouldn't have the power to worry him after what she had done.

"I don't think this is her fault," Hannibal's words were almost a whisper.

Ink slammed his first on the bar. "Not her fault? We all have choices in life. She chose to help that piece of shit Eric over us."

"Maybe, or maybe they threatened her with something else. We won't know unless we ask her."

"What else could they threaten her with? She told us she

doesn't have any family or close friends. If she was the one in danger, did she think we wouldn't protect her?"

"Jesus Christ, Ink, listen to yourself. We've only known her for less than a week. Yeah, we shared more with her than we usually do with any woman we're with. But it's not like we told her about the darker stuff. Or that our Brothers handle threats every day. All she knows is that we're tattoo artists who used to be in the military. She has no clue what being a Dark Son means."

Ink grunted, not wanting to acknowledge that Hannibal had a point.

"For all we know, they could've threatened to hurt us if she didn't do what they said. And she might have been dumb enough to fall for it."

Ink leaned back in his chair and closed his eyes in frustration. He didn't want to see the sense in Hannibal's words. It was easier to hold on to the idea that she'd betrayed them for no good reason. If she was a conniving bitch, it would kill that sense of hope that kept trying to rear its ugly head. Hope was nothing but a poison pill for the soul.

"So what, if she gives us a good enough sob story, you expect me to take her back with open arms?"

"I don't know." Hannibal ran a hand over his tight cropped hair. "But I do expect you to be willing to listen."

Ink shook his head. He couldn't imagine a story that would give him back the ability to trust her again.

"I've got her location," Tek called out to the room of men. "She was parked about ten minutes away for the last hour. About five minutes ago, she started moving towards Denver. I'm able to track her real time now."

Hawk stood up and looked around the room. His gaze stopped on Hannibal and Ink. "This could be a trap set by Petrov to get us to follow her. We need to be alert for an ambush en route or wherever she leads us. I want every

Brother available on this ride. Keep your heads on a swivel." He took a breath, as if hesitating. "The plan is to give her a non-negotiable invite to talk to us and give us the full story. Don't hurt her unless it's necessary."

Ink swallowed, his President's cold words driving home the stark reality of what might happen. He nodded his acceptance of them.

Hannibal gave him a disgusted look and shook his head. "You might not be willing to listen, but I will."

The coldness inside of him grew. "And if after she tells her story I still don't want to trust her?"

"I guess then we'll see."

Ink watched as his closest friend, for over a decade, walked away from him without a backward glance. Hope really was the ultimate poison. It might destroy every good thing in his life because he'd been stupid enough to take a chance on it.

Chapter 28

When I was a child I played 'the floor is lava'. Parkour just took that to the next level.

Jade

J ade pulled herself up onto the roof, praying, as cement shattered around her from a gunshot. She had to get out of their range. More shouts sounded from behind her, more than the two voices she expected. Damn, there were more of them.

She took a chance and peeked back over the edge once she was over. One of her original chasers was climbing up onto the dumpster and at least five men were running into the alley from the parking lot. One of them took a shot at her and she ducked down with a curse.

She took a deep breath and scanned the area. There were several buildings close enough to be a possible escape. She sprinted for the far edge of the building towards the closest building. Her heart raced and adrenaline flooded her system as she hit the edge and pushed off the distance only a few feet. She came down in a controlled roll on the other side and kept moving.

A quick glance told her one man was pulling himself up in the same spot she had. There wasn't anywhere to duck or hide on this roof. Men's shouts came from below and she had to guess they would follow her on the ground. There was a U-shaped building off to her right that looked barely close enough to several more buildings down Logan Street. At the end of the street was the giant cathedral, she had noticed before. Its spires rose up into the night.

Trying to make her way back down to the street would be dangerous. She didn't think her chances were very good at outrunning men with cars and bullets. She looked back at the church, tried to gauge the run and path to get to it. She could climb and try to get in the bell tower, but if they broke into the church, they would be able to get her there.

If she went all the way to the top of one of the spires, then the crenellations at the top would protect her from gunfire from below, and she might be able to hide out until the police came. If she made it without dying or falling on one of the many jumps. She ran before fear could steal her will.

The man behind her must have gotten to his feet, because the sound of a shot sent her pulse racing. The world grew small in her mind as she focused down to finding her steps, and the buildings in front of her. The shadows surrounding her would mask obstacles, and she couldn't risk a single stumble. The scattered streetlamps barely illuminated enough for her to find a path.

She ignored the sound of gunfire coming now from not only behind, but below her except to pray the sound brought the police faster. They would either hit her or not. Her moving as fast as possible was her only chance of survival.

She vaulted an air conditioning unit and continued her

sprint. Each gap between the buildings was easy, no harder than the jumps she did every day at her gym. She hit the fifth building, her breath coming hard. The jump to the church's main building was longer than she expected. It would take all of her speed to even have a chance of making that.

She forced her muscles to go faster and ran for all she was worth. Jade swore she would make this jump or die trying. The impact of the edge of the building against her foot was just slightly off, but she didn't hesitate. She exploded upward and leaped into the dark.

There are moments during stunts where there is no safety net or wire and nothing keeping her from flying away except gravity. Time seemed to pause, and she was suspended in the air between buildings. In the middle of all the chaos and gunfire, the pain of her body disappeared, and she felt joy for a brief moment.

The roof of the cathedral hit her in the stomach, its slanted exterior caused her to slide down a few feet. She scrambled, using her nails to dig into the rough material tearing up her skin. She heard men cursing in Russian as she finally pulled her bruised and battered body onto the roof.

Everything hurt, and she knew she was going to be badly bruised. Stopping now would be suicide. A roof shingle exploded next to her. She glanced back. The man who had been chasing her hadn't continued past the third building. He stood in a shooter's stance and fired at her from a distance.

She scrambled across the tilted roof, pulling herself up onto the next level, until she reached the main part of the cathedral's roof and the attached towers. Jade refused to think about how dangerous climbing up an old building in low light while people shot at her was. She grasped the stonework and pulled her way upward. Her grip slipped, and she swung to the side, barely gaining purchase with her other hand before falling.

Time after time she moved upward, praying the stone wouldn't give under her hands or feet. Rock and stone pelted her, both from the crumbling exterior and from the gunshots now coming at her, from both on the ground and behind her. Bile rose in her throat as she grasped onto the edge of the window of the bell tower and realized there were metal bars blocking the entrance.

She couldn't stop here even if she wanted to. Jade pulled herself up higher and higher, not daring to look down, or even guess what would happen if she fell. Finally, she gripped the thick top of the bell tower and pulled herself over and collapsed behind the crenellations and the thick stone.

She was alive, by some miracle neither the gunmen nor the climb had killed her. How long she would stay that way was still uncertain. Her heart slowed and everything from the night came crashing back at her.

Eric was dead, and she would probably be next. These men didn't seem concerned about flagrantly breaking the law. Her death wouldn't be more than a blip in their lives. She regretted so much. Not seeing that Eric was in trouble sooner. Allowing him to take advantage of her for so long.

But more than anything else, she regretted not telling Hannibal and Ink how she felt about them. Not giving them the opportunity to help her find her way out of the mess she was now in. They probably hated her and she couldn't blame them.

A short blast of a siren sounded from below and gave her hope. She peeked out over the edge of the stone tower. A police cruiser pulled up on the road outside the church. Four of the men pursuing her approached the police car.

Their guns were in their hands, and they did not try to conceal them. Were they going to kill the police officers? She scanned the strip below and saw ten people who were now staring up at the place where she was hidden.

She didn't know what the men said to the police, but the cruiser pulled away, leaving her alone in the tower. So much for her rescue. Would the Russians now try to climb up after her? If they didn't, would she be safe to try to climb down in the morning? The crowds and the morning traffic would have to force them to give up their hunt for her.

Hope was a vicious thing. As soon as you had it, it could be ripped away. Three men broke off from the others and headed towards the doors of the church. She didn't know what their plan was, but guessed they were probably going to try to get as high as possible. And then come drag her out of her hiding spot.

They had hours before they had to worry if the police weren't an issue. She wouldn't submit quietly to her fate, but knew that she was only stalling for time. If she only had a short time to live, then she would make right what things she could.

The one mistake she truly regretted was hurting Hannibal and Ink. The idea that she might die with them still hating her tore at her heart. They were unlikely to forgive her, but she owed them the truth. All of it.

Jade pulled her phone out of her pocket and stared at the screen. Which one should she call? The twenty missed calls from Hannibal told her he at least might be willing to listen. She clicked on his name and hit the call button.

Chapter 29

A man might fear to stand alone, but a Brother never has to.

Hannibal

The midnight black sky was an endless field of stars above them as the thirty Dark Sons sped down the highway, ready for war. Hannibal usually enjoyed being surrounded by his Brothers no matter what the mission was. Unfortunately, for his heart, it wasn't possible to get behind their current objective.

The idea of forcibly dragging Jade back to be questioned and possibly tortured tied his stomach into knots. He was in love with her. It was fucked up in so many ways. But even knowing she had betrayed them, possibly from the start, didn't change the fact that the woman had taken possession of his heart.

He'd suspected that was the case at breakfast that morning, but it had solidified into undeniable truth when his heart had shattered when she drove away crying. That didn't change what he had to do. They needed to find out what information she had.

Every Brother had been issued a Bluetooth earpiece that allowed them to communicate even when riding. Normally there would be lots of chatter while they psyched themselves up for possible combat. But everyone remained silent, leaving him wrapped in his own thoughts and state of mind.

Ink rode in his usual spot at Hannibal's side, his face grim. Trust wasn't something his friend often allowed himself to indulge in. So when Jade betrayed them, the blow had been devastating.

Would his Brother forgive her? Hannibal wasn't sure he would, no matter what her reasons. The man might appear easygoing to those who didn't know him well, but his past had made him unwilling to let people in close. His temper was quick to ignite and slow to cool.

The anger simmering through the Brothers over what Jade had done was understandable. The dangerous games between the Club and the Russians had been going on for far too long. Most of them still harbored a barely contained rage over Max's kidnapping, and supposed death two months ago.

Anyone who associated with the Russians, in any way, was seen as the enemy. But Hannibal believed Jade was their victim, not their ally. He had faith that once she told her side of the story, his Brothers would come around. Unfortunately, he wasn't as sure about Ink.

If the frustrating woman had picked up a single one of his calls, they could have avoided this entire thing. Instead she had run, without any explanation except the stupid bag of listening devices she had thrown at him. If onlys were a waste of time.

"It looks like she's heading into downtown Denver." Tek's voice was clear across his earpiece.

Acting as coordinator and recon for the mission, the man was secured inside the black van at the back of the procession of bikes. Several of the prospects were in there with him to act as driver and protection, allowing the man to focus on using his gear to track Jade.

Disappointment was a leaden weight on his shoulders. Jade lived outside the city in an apartment near her gym, so she wasn't heading home. Why was she heading into downtown Denver at this time of night?

The Russians had control over several areas of downtown. Was she heading to one of their businesses? Would she be dumb enough to head right into the center of their territory and tell them she had failed?

They would kill her. If for no other reason than to remove the proof, they had been the ones to break the treaty. Or was this a trap?

When Hawk had first suggested she might be bait for them, Hannibal had dismissed the idea. But maybe the Russians had counted on her getting caught and leading them into the middle of the Russians territory.

He didn't think that was the case. The pain and tears had been real. He would swear the impulse to give him the bag of devices had been a spur-of-the-moment choice.

Jade couldn't fake that kind of emotion. She was an open and honest person, almost to a fault. Her mouth had given away her feelings on more than one occasion.

Highway turned into city streets as he circled in his own thoughts. He see-sawed between worry for her and wild theories on what she was doing in the city.

"Looks like she's parked about two blocks away from Petrov's headquarters. We're about ten minutes out from her location." Tek's information killed the wild hope Hannibal had that she was only trying to find a bar to drown her sorrows.

"All right." Hawk's voice was deep, the static from his bike only slightly distorting his words. "We're going to pull over at the civic center and strategize what we're going to do. I'm not stumbling into a trap or kicking off the war tonight unless there is no other option. We'll wait and see if she moves again."

Hannibal wanted to protest, but the argument would be a waste of time. She wasn't their Old Lady. So none of them would be willing to go in and risk their lives for her. He couldn't ask them to when things were still so uncertain.

That meant he might be sitting nearby doing nothing while the Russians killed her. He didn't think he would be able to live with that decision. He might have to go in alone.

A few months ago, he had cursed Max for doing something exactly like that. Hannibal hadn't understood at the time why his Brother had been willing to risk his life and problems for the Club, for the sake of a woman. Now he got it.

They were parked in the location Hawk had chosen and Hannibal had shut down his bike. Tek's voice came over the headset. "She's moving at speed. She may have gotten back in her car."

Everyone paused, waiting to see if they would be moving out. The silence of the city was unnerving after being in the middle of the loud noise of the procession for so long. Turning off the bikes meant they would be slower to respond, but lessened the possibility that locals would call in a noise complaint and they would have to deal with cops.

"Was she in the Russians' headquarters?" Hawk asked.

"Not from what I could tell. I'm trying to make sense of the location, but she seems to have stopped again and settled at the Cathedral Basilica a few blocks away."

"Does Petrov control the church?" Sharp's question echoed Hannibal's own thoughts.

"Not according to our Intel. It's actually a Roman Catholic Cathedral. No ties in our system to anything criminal. Wait. I've got police reports coming in of gunfire in the area. They're dispatching a unit to check it out."

Every muscle in his body clenched with the urge to start up his bike. Jade might be in danger. He needed to do something. A heavy grip on his shoulder made him jump.

Hannibal glared at Highdive, who gave him a cold shake of his head and kept his hand steady on his shoulder. He understood the message. He wasn't allowed to ride off.

Looking over at Ink, Hannibal saw his Brother was struggling as well. They needed to make a decision that would have long-standing consequences.

"Cops are on scene and reporting that it was a false alarm. Kids with fireworks." Tek's voice didn't hide his lack of faith in that report.

"Petrov has the cops in his pocket," Ink growled next to him.

He couldn't sit there doing nothing. Even if he was too late, he needed to find out what was going on and if Jade was in trouble

Hannibal's phone rang in his pocket and he pulled it out. Jade's name flashed like the answer to a prayer across his screen. He took a moment to tap his earpiece. "I've got Jade calling me on the phone."

Hawk's voice came back almost immediately. "Tek, patch it through. I want to hear what she has to say."

Hannibal answered the phone on speaker, not waiting to hear how the guy was gonna manage that.

"Are you okay, Jade?"

Her small sob shot right into his heart. "I'm sorry, Hannibal. I want you to know that. I never meant to hurt you or Ink."

"What exactly are you sorry for, *cher*?" Hannibal tried to

keep his heart out of his voice, but wasn't sure he was succeeding. Ink got off his bike and moved to stand next to him.

"I don't want to die without telling you everything."

Tek's voice came over the earpiece, "Ask her when—"

Hannibal pulled out the annoying distraction from his ear and focused on the phone. "What do you have to tell me?"

"I planted three of those bugs in the Clubhouse. One under the bar and one in the ladies' room and one on the pool table. They shouldn't be hard to find."

Disappointment settled in his heart. "We already found them."

"Good. I don't want that bastard to get anything he wanted."

"Why did you do it?" For him, nothing else mattered than the answer to that question. He would forgive her if her motivations hadn't been money or protecting that prick who had spent years taking advantage of her.

"Petrov threatened to hospitalize either someone from my staff or one of my students if I didn't help him. He made it clear that even the kids wouldn't be safe."

"Why did he target you?" Hannibal thought he knew the answer, but wanted to see what she would say.

"Turns out that asshole Eric owed him over $100,000. I stupidly thought he only owed him $10,000. So I agreed to buy Eric out so he could pay it back. Petrov said that meant the debt was now mine. That he owns me."

Ink's growl echoed his own. "Why didn't you tell us?"

"This guy is scary. I recognized some of his tattoos as marks of the Bratva. That's like the Russian mafia," she explained like they wouldn't know. "I couldn't drag you into that. I didn't want you guys to get hurt as well. There was nothing you could do against someone like that."

Hannibal wanted to reach through the phone and either strangle her or kiss her for her naïve assumptions. "Where are you now?"

Her laughter had a slightly hysterical edge to it. "You wouldn't believe me if I told you."

"Try me. Wherever it is, I'll come and get you." Hannibal ignored Highdive's annoyed growl.

"No. They killed Eric. I saw his body. I came into Denver to track him down using the stupid 'find a friend' app and stumbled like an idiot right into them cleaning up his blood from the pavement."

"What happened?"

"They saw me and I ran."

"Where are you now?"

"Know that old Cathedral on Colfax and Logan?"

"Yeah."

"I'm on top of one of the spires. They know where I am. They've got at least ten men with guns on the street and I'm pretty sure more are climbing up to get me. I was hoping they wouldn't be able to get me up here, but…" There was the sound of some rustling and then a gunshot rang out both over the phone and through the night air.

Hannibal's heart froze for a minute. "Jade!"

"I'm okay. It looks like they're on their way up here. There are three guys on the roof, so I guess it won't be long until they get up the nerve to climb up here. Maybe they'll blow up the tower with me on it. Do you think gangsters have explosives?"

Her mind was obviously traveling down some very dark roads. "Probably not on hand."

They had some hidden back at the compound but he hoped Petrov wasn't as prepared. Or that the difficulty of covering up destroying a church would deter them.

"That's good to know," she said.

"Why did you call me, little Jewel? Were you hoping I would come and rescue you?" He knew he would try, but thirteen gunmen alone was a tall order even if Ink helped him.

"No." The word held a soft acceptance that Hannibal didn't like. "You're too far away to save me. Is Ink there with you?"

"Yeah, I'm here darlin'." Ink's voice was tight, but his use of an endearment gave Hannibal the first spark of hope that his Brother had heard her explanation and might consider forgiving her given time. Time which they didn't have.

"Good." Her shuddering breath was audible even over the phone. "The two of you coming into my life was like a dream I wish I'd never woken up from. I'd imagined what you would be like, since I stalked you online for years. But the reality was so much better."

"Darlin'—"

"No, let me finish. It may have been only a week, but I know from the core of my heart that I love you both. Hannibal, I love the way you notice every tiny detail about everything and everyone. How you give your whole heart to everything you do without reservation. Ink, I love your many layers from the man who fools everyone with his sweet southern looks to the prickly cactus who pushes everyone away. But under it all is the man who dreams of beauty and brings fantasy to life."

Her words were filled with tears now. "I love how loyal you guys are to each other and your Club. I even love your Brothers, though some of them are as intimidating as shit, because they love you. And because as badass as they may be, they love and nurture those wild, wonderful, and completely insane women I've come to call friends."

Her voice caught, and she cleared her throat. "That doesn't make up for what I did. I wish I'd been stronger so I might have someday been an actual part of that family. I hope someday you can forgive me."

Her words seemed to hang in the night air. They were her final wish, and everyone listening realized she didn't expect to survive the night. How the hell was this happening?

She was only blocks away and there wasn't a damn thing he could do about it. Rushing in there to try to save her would only get him killed and finally spark off the war that would cost many of his Brothers' lives.

Around him his Brothers' faces were grim. They'd been by his side, and he'd been at their backs more times than he could count. All he wanted to do in this moment was start up his bike and rush over and try to save a vibrant, wonderful woman on the other end of the phone.

To do that, he would have to renounce the Club to prevent blowback. Could he do it? Could he step away from his brothers and put everything on the line for her?

Hannibal looked over at Ink, and in that moment, they were both in sync.

"Let's do this," Ink's voice was a harsh growl.

"Hold on, baby. We're coming for you." They gripped their cuts, ready to hand them in before riding away.

Hawk's bike roared to life. "Fuck it," their President growled. "Let's go get your woman."

The cheer that sounded from every Brother's voice as they kicked their bikes to life lifted Hannibal's soul and echoed into the night.

Chapter 30

If you back me into a corner you're going to find out I'm five pounds of crazy and you only have a one pound bag.

Jade

"Hold on, baby. We're coming for you."

Jade wanted to shake her head at Hannibal's crazy proclamation. The sounds of motorcycles through her cell phone were so loud it seemed to echo out into the night.

The call cut off and the sound of motorcycles continued. She wasn't an expert on sound, but it seemed like they couldn't really be that close. Forgetting the fact that he shouldn't be anywhere close by, what did he think he could do against more than ten armed men?

A quick peek over the edge of the spire was enough to see that one of the three men who'd been on the roof had climbed about a quarter of the way up the tower. The man had his feet on an outcropping and was gripping onto a decorative element with all of his strength while he looked around and searched for another place to grab on.

Jade shook her head and pulled back before any of them started shooting. She had a bit of time before the guy realized he had to come up from a different side to get better handholds, or attempt the jump over to the next place with a viable handhold. If he did jump and wasn't used to the slippery texture of stone, he was as likely to fall as to stick to the landing.

It wasn't a nice thought, but she really hoped he would slip. Her talk with Hannibal and Ink had settled something inside her. Letting them know how she felt freed her in a way she hadn't expected. That they'd accepted her words and were even going to attempt to help her created a sense of peace in her soul.

Not that she was ready to die. Far from it. But if she did, it was nice to know that she wouldn't have left things unbalanced between them. Could they love her the way she loved them? The declaration they were coming, even if they wouldn't arrive in time, gave her hope.

Jade clenched her fists and punched down on the stone floor. The space around the spire she was curled up in wasn't big enough for a fully grown man. She tried to picture what would happen once one of them got up here. With time and the calm her men had gifted her, it was easier to think.

She heard a grunt and scrambling of footwear not designed for climbing against rock. She looked down and saw that the man had made the jump over to the window and was hanging from its ledge. If he pulled himself up, it wouldn't be long before he was at the edge of her hiding place.

She pulled her head back at the sound of a gunshot. The rumble of motorcycles seemed to be getting closer. The sound was so loud. Was all that noise from only two bikes?

Was she crazy to pretend it was her men coming to get her? Maybe it was a cosmic coincidence that she heard a group of bikers at the same time Hannibal and Ink were racing the thirty minutes from their Clubhouse to reach her.

She needed to focus. In order for the man to get up to her hiding spot. He was going to have to grip the edge and pull himself up. There was no way he would have a weapon in his hand. At least not at first. She bit her lip.

When he first got a grip, or even as he was pulling himself up, he would be completely vulnerable. She could push him off. It was a horrible thing to do, but there was no pleasant way to stop him. The fall from this height guaranteed, if not death, then a paralyzing injury. Could she do that to another human being?

Would she be able to live if she caused someone's death? She didn't think so. If she pushed him toward the main building, then he might only fall as far as the roof below. That was a little over a two-story fall and he might survive. No, she wouldn't lie to herself. If she made him fall, she would have to live with the consequences, regardless of intent.

These men had killed Eric. Not that her friend had been a good man anymore, but despite all of his flaws, he hadn't deserved to die. The man climbing up to her would probably be one of the ones who Petrov would have sent to hurt her staff or students. Men like that wouldn't hesitate to kill her. So why was she hesitating about killing them?

Time had run out. Large hands gripped the edge of the stone, and she only had a few seconds to decide. Terror caused her limbs to shake. She didn't want to die. Jade brought her hands up and slammed them down onto his fingers as he levered himself upwards. His scream of pain slid into one of terror. The sight of him falling down backwards, slamming into the tilted roof, froze her in place. He tumbled off the side of the building, his body limp before he even hit the ground. His friends scrambled, as if they were going to try to catch him. But there was nothing they could do.

She watched in fascinated horror as he impacted the ground in the side yard of the cathedral. His body splayed in such a way that there was no question he was dead. She'd killed him. Horror and disgust swirled in her stomach.

She fought back nausea, thankful she hadn't eaten anything all day. *Murderer*, her mind shrieked. It might have been self-defense, but that was what she was. Right up until the moment she acted, she hadn't believed she would do it. Her survival instinct had overridden logic and compassion.

Her muscles trembled as she remembered how her body moved without thought or conscience. The roar of motorcycles echoed around her in a wave of noise that must be a result of the surrounding buildings. It was like she was standing in the middle of them. She took a chance and moved to the other side of the spire and looked down Colfax Ave.

It was like something straight out of a movie. Motorcycles lined up in rows, their headlights illuminating the entire street in front of them as they crept down the street towards her. There had to be at least twenty-five of them. Had Hannibal and Ink brought all of their Brothers?

How the hell had they gotten here so fast? Only ten minutes had passed since she'd hung up from the call with them. Their compound was a good thirty-five or more minutes away.

Jade looked back towards the two Russian men who had her penned up on the roof. They were looking down at the street as well, guns drawn. She didn't know any of the Brothers, well enough to recognize them at a distance with only headlights and streetlights to make their features visible.

Nowhere in the group of bikers did she see Hannibal's gorgeous dark skin, or large bulk. She thought she recognized Ink in the front line of bikes, but she wasn't sure. Movement near the back of the roof caught her attention, and she wrapped her hand over her mouth to hold back the shout of joy.

Three men crouched, sneaking across the roof. She recognized at least two of them. Hannibal, and the tall, muscular Native American looking brother named Dragon. The third man, she'd seen around but hadn't really met, but he moved with the same deadly grace as the other two. The two Russians were so busy looking at the commotion down below, they didn't notice until too late that they weren't alone.

Jade watched as Hannibal and Dragon slipped up behind the two men with knives. These men didn't have any of her hesitation, and in a motion she could only guess was slitting their throats, the Dark Sons pulled the Russians backwards.

They carefully draped the limp bodies across the roof and away from the sight of the people below. Not willing to wait another minute longer. Jade scrambled down the tower, only slowing enough to be careful not to fall. She was about to make the last jump down when powerful arms plucked her off the wall.

She was in Hannibal's embrace, where she belonged. It should have bothered her that he'd killed someone so brutally, but it didn't. Hell, she was a killer, too. Instead, all she could think of was how wonderful it was to be safe in his arms. She never wanted to let go.

Hannibal's hands wrapped into her hair and pulled her in for a kiss. She lost herself in the heat, passion, and joy that being alive gave her. She loved the taste of him and never wanted this moment to end.

"I hate to break up this party. But we've got to get out of

here before they realize their men are down." Hannibal pulled away and looked at the man whom she'd never met.

She could just make out in the dim light that the leather vest he wore had a patch with the name Highdive on it. "Of course, I'm sorry." She unwrapped her legs and Hannibal lowered her to the roof. Something oddly bulky under his shirt kept her from feeling all the wonderful muscles underneath. She shook her head and tried to focus. "What about Ink? Is he going to be safe down there?"

Hannibal chuckled. "Yeah, he's helping Hawk deliver a message to Petrov." He took her by the shoulders and looked straight into her eyes. "You need to understand, little Jewel, that this is going to mean war between our two groups. And there's a whole lot you're going to have to come up to speed on really fast, if you're going to stay with us."

Fifteen minutes ago, she didn't think she was going to survive the night, and that she'd lost everything. Instead, she'd been rescued. And by all appearances, Hannibal had forgiven her. She didn't care what obstacles were in their way, hell that was her specialty. She would find a way around, over, or through them, if it meant being with those two men. She gave Hannibal a smile. "As long as I have you guys, that's all that matters."

Chapter 31

*If they stand behind you, protect them. If they stand beside you, respect
them. If they stand against you, destroy them*

Ink

I t felt odd riding in the front line with the officers down
Colfax street. Ink tried not to think about Hannibal,
Dragon and Highdive, racing through the back streets
to come in at the church from another direction. It was a
solid plan considering they had made it up on the fly.

Those three men would go and rescue Jade off of the
church roof. While Ink and the rest of the Brothers played
distraction and delivered a message. He didn't envy Hawk.
Having the weight of this kind of decision squarely on his
shoulders must be exhausting.

It was still unbelievable that they were here for him.
Overwhelming pride of being part of this Brotherhood was
one of the many emotions churning through him. No
matter how many times he had ridden at their backs,
during missions both dangerous and boring, for some

reason, he had never considered they would back him like that.

They hadn't yet even asked Jade to be their Old Lady and every one of his Brothers were willing to risk their lives in order to back him and Hannibal up. Hearing their little Jewel's voice over the phone had crushed all the ice that had been building up inside him.

Her declarations of love had been exactly what he needed. That she called expecting that she wouldn't survive the night but needed to talk to them before she died had unleashed an inferno in his soul which had burned through all of his worries and doubts. He loved this woman and he would sacrifice anything in order to keep her safe.

Six men strode out into the street to block them, and it was clear they were in the right place. Each man held a gun pointed straight at the lines of Dark Sons. It was a stupid move. Even if they fired and managed to take some of them out, the numbers meant their situation would be hopeless.

Ink's hands twitched with the urge to go for his own gun, but he followed Hawk's lead. Their President parked and turned off his bike. Every one of the twenty-seven brothers with them followed suit. It was like an old-fashioned standoff.

The group of Russians stood in a row, and Ink recognized most of them from their different dealings over the years. Petrov wasn't among the crowd, nor was his second in command.

Ink was at Hawk's back as he stood at the front of their formation, his arms crossed, and glared at the men. He didn't even seem to notice all the weapons. The man had a spine of steel. Most of the drawn guns were pointed at him, but you wouldn't have known it by his look.

Several minutes ticked by in a strange silence as the two groups just glared at one another. Ink could see the arms of the men holding guns shake with fatigue. A door slammed somewhere nearby and Petrov strolled up the street from the direction of his headquarters. His men parted to let him through.

"How dare you come into my territory?" the Russian snarled.

Hawk tossed the bag that he had been palming in his hand to the ground between them. It held the listening devices Jade had been given. "You broke the treaty. Why am I not surprised that you did it like a coward? Couldn't man up enough to try something on your own, so you terrified a woman to do your dirty work on the miniscule hope that she might be able to get you some information. I knew you were desperate, but I didn't think you were pathetic."

"You are pathetic one." The Russian spat at the ground. "That's what I think of the treaty. And that's what I think of you. Why she thinks you're a better man than me, I'll never understand."

Ink could have sworn he saw surprise on Hawk's face. "Is that what this is about? Akula?"

"Alena was supposed to be mine."

Ink didn't understand what was going on, but it seemed like this was much more than a territorial dispute over business in Denver. Was the man implying that the years of hostility between them were over a woman?

He had met Akula, the woman in question. The assassin, whose real name was Alena, was a dynamic sort of crazy and somehow involved with their President. Was she really worth going to war for? Ink chastised himself. He had been willing to go to war over Jade. What right did he have to question anyone else's motives?

His President being hooked up with the Russian assassin wasn't as out of the realm of possibility as he'd thought when they first met. Honestly, most people believed the stoic man was celibate since he never showed even the slightest interest in any of the many women available to him. He'd discounted the rumors going around that the two of them had a relationship. He would have to reconsider that.

"Alena is her own woman. If she wanted you, then she would have had you." Hawk's glacial mask was firmly back in place.

"She was engaged to me before you took advantage of her."

Hawk shrugged as if he didn't care. "There are so many times I've fucked her or she's fucked me. Which one are you claiming was me taking advantage of her?"

His words lit a fuse within the usually cool Russian and he exploded into Russian curses. Petrov had become more and more hostile over the last few years since he had taken charge of the Bratva in Denver. It was easy to see something unhinged the man when it came to this woman. "Nineteen years ago in Afghanistan. Does that ring a bell?"

"Sure, I remember. What's your point?" Ink didn't know if Hawk was purposefully baiting the man or if he really didn't care.

"My point is she and I made a deal. She would marry me and be able to get out of the assassin business. She would be my ticket into the inner circle of her family. Your bastard spawn ruined all of that."

For the first time in his life, Ink saw Hawk stumble back, as if he had taken a blow. Horror and an icy rage seemed to wash over him. "What the fuck are you talking about?"

Petrov's laugh was wild. "I wondered if you knew. I guess she doesn't really love you either. Yes, your daughter gave her father the perfect leverage to keep her killing for them. They've held your child hostage and forced her to be Akula, their killing blade. Since there was no way for her to get out of the business, she no longer had an interest in me. She was more than my fiancée, she was my friend and you destroyed both of our lives."

Hawk looked terrifying as he glared at Petrov. "I have a daughter?"

"Yes. But you know what? After I heard she came back to your bed last month. I don't care anymore why we go to war. So long as I get to take you out."

Before any of them could react, Andrey Petrov pulled his gun and fired. Chaos erupted around them. Able to keep their heads during the drama, the Dark Sons were the first to react and several Russian men went down in the next round of gunfire. Ink was going to pull his own gun, but he saw Hawk collapse backward onto the cement and grabbed him instead. He dragged him out of the line of fire as Brothers closed in around them.

He got him behind a vehicle, then took the time to examine him. Hawk coughed and bucked. Ink lifted his shirt and was relieved to see that the bulletproof vest had done its job. Hawk gasped a few more times.

"Fuck, that hurt." The man rolled to his knees and pushed Ink away as he caught his breath, then stood.

The Dark Sons were all behind cover now and the Russians were retreating down the street at top speed.

"Did anyone get Petrov?" Ink heard Hawk's voice in front of them, as well as over their comms.

"No," Sharp replied. "Glad you are okay. He ducked behind his men after shooting you and ran like a coward."

"Can you ride?" Ink asked his president.

Hawk nodded. "Is there anyone too injured to ride?"

"Only minor injuries on our side. Our gear did its job."

Hawk's expression held its usual calm, but his eyes said that Ink didn't want to dig too deep. "Everyone meet back at the Clubhouse." Ink moved towards his bike and barely heard him mutter. "I have to make some phone calls."

He couldn't stop the question that came out of his mouth. "Do you think he was telling the truth about you having a daughter?"

Hawk's eyes blazed as he glared at Ink. "I don't know. But we're at war. Keep your head in the fucking game."

Ink nodded, got on his bike, and kicked it to life. He wasn't dumb enough to push again. Hannibal's voice came over his earpiece. "Jewel acquired and safe. On our way back to the Clubhouse." Ink's heart soared at the wonderful news.

"Understood," Hawk's response was curt. "Right behind you, I want all Brothers and their families pulled in. We're going on full lockdown until we know what Petrov's next step is."

It was after one o'clock in the morning, but the night was nowhere near over for them. There were too many things to be done. So many things to prepare for, but nothing, not even facing Hawk's wrath, would stop him from first making sure that their Jewel was all right with his own two eyes. Once they claimed her as their own, it wouldn't matter what else was going on. They could and would face it together.

Chapter 32

Sometimes the path to forgiveness requires you to admit you were an idiot.

Jade

J ade sat up, her whole body trembling from a nightmare. She stared up at the ceiling, trying to clear the images from her brain. In her dream, instead of pushing some random man off the side of the tower, she looked down and saw Ink falling to his death. It was a miracle she had even fallen asleep last night with everything still going on. She had only gotten a quick check-in with Ink before both men had disappeared into war conferences. While the confirmation that he wasn't hurt was nice, it hadn't settled her nerves at all.

They'd set her up in her bedroom in the upstairs of the Clubhouse and told her they wouldn't be able to be back for hours. Other families had been settling in as well, and they were getting ready for the long haul. Her men had asked her to stay put, and she would not argue after what the entire Club had done for her.

Exhaustion from the day must have overwhelmed her, because the minute she lay down on the bed, she'd been drawn into a nightmare. By the light streaming through the window, she could tell she had been asleep for a while.

"Everything's going to be okay. Go back to sleep, darlin'." She looked over to her left and her body relaxed. Ink's sleep tousled hair was on the pillow next to hers. She looked to her other side and saw Hannibal's dark gorgeous features relaxed, asleep on the pillow on her right. At some point, both men must have joined her in the bed.

Both men looked exhausted, even in sleep. Ink hadn't even seemed to have woken up to whisper his comforting words. She lay back into the center of the bed, both men on their sides facing her. Their breath was warm on her shoulders and her body tingled to life.

They were so physically perfect it was painful to resist reaching out to touch them. Hannibal's dark skin and large, bulky muscles were a contrast to Ink's pale tone and sleek, defined form. They were a perfect complement to each other in all things. The intricate art on both of their bodies called out to be traced and studied. She should probably let them sleep.

It was light outside, and they were still completely out of it. Even her sitting up in bed hadn't woken them, which meant they probably needed the sleep. But even with them bracketing her naked in the bed, she needed more. Needed the physical closeness of both of them, not only around her but inside her.

She needed to know they had forgiven her, and were giving her another chance. Unable to resist, she slipped her hands lightly down their bodies. The small muscle twitches that followed her touches made her smile. To reach their cocks, she had to slide down a little. Jade wrapped her hands around them in a gentle grip.

She kept her motions slow at first as she enjoyed the velvet soft skin in her hands. Hannibal woke before Ink and started thrusting into her hand. She tightened her grip, and both men woke with a groan. Their sexy smiles were like sunshine against her skin.

Hannibal thrust forward into her hand. "I think our little Jewel is trying to tell us something."

Their hands moved almost as one and cupped her breasts. She groaned as each man rolled out of her grip and locked their lips around her nipples. The joint pulls on both of her breasts at once, caused liquid heat to gush out of her core. They increased their suction and soon she was scissoring her legs, trying to get friction on her clit as they teased her almost to the point of orgasm.

She didn't know if coming from playing with her nipples alone was possible, but with these two, she didn't doubt they would find a way, if given time. It was tempting, but she needed more from them than pleasure.

"I need to feel you inside me," she moaned, and Hannibal and Ink bit her nipples. Lightning shot down her spine.

She bucked up against them. The weight of their bodies made all but the smallest movement impossible.

"Is that so?" She loved the way Hannibal's accent almost dripped with honey. His slow southern drawl of Louisiana.

"What if we want to play?" Ink's Texas twang was always strongest when he was tired or excited.

How had she gotten so lucky? "I want you to come inside me. I want you to mark me as your own."

Both Hannibal and Ink paused in their teasing torture and looked up at her. Her blush heated her cheeks. She gave them a naughty smile. "I got tested earlier in the week. Everything came back clean."

The men looked at each other and then back at her. "So did we," Ink said with a grin. "You sure about this, darlin'?"

"Yes."

"You want nothing between us anymore?" Hannibal asked.

"From now on I promise, no secrets, no lies, nothing between us, but us."

Hannibal growled and grabbed her. He rolled her on top of him and took her mouth in a passionate kiss. Ink rolled off the side of the bed. Jade couldn't concentrate on what he was doing because Hannibal's talented mouth was exploring hers as his hands ran up and down her back with possessive strokes.

She ran her wet pussy up and down his long, thick length, and teased herself against him. The sensation of his piercing as it moved against her clit was amazing. Something cool dripped down onto her ass and made her groan.

Ink's fingers slowly circled the tight rosette of her ass. He slid one finger inside her and she moaned against Hannibal's lips, nipping him in her pleasure and pushing back against the wonderfully naughty sensation. He seemed to be in as much of a hurry as she was. Because it was only a few seconds before he slipped a second finger in alongside the first.

The slight stretch and burn had her grinding her clit down against Hannibal's cock and both of them groaned at the wonderful sensation.

"God, you're beautiful." Ink's voice was a reverent whisper from behind her. "I've never taken a woman bare, darlin'. I can't wait to fill you up with my cum. Mark you as mine."

"Yes," she moaned and reached down between her legs

and guided Hannibal to her entrance. She lowered herself slowly, her whole body tensed for a moment before adjusting to his size. Without the condom, his piercing was a wicked delight as it stroked into the deepest parts of her.

Ink's fingers in her ass scissored, and she pushed back, wanting him to stop playing and take her. Ink smacked her cheeks once, twice. Each spank shocked her nerves and brought them to life. The pain wasn't enough to hurt or to push her into that other headspace where she enjoyed their punishment.

Right now, she didn't want that. All she needed was to feel them inside her. To feel their desire and acceptance. She hoped and prayed that they felt her love in return. The tip of Ink's cock at the entrance of her ass made her still. He breached the tight ring of muscles and she couldn't help but clench around Hannibal, causing him to echo her cry of pleasure with a deep moan of his own.

"Fuck, you feel so perfect around me," Hannibal moaned. "I can feel every twitch of your pussy."

"Christ, Jade. That's right. Pull me in," Ink moaned as he slowly inched his way inside her.

She wanted them to speed up, but also wanted this to last forever. This perfect first moment when the three of them came together with no barriers between them. Hannibal gripped her nipples, twisting and pinching them, causing her pleasure to spiral upwards. Her pussy clenched and both men groaned in response.

"Please, mark me, claim me," she cried out. "Masters. I love you. I need you."

She didn't know if it was calling them Master or her proclamation of love, but both men thrust harder and faster. It was all she could do to hold on and ride her pleasure to its inevitable crescendo. Hannibal thrust up into her with slow snapping strokes while Ink slid in and out of her in a smooth, but fast rhythm that matched every single swerve of his hips.

The rhythms were so different, but worked perfectly together. Her orgasm built at the base of her spine, and she knew this was going to be explosive. "Yes! Love you, Hannibal, Love you, Ink."

Hannibal snapped his hips up and hit that spot inside her that had stars exploding across the backs of her eyes and she screamed her pleasure out to the room. Her orgasm barreled over her and washed through her skin like a tidal wave. Her men held on for a few seconds, their strokes continuing and drawing out the orgasm.

Then they both seemed to have reached their limit. The rhythms faltered and their breathing became jagged and rough. They bathed the inside of her in hot cum, and their shouts were louder than hers.

She let her head fall onto Hannibal's chest, as she panted, Ink's body pressed them all down. A smile she couldn't hide tipped up her lips as she placed a small kiss on the center of his chest. It was like their love wrapped her up in a safe cocoon. They hadn't said the words with their mouths, but she could feel it in their touches.

She knew there would still be problems and worries in their future. But here, between the two of them, she was safe, cherished, and loved. She traced a little circular pattern over the defined muscles of Hannibal's chest.

"What are you thinking about, precious little Jewel?" Hannibal's words rumbled through his chest and into her ear, making her giggle.

"Nothing. It doesn't matter."

Ink pulled out of her and rolled them so she was on her side, pinned between them with him as the big spoon behind her. "None of that. What were you thinking?" Ink spoke directly into her ear.

"I was just wondering," she paused, not wanting to break the moment. But also needing to hold up her promises of not keeping secrets between them anymore. "If someday you might want to claim me for real."

Hannibal's frown made her smile, and she lifted her hand to smooth out the lines on his forehead that the expression created.

"What do you mean, for real?"

She shrugged and wished they would drop the whole topic. They wouldn't, and she didn't want to fight. "I mean, claiming me as your Old Lady. Is that something you might want to do someday?" Her voice was small. It was a silly dream. And she knew she had a long way to go to gain back their trust.

Becoming an official part of this bigger family who had come to her rescue last night was something she really wanted. She was willing to wait, but she wasn't gonna hide what she wanted.

Ink snorted and rolled off the bed. He pulled on a pair of jeans without bothering with underwear. She sat up, concerned. "I'm sorry. We don't have to talk about it. I didn't mean to push you. You asked what I was thinking about and I told you. I know, I have a long way to go to gain back your trust."

Hannibal rolled off the other side and copied Ink's actions, slipping on his own jeans with haste. Were they both leaving her now? Had she been wrong about what she had felt? She reached out her hands in a pleading gesture, not knowing what she could possibly say or do to fix things.

Hannibal grabbed the sheet off of the bed and tackled her. She struggled as he wrapped her up in the fabric, not understanding what was going on. Ink joined in the struggle and between the two of them, they had her wrapped up in a cocoon of white sheet. Hannibal picked her up without a word.

His shoulder was hard against her stomach. "What are you doing?"

They were silent as they strode down the hall. She would have struggled, but they had managed to wrap her up so tight that even up and down movements were hard. All she could see was Hannibal's ass, and an occasional glance at Ink. The big man strode down the hall with purpose.

She didn't know if she should scream or cry. Were they going to dump her outside in only a sheet? When they hit the stairs, she got a good look at Ink and his smile and the mischief that lit his eyes confused her.

What the hell were they doing and why were they heading downstairs? They passed through the main room and she saw that there were people there. Feminine laughter filled the room as the two men walked through it, and Jade recognized Val's musical laugh, but she couldn't tell who else was there. Men wolf-whistled, and a few people clapped as they hauled her down a hallway.

Was this some strange form of punishment for betraying the Club? Hannibal knocked at a door. "Come in." She recognized Hawk's gruff voice.

The door behind her opened. Jade gasped as she slid down Hannibal's body and she ended up facing Hawk, who sat behind a desk in some sort of office. Several men she recognized as the Officers of the Club were sitting in chairs around the room. Embarrassment overwhelmed her as she realized she was standing in a room full of men with a sheet wrapped around her like she was some sort of trapped butterfly trying to escape its cocoon.

Ink stepped up beside her. "Hey, Hawk, we just wanted to let you guys know that we love our Jewel and we're claiming her and putting our patch on her back."

"I love her too and want my patch on her back as well." Hannibal grinned.

She was going to be their Old Lady? She looked back and forth between her men. "That's how you tell me you love me for the first time?"

Hawk smiled, even if the expression didn't quite reach his eyes. "Do you swear to be loyal to your men and the Club?"

It took her scattered brain a moment to understand he was talking to her. "Yes, I swear."

"No more keeping secrets or hiding anything from them or the Club?"

"Yes, I swear." She repeated, not sure of what else to say.

"All right. Good enough."

The Officers in the room chuckled. Hannibal and Ink shouted, "Dark Sons for Life!"

All the men in the room, plus the men who apparently had followed them in the hallway, echoed her men's proclamation.

"Dark Sons for Life!"

Epilogue

Up, Up and Away!

Hannibal strode into Jade's gym, Ink at his side. The past month had been hectic. Small skirmishes with the Russians broke out whenever the assholes thought they would get away with it. Striking at the Dark Sons' businesses in cowardly ways.

The security detail stationed at the door was one of the many precautions they were taking. Mixed in with his Dark Sons' Brothers were professional bodyguards hired from Tek's friend Kane's company. They increased the number of guards whenever the Old Ladies were here. They didn't want to scare the women, but there was no way any of them were taking chances with so many of them in one place.

Leap was a good outlet for their energy because they could secure it during the off hours. Jade's passion for the wild stunts and obstacles had spread. Watching her share something she loved was an amazing experience.

Hannibal couldn't wait to see her. They came bearing good news. It had devastated her when the loan she'd been hoping for from the bank had been declined because of lack of collateral. His Brothers had voted and agreed to give her the money she needed for the expansion.

When they'd first suggested it, she'd balked, not wanting to accept charity. But he'd explained how the Dark Sons invested in businesses all the time, and she'd listened. His Club would pay for the expansion in return for a 25% interest in her company. He was glad that she had seemed excited by the prospect, even if she was skeptical that his Brothers would want to invest in her gym. His favorite part of the deal was it would put her business under their protection, and allow them to spend resources to help in tough times.

He hoped that protection was never needed. Petrov had seemed to lose interest in Jade. Maybe it was because he was focusing his attention elsewhere, but this agreement meant they could continue to justify the cost and resources to protect the thing their woman loved.

Where was their little Jewel? Hannibal spotted Jade at the bottom of the Salmon Ladder in the center of the room. Cami was in front of her with the obstacle bar set on the bottom rung. Tek's woman gripped it and hopped the metal up one rung. She swung wildly, trying to move it a second time, but it slipped and didn't catch and she fell to the padded ground.

Jade smiled encouragingly at her. "It's not only about strength." Her voice was sweet to his ears. "It's about getting a rhythm with the rocking of your body." She settled the bar back on the bottom rung. "You need to rock your body and explode at exactly the right moment."

Ink and he watched. They had heard tales of their Jewel and the Salmon Ladder. It looked like they were finally going to get to see her in action.

Jade jumped up and gripped the bar. "Now watch my

body on the backswing, notice where in the motion I pull the bar up and get it to the next level."

It was startling the speed at which her body exploded into motion. The steady rock, click, rock, click as their beautiful, powerful woman worked her way all the way to the top of the ladder was like a metronome. She didn't pause on any of the ten rungs.

She held steady for a moment, then dropped down onto the soft, thick mats. "Do you see what I mean?"

"Seeing what you mean and doing what you mean are two vastly different things."

"I think that has to be the sexiest thing I've ever seen." Ink's voice must have been loud enough to carry, because Jade looked over with a smile.

She ran towards them at full speed and jumped into Ink's arms. He spun her around as she gave him a kiss. Then she leaned backwards, letting Hannibal take her mouth with his.

"Dang, that is hotter than the desert sun in July," Val catcalled at them, interrupting their kiss. "I guess the appearance of your hotties means the lesson's over for today." She smiled at the three of them and waved to the other Old Ladies to let them know it was time to leave.

"I didn't know you guys were coming." Jade smiled at both of them as she lowered herself to the ground.

"We have some good news for you." Ink's smile showed he was as excited as Hannibal was. "The Club approved the deal."

Her jaw dropped, then she squealed and did a little jump. Hannibal loved how every emotion was always clear in everything their woman did. True to her word, the day they claimed her, she now practiced an almost extreme form of honesty.

Occasionally, she would hesitate briefly when they asked her a question that she found embarrassing or when the answer might upset them. But even then, she told them exactly what she thought in the end. It was a wonderful and refreshing part of their life.

She created a perfect balance between Ink and him. His Brother had finally gotten to show her his whips last week, and she'd enjoyed every kiss of the leather. At the end of the intense scene, she had spent almost an hour floating in subspace, and came out of it giggling.

"I think this calls for a celebration." The sexy smile that crossed her face had Hannibal curious.

"Is that so? Did you have something special in mind?"

She blushed. But then looked over at the mountain climbing wall. "Maybe."

Ink looked over at the same wall, then back at their woman. "What's going on in that pretty little mind of yours?"

"I had this dream last night. And since I have all of these fancy harnesses and belaying gear. I thought you guys would be interested in making it come true."

Hannibal tried to imagine what she could possibly be imagining. It couldn't just be about suspension, they had a wonderful sex swing at home specifically designed for that and had made excellent use of it. On multiple occasions.

"We're always happy to make your dreams come true, *cher*. What were you thinking?"

She smiled and looked between the two of them. "Have you ever thought about fucking while flying?"

Ann Jensen

I'm a snarky Jersey Woman who dreamed of one day becoming an Author. I write Romance with bigger than life characters who have to dodge every obstacle I gleefully throw in their paths. Somehow my characters also find time for steamy fun on their way to their HEAs.

I'm an avid reader, engineer, photographer, and a proud Bi woman. My life is a journey that I hope never stops in one place too long. I fill it with love and laughter whenever possible and when I can't, I pull out my clue by four and use it with deadly precision.

https://annjensenwrites.com/

Dark Sons Motorcycle Club
Saved by the Dark
Lost in the Dark
Caught in the Dark
Undercover In the Dark
Leap Into the Dark

Blushing Books

Blushing Books is the oldest eBook publisher on the web. We've been running websites that publish steamy romance and erotica since 1999, and we have been selling eBooks since 2003. We have free and promotional offerings that change weekly, so please do visit us at http://www.blushing-books.com/free.

Blushing Books Newsletter

Please join the Blushing Books newsletter
to receive updates & special promotional offers.
You can also join by using your mobile phone:
Just text BLUSHING to 22828.

Every month, one new sign up via text messaging will receive
a $25.00 Amazon gift card, so sign up today!